CLAIMED FOR THE HIGHLANDER'S REVENGE

Millie Adams

MILLS & BOON

First Published in Great Britain 2020
by Mills & Boon, an imprint of HarperCollins*Publishers*
1 London Bridge Street, London, SE1 9GF

© 2020 Millie Adams

ISBN: 978-0-263-27708-1

MIX
Paper from
responsible sources
FSC www.fsc.org **FSC™ C007454**

This book is produced from independently certified FSC™ paper
to ensure responsible forest management.
For more information visit www.harpercollins.co.uk/green.

Printed and bound in Spain
by CPI, Barcelona

To Harlequin,
for being my dream come true in so many ways.

Chapter One

England—1818

Lady Penelope Hastings was sitting in the drawing room, eating buttered toast, when she discovered she had been sold to a barbarian.

'I'm afraid there's nothing to be done.'

That was all the explanation offered by her father, Lord Avondale.

If there was one thing Penny knew from experience, it was that the situation was never ideal when her father began by stating how limited the options were. When her mother had died there had been *nothing to be done*. When he had dismissed her favourite governess—the only person in the household with whom she shared a connection—there had been *nothing to be done*.

When she had been young and full of dreams, and she had brought him a small, wounded bird in the hope that she might save it, he had barely given her a glance.

There is nothing to be done.

She felt a bit like that wounded bird now.

'I'm not quite certain I understand the full implications of the situation.' She looked at her toast and found it was no longer appealing. She set it back down on her plate.

'You are no longer to be married to the Duke of Kendal. There is… It is only that I thought the man dead and I did not imagine I would have to honour any prior agreements.'

'This is the first I've heard of any agreements.' She folded her hands in her lap and affected a bland expression. There was no point or purpose to arguing with her father. At best, protestations fell on deaf ears. At worst, she often caught the edge of his temper.

Penny had no wish to engage with her father in either state. And so, it was best to remain bland. Her emotions upset him. So much so at her mother's funeral that he had locked her away for days after.

And so she had learned to lock her feelings away. She felt them still, echoing inside her chest like a cry in an empty room. But no one could see them. No one could use them against her.

Later, she had learned this particular method of dealing with him. Rational responses. Forcing him to repeat his statements multiple times. She'd read once about negotiating tactics in war and had internalised the lesson.

Her father's one virtue was that he was in possession of a rather good library. More for vanity than his actual use, but she'd made use of it and often.

Books had been her companions growing up in this house where her father was rarely in residence and staff came and went like spirits in the night.

She'd long suspected the disappearance of staff was due to lack of payment, for she knew they had joined the ranks of the peerage who had title, reputation and a position in society, but no money to support any of it. Their home was a metaphor for the position. Stately, large and crumbling inside.

The ornate, tarnished gold that adorned the ceilings and door frames seemed a mockery of what they were now. All gilded with no substance.

The paper hangings in the drawing room had been a rich blue once, faded now to a mottled navy. What had formerly looked like expensive, damask silk now looked like worn paint. It didn't much matter, as her father hadn't entertained here since her mother's death when Penny was five.

Her father didn't have to announce their dire straits for it to be obvious to Penny.

Penny wasn't a fool. She spent her hours reading and watching. When there was someone around she talked to them. Servant, chaperon, even the falconer who lived on the estate. She would talk to anyone. She hated silence. Silence created fertile ground for terrible memories and awful feelings to rise up to the surface, and that didn't accomplish anything. However, asking endless questions was the simplest way to find common ground with a person and she'd discovered that not everyone was like her father. Not everyone told her to be quiet the moment she made a noise. And so, she asked. And asked and asked.

How the household worked. What London society was like. How long it took for an egg to become a chicken.

She remembered everything.

It might not soothe her loneliness, but it helped her put together a clear picture of the world. Of the reality of the situation she and her father were in.

'I did not require your opinion to be given, Penelope, you did not need to be consulted. But you will marry the Scot.'

She was in disbelief. Her face was hot, as if she'd stuck it in the fire where her toast had just been made. Her hands were cold as ice, as though she had some grave illness.

It felt a blessing because it was better than the absolute despair that was just beneath it. But there was no point giving in to that, nor the rage she could feel beginning to churn inside her.

She didn't know what horrified her more. The fact her hopes were being burned to the ground before her eyes, or the fact that she was having difficulty controlling her response.

If she spoke out of turn, her father would fly off into a temper and then not only would she be less an engagement to a duke, she would know nothing of her current situation.

Her father, when challenged, was all bluster and rage and no useful information at all.

'Have you spoken to the Duke of Kendal, Father?' she asked, choosing her words and tone carefully.

She wanted to yell. To scream and cry and fling herself on the ground like a child denied a sweet. But being a child, free to release emotion whenever it welled up in her chest, had ended when her mother had died.

Mourning was supposed to be worn on your body. Signified by the colour. It wasn't supposed to overtake who you were. To run rampant through your chest leaving jagged, painful wounds that felt as though they would never heal.

She had learned to keep her feelings hidden away. She had a jewellery box that had been her mother's and, while she'd inherited no jewellery—all sold to pay the estate's debts—she'd treasured the heavy wooden box with its gold lock since she was small. She kept stones and feathers inside, little trinkets she'd collected on the grounds. Treasures her father couldn't sell, but that marked the years of her life, years spent wandering the grounds alone. Things that mattered only to her.

When her mother had died, she hadn't understood. One of the boys who worked in the stables had told her it meant her mother was being put in a wooden box under the ground. She'd started to wail. A deep, painful sound that had come from the depths of who she was. And her father...he'd been so angry. He'd screamed at her to stop. Uncaring of all the servants who witnessed it. He'd carried her into the house and set her in the centre of the great hall and yelled at her, but she hadn't been able to make her tears stop.

He'd banished her to her room, and roared at the staff she wasn't to come out until she'd stopped crying.

And there she'd stayed. For nearly three days. She'd felt as though she was in that wooden box the boy had said her mother was in. She'd felt buried in misery. And then she'd taken her mother's jewellery box down from her vanity and had brought it into bed with her. Held it close against her chest. And when she'd had a feeling that was too big, too bright and sharp to be contained in her chest, she'd imagined locking it away in that box.

She hadn't cried since then. Not for years. She simply put her feelings in the jewellery box.

With all the stones and feathers and other precious things she could not afford to let her father touch.

It was what she did now. She imagined locking all of her fear, her anger, her sadness, away. Those feelings wouldn't help her now.

'No,' he said. 'Not yet, but there is nothing—'

'Only,' she said, cutting him off, trying to disguise the desperation in her voice, 'I am certain the Duke will know what to do and will have some means of assisting us as our engagement is common knowledge. And I have purchased my trousseau.'

Paid for by the Duke, of course, as her father could never have provided her with the trappings required by a duchess.

And the Duke's family...his sister and his ward, his mother. She was supposed to live with them. She was supposed to have real friends.

The bit of toast in her stomach was now sitting heavily.

Penny's engagement to His Grace, the Duke of Kendal, had been her father's greatest triumph. It had been evidence to him that perhaps having a daughter had some value.

For him to dissolve such an arrangement and offer her hand to a soldier, a Scottish soldier at that, spoke of a situation so desperate she could scarcely fathom it.

She loved the Duke and everything he represented. Everything about him. From his lovely manners to his exquisitely formed face and his perfectly manicured manor. The one good thing her father had ever done was put her in the position to secure the match.

It had come as a shock to her. She'd never been given a proper debut. It was a match borne from geographical luck and she was not foolish enough to think otherwise.

The Duke's grand country estate was only an hour's ride away. One day when she'd been out walking she had discovered the Duke's sister, lost and covered in mud. She'd brought her back to the house and given her tea and toast.

It had been a great shock when the Duke himself had appeared to ferry his sister home.

His mother had sent her thanks and an invitation to tea.

It had been the beginning of something Penny had never even dreamed of. A fantasy too fine for her to have ever spun for herself. Perhaps, she might have dreamed it, but only if she imagined first that she were someone else and not simply Penelope Hastings.

She would never know the full circumstances of why exactly the Duke had chosen to marry her rather than a girl who had graced London's ballrooms for the Season. Though as she had got to know him she had made some guesses as to why.

Penny knew she was beautiful. Along with that empty jewellery box, beauty was the only thing her mother had left her. She knew, though, that it was not her beauty that appealed to the Duke of Kendal. Rather she imagined he took great pleasure in circumnavigating the rabid mothers of the marriage mart and finding himself a wife who was respectable, free of scandal and entirely his choice.

Her father's pleasure in the match was self-serving on his part and she knew it. She also didn't care. Without a good marriage she would be left with nothing. It was a matter of survival. She had expected to be forced into marriage to a toothless old man whose lack of hair on his head was to be compensated for by the gold in his purse.

She had expected something like *this*.

And to be given the Duke, only to have him *replaced*, was a blow to her heart, her hope, her pride, that she had not expected.

Her father had found a way to be worse than her every expectation.

Because he had given her something sweet, a dream spun from sugar and gold, then burned it to dust before her.

She'd been sure her father had lost the ability to hurt her. Disappoint her.

She'd been wrong.

'He has informed me that he will be procuring a special licence. And after that, you will return with him to Scotland.'

Without thought, Penny pushed herself back from the table and sat for a moment. Then she stood slowly, the room tilting as she did, though her feet remained firmly planted on the ground.

She was not only losing her future husband, but also the plans for her future. The beautiful jewel box of a withdrawing room at Bybee House was not faded. Rather the paper hangings were a cheerful pink, with gold detail and ornate marble like twisted vines over the walls and ceilings. She'd already imagined sitting there for hours and sewing, reading, petting a cat.

She had planned on getting a cat. One she would keep in the house and not out in the barn simply to trap mice.

To say nothing of the Duchess of Kendal, the Duke's mother, who had become so dear to her. His younger sister and his ward, who had become such good friends to her. Who had made her feel as though she might not have to be lonely any more and she could have friends that existed outside the pages of a book.

She hadn't felt like that in a long time. Not since…well, not since Lachlan. A servant who had worked on the estate. He'd been nearly ten years her senior, she was sure of it. But he'd been kind to her. Her first experience of a friend.

He'd once helped her save a bird. He'd let her trail after him and ask endless questions that would have caused most men to be sharp or short with her. He'd been there. A place for her words to go so she didn't have to sit in silence.

Then one day he'd gone. No explanation. No goodbye. It might as well have been death.

She'd mourned him.

Only this time she'd done it inside. For she knew better than to ever show her pain.

She did the same now, her hands folded in her lap, her face betraying nothing as the vision of the life she'd hoped for burned before her. And she had no idea how she might make it right.

Lachlan Bain was a patient man. The years had hardened him, changed him. Battle had scarred him. Destroyed what had once been good inside him.

But it had also sanded away the edges of youth. Impatience, hot-headedness. Like a broadsword made in fire all that remained was sharp, cold steel.

For years he had carried his rage inside him, a reckless heat that had driven him in battle. Had driven him beyond. The years had dimmed the motivation for that rage. Somewhere on the muddy battlefields he had forgotten where his anger had come from. It had spilled over into all the things around him, the atrocities of war.

The innocent lives he'd failed to save.

But he'd learned to harness it. Honed it into a sharpened blade he'd used to cut down the enemy.

He'd let the memory of the enemy who had ignited the rage in the first place fade.

But when news of his father's death reached him, he was reminded. It had taken him six months to ready his business to function without him. Six months to begin putting his plans for revenge in order.

And his blood burned with all the red-hot rage that had existed inside him these long years. It had not truly gone away. The fire had only been banked. And now it glowed red.

Before he returned to Scotland, before he returned to the Highlands to restore his clan to their former glory, he would collect the debt owed him.

He had heard whispers among London's high society, happy enough to share the tables in the gaming hell with him though he knew he would never be invited to any ballrooms, that the Earl of Avondale had made himself a prestigious match for his daughter.

A match that was far above what an impoverished man with his reputation should have been able to manage.

A duke.

The man was puffed up in his pride over his triumph.

Lachlan knew the Earl had nothing else of value. Nothing but his daughter.

He remembered the girl. She had been pretty in that way a doll might be, but had looked terribly fragile with her blonde hair, so light it was nearly white, and her wide, blue eyes the colour of a robin's egg. He had felt pity for her. As much of a hardship as it had been to work for the Earl as a lad, he imagined being a child in that mausoleum that passed for a manor house was worse.

Lachlan knew all about useless fathers. And he had deemed the Earl worse than useless.

He had felt pity for the girl then and he might have felt guilt for using her now if he were a different man.

But he was not.

He was a man of battle. A man who had the courage to be all his father could not. A man who refused to sit back and fill his pockets while his people went without.

He had gone into battle to fight. He had gone into battle to die.

But over the near decade he'd spent fighting, he'd gone from being a boy who'd been beneath the contempt of the Englishmen around him to a brother in arms.

The necessities of war, and his own skill, had found him advancing through the ranks until he was a captain. He'd been in command of a group of men, most Scottish like himself, and they had fought hard, in kilts, for their oppressors. And through those acts had earned respect none of them had even wanted.

But in war, they'd all become the same. He could not stomach the death of a young man any easier if he was English. Covered in mud and blood, they were the same.

And when he'd saved a young peer who'd been injured in a battle, had stayed with him in a ditch all night while gunfire exploded around them...

He had found himself a decorated war hero and a very rich man. Which made his options when it came to revenge that much richer. It also presented the possibility of being able to restore that which his father had nearly destroyed.

He had a plan. He could not afford guilt.

Guilt was a luxury afforded to men who were both rich and titled. Of course, men less likely to feel guilt did not exist, as far as Lachlan could see.

The girl's father was only lucky he'd decided on this action, rather than separating the man's head from his shoulders.

When he had ensured that his horses were secured in the stable—a stable that was all too familiar to him from his time spent on the Avondale estate—he made his way to the house.

It stood as grim and imposing as it ever had. An English manor house was a far cry from the impassable stone keeps in the Highlands, where he had been the son of a chieftain. Disgraced though he was in Lachlan's eyes, his father had been a man who retained an air of power. And in his homeland, no door was ever closed to Lachlan.

In England, it was another matter.

Though the years had shifted English sentiments on the Scots, after seeing how bloody well they fought, it was still clear he wasn't a member of the upper echelons of society here. War hero or not.

For three years he'd been building his shipping empire and he could buy access into any London club he chose, but like many merchants…he would never be considered on equal ground with smart society. He'd no mind to try. He enjoyed frequenting the gaming hells and putting more coin on the table than the peerage could.

Enjoyed forcing them to interact with—and lose to—a man so beneath them.

A rebellion against his father and his fascination with the English.

But the time for games was over.

It was time for him to leave. Time for him to go back home.

Though, perhaps the memory he had of his homeland was one that wouldn't stand all these years on. If he were greeted by swords and pitchforks, he wouldn't be terribly shocked.

If the clan imagined he were anything like his dead father, he wouldn't blame them at all.

His father had squandered his money, the money of the clan, the money of his people, trying to live life like the English peerage, drinking it away in pubs in Edinburgh while those they were sworn to protect starved, their ancestral homes falling down around them in disrepair.

It might be too late and there might be too little left for him to bring salvation now.

But defeat was not in his blood.

For good or ill.

Neither was mercy.

As the Earl of Avondale was discovering.

It was time for Lachlan to go home, but he would bring with him a souvenir. The greatest prize of the man who had nearly destroyed him.

He could think of nothing sweeter.

Lachlan's mother had sent him to England, using a connection forged by his father, to gain him a position with the Earl. She'd sent him without his father's knowledge or permission. A great dishonour, his father would think. To send his son to make money to replace the money he was squandering.

But the Earl had cheated Lachlan. Left his labour unpaid. And he could not return home a failure. So he had stayed. Waiting for the man to make good and in that time his mother…

She had given in to despair.

She had taken her own life.

His father bore the brunt of that guilt. But the Earl of Avondale had played a part in it and he would pay for that part.

Lachlan went to the door and knocked. He could have barged in. He had no patience for waiting around. But he would be let in here. Admitted by servants. A station he no longer held.

He could buy this manor, he could buy the Earl of Avondale, twice over. He bowed to no man.

Their fortunes had reversed and he intended to make the other man feel the weight of it.

The butler who answered the door was the same man who had been here when Lachlan was a boy of fifteen. He remembered him as being rather imposing. A hawkish face and broad shoulders, which Lachlan recognised now were padded.

The man's black eyes no longer looked intimidating, rather Lachlan could see a depth of exhaustion there he would not have appreciated as a boy.

He felt no pity. It was the price to pay for working for the devil.

He didn't judge the man, either, as Lachlan had once found himself in the Earl's employ.

'Mr Bain,' he said. 'The Earl is expecting you.'

'Captain,' he said. 'Captain Bain.'

His ranking in the British Army, which he used only because it gave him some satisfaction to exceed the position this Englishman insisted on placing him in.

The man's lip curled ever so slightly. If the man recognised him as the boy he had been, Lachlan couldn't be sure. But he recognised a Scotsman and it was clear he found him beneath contempt. Yet the man had no choice but to admit him entry and so he did. Lachlan looked around the entry that he knew at one time had been grand. Now the wallpaper was stained and peeling, the flowers warped and swollen from moisture that seeped into the walls here. Apparently even aristocrats could not find insulation from the damp.

Before he could take another step, a door flung open and a woman all but tumbled into the space in which he was standing. She straightened, pressing her hands down over her skirts. Hands that were clearly shaking.

'Steady, lass,' he said.

His voice clearly provided her with no comfort. Wide, blue eyes met his and he could see fear there. He was used to men looking up at him with fear. He was quite accustomed to being the last thing a man saw. He had a reputation for being brutal in battle and it was well earned.

But he derived no joy from frightening small women.

It took him a moment to realise that this woman was his newly betrothed. He had not seen her since she was a girl. But he could see traces of the child she had been then. She still had a small frame, delicate. Her cheeks were no longer round, but her eyes were the same blue and the stubborn set of her chin remained.

Her dress was a simple, pale shift, the same milk white as her skin, the neck low and wide in that way that was so fashionable. He had wondered more than once if men were responsible for the current sensibility since it offered a tantalising view of female flesh.

He had not expected her to be *beautiful*. Beautiful seemed too insipid a word.

She was like a faery. It seemed that gold glowed beneath the surface of her skin.

She was infinitely lovelier than he had imagined she might be. He had not thought the collection of limbs she'd once been could be reassembled into something quite so pleasing.

She was still slim, her pale blonde hair like gold, her eyes the sort of blue found in the deep part of the sea. Mysterious like the ocean, too. He could see her fear, but there was more. A strength and stubbornness and something he could not define.

A depth he had not expected.

That, he supposed, had always been there. The magic behind her stubborn bearing. Most vulnerable beings would find themselves crushed living with a man such as the Earl. Yet she had seemed to retain her stubbornness and he found it admirable.

But while he could see her defiance, he could also see her fear. A pulse racing at the base of that delicate throat. It angered him for a moment, that her body betrayed her in such a way. The source of her life there to be seen. So easily crushed if a man was of a mind.

Had he been a different man he might have felt pity for her. But he was not a different man and pity had no place in his life.

'*You,*' she said, her expression changing from one of fear to shock.

That one word contained many.

'Aye,' he said. 'You've spoken to your father, then.'

'That's not what I mean,' she said. 'It's you. You're the boy.'

She did remember him. He had wondered if she might when he had wondered about her at all and it had been only for the briefest of moments.

He had thought of her only in terms of a tool he might use to exact revenge.

A might bit more difficult now that she stood before him, clearly a woman and not a chess piece.

Most women, he found, displayed what they wanted from him, or didn't, with immediate clarity. Fear, lust or greed an immediate flash in their eyes and smile, with nothing else beyond.

But not this woman.

He knew what manner of man her father was. Living beneath this roof would have been enough to break even the strongest of men, yet here she stood, her back straight, her shoulders square.

She was unexpected in every way, though she should not have been.

A neglected child with a broken wing of her own, she had occupied herself saving animals on the estate. Curious, he'd thought at the time. For she so clearly needed rescuing, yet she concerned herself with the plight of other small, vulnerable creatures, not seeming to recognise she was kin to them.

Recognising that did not change his intention.

Though the flare of lust he felt when he looked upon his future bride was a welcome and unexpected addition to his revenge.

'The boy who used to talk to me. The boy who helped me save the bird,' she added.

'Yes. I suppose I should be flattered that you

remembered. But you will find that I'm not a servant any more. Neither am I a boy. I'm Captain Lachlan Bain, Chief of Clan MacKenzie. And you are to be my bride.'

Chapter Two

Penelope had run straight from fireplace and... well, right into the enemy.

Except, the enemy was a man she had once considered...nearly a friend. Her only friend in the whole world, once upon a time. Oh, if her father had known it would have meant disaster for them both. But he hadn't. She had been careful, sneaking out of the manor during the day when her father was otherwise occupied. When he had left her to her own devices, left her without a governess, she had nothing else to do.

So, she had made the hours pass picking across the fields that surrounded the property. And she had often rescued wounded animals she'd found there.

Lachlan had helped her.

She'd thought him an angel. She'd loved his funny accent and the way the sunlight caught the curls in his hair. She'd loved the way he'd smiled at her.

She'd been quietly destroyed when he'd gone. Another brush with grief.

It was tempting for a moment to think he'd come back for her. He *had*. But she knew it wasn't like that. She could look at him and know.

There was almost nothing of the boy she'd once known left in him.

She didn't remember him being quite so tall. But then, she'd been a child when he was here and to her, everyone seemed tall. That he still towered over her now seemed notable.

She knew for a fact he had not been quite so broad.

His hands were battered and scarred, a great, raised slash extending from his neck down beneath the collar of his white shirt. A shirt which was open at the neck and revealed quite a bit more of his chest than was at all decent.

He wore a kilt with a green tartan, a sword at his hip, and a sporran clasped with a badger's head.

She knew that the kilt was common dress for Scottish soldiers, but it was very rare to see a man wearing one for a social call.

She looked to his face, hoping to see someone she recognised. Hoping to see Lachlan as she'd known him somewhere in those eyes.

But they were hard as flint, his mouth set into a grim line. As mysterious and frightening to her as the Highlands themselves.

If she had hoped to find an ally in him, she suspected she would be disappointed. Because this man was not soft. She couldn't imagine him bending down to help a small, distraught child save a doomed bird. No. Instead, she could imagine that large hand wrapping itself around the vulnerable creature and crushing it.

She thought to use the same tactic with him that she used with her father. Rational, reasonable negotiation.

'I am engaged already,' she said, trying her very best to look beset by regret. 'A sad truth. But that will make a betrothal between you and me quite difficult.'

'Nothing difficult about it, lass,' he said, his voice rich and low. She remembered the accent, but the voice had definitely changed. She could feel it echoing inside her chest and she did not like it.

He had come into her home and filled the space here. Now he was invading her as well.

'Your father owes me a debt. And money will not suffice.'

'I don't understand.'

'It's not for you to understand. It's for you to do as you're told.'

Well, rational did *not* seem to be working. He certainly wasn't giving her any answers that she could hold on to. Nothing about this made sense to her. He had been a boy, a servant when he had left, and now he had returned, saying that he had some sort of hold on her father.

'I'm not certain I understand,' she said, keeping her tone exceedingly patient. 'You see, when you were here last you were a servant. You can see how I might be having some difficulty connecting how you went from there...' She circled her hand and then pointed at the floor. 'Here.'

'I saved the neck of the right rich man while fighting in the war. His parents were exceedingly grateful. They gave to me what your father promised and did not deliver.'

'What?'

'I worked for your father for years. Sweat and blood, lass. There were no wages paid. I was nothing but a penniless boy in a foreign land unfriendly to me based on my origins. I had few options when I arrived, less after I'd spent a year here, with all the money sent by my mother long since gone. And when I approached your father about the lack of payment, he promised me a merchant ship, if only I were to work three more years.'

'That's... I can't imagine that my father would pay a boy something with that sort of value.'

'He didn't,' Lachlan said. He smiled, but there was nothing at all nice in that smile. 'He lied. And he sent me off with nothing. After years of promises. Years of working for nothing. I had no means of getting home and, by the time I was through here, by the time I realised that nothing would come of this, that I had wasted those years, my mother was dead.' His lip curled, the expression savage. Thunderous. 'And there was nothing I could do to save her.'

'I'm sorry about your mother,' she said. 'Really. I know what that's like. My mother's dead, too.'

'Are you trying to appeal to my softer side? Because you're wasting your time, lass. I haven't got one.'

'That's not true. You did.' He had and it had meant everything to her at the time. Everything to a girl trapped inside herself.

'That boy you knew is dead.' Those words were haunting, but had they been spoken in anger, had there been some discernible emotion on that face of his, they might have been less terrifying. But it was the emptiness there, the way his face seemed carved directly from rock, as immovable and unreadable as a sheer cliff, that made her soul turn to ice. 'He died somewhere on a battlefield in Belgium. The man who stands before you wants nothing but revenge before he returns home for absolution. I got my ship, but I paid for it with blood. And I've made my fortune. Which means I have the power now. And your father has none. He has nothing. And I've purchased his debts. Sadly for him I've made you the price.'

'But why?' she asked. 'If you have the money, then what difference does it make?'

'My mother is dead. And I would have your life for hers.'

Fear rioted through her. 'You don't mean to… You don't mean…'

'You're no good to me dead.'

'Honestly,' she said, losing track of strategy altogether, 'I probably wouldn't be any use to you alive. My father often tells me that I'm useless. Save my beauty, of course, which I find to be quite a hollow comfort.'

He stared at her, his eyes cold, and she realised it was perhaps not good of her to speak of her own beauty. But truly, now, it meant nothing to her at all.

She cleared her throat and continued. 'It must be said, I accomplished some sort of usefulness when I secured an engagement to the Duke of Kendal.'

'If Kendal found you useful, I imagine I can find something to do with you.' The words were rough and hinted at a mystery she didn't fully understand.

One that made her stomach shiver and the hair on her arms go up on end.

She pushed the unwanted sensations down deep. 'I'm not entirely sure he found me useful. But his sister likes me quite a lot and so does his mother, and...'

'I'm not interested in the particulars of an engagement that no longer exists.'

'Then perhaps you would like to tell me about the particulars of this one.'

He took a step towards her. 'You are right. Your father was very proud of your engagement to the Duke. His highest achievement. And a pathway out of debt. It brings me great joy to deprive him of both of those things.'

'So I'm...simply revenge to you? A pawn? No regard whatsoever for the fact that I had plans. For the fact that I'm supposed to be getting married to somebody that I'm actually quite fond of. It doesn't make any sense. You...' She sputtered, trying to think of some way she might appeal to a humanity she wasn't certain he possessed. 'You *saved a bird*.'

'That is the second time you've mentioned the bird. I confess I don't remember much about you as a child, but I do remember your chatter and I had hoped you'd grown out of that.'

'It's not chatter!' she protested. 'The bird matters.'

She was no longer able to keep her feelings, her frustrations, wholly locked away. The bird, the truth about Lachlan as she'd known him, had been her only hope.

She was so very tired of glimmers of hope, faintly shining in the distance, only to be snuffed out.

'You *helped* me save the bird,' she said again. 'I came and I found you and you were working in the stables. I had found a small bird that had fallen out of its nest and you helped me save it.'

'You are applying far too much meaning to it. I was simply a servant doing his best to keep the mistress of the house from reporting to her father that I'd disappointed her. I still thought I was saving my family then, my clan. I still had a heart in my chest. I think what you'll find is that what war can do to harden a man, to change him, is beyond understanding. There is battle, yes. But what happens in that battle turns men into beasts and what those men will do to the innocent is beyond comprehension.'

There was something utterly cold and desolate in that tone, something that chilled her from the inside. But she refused to back down. She met his gaze, hard as it was, and would not look away. 'I don't understand how the same boy who could help me save that bird would do something so utterly barbaric as to force me into a marriage that I don't even want.'

'You haven't even seen the beginning of how barbaric I can be. And if you think I care about your feelings any more than I care about the plight of a bird, you are gravely mistaken.' His tone was laced with iron and there was a promise in those words that she could not quite untangle. It made strange waves of tension begin to radiate low in her stomach, spreading out through her limbs. 'I care about two things, lass, and your feelings are not among them.'

His eyes were green. Deep and dark and unfeeling. When she had seen him standing there she had been struck by a sense of the familiar. But the longer she looked, the more that feeling drained away.

Until all she could see was a stranger.

He was right, he wasn't the boy who had helped her. The boy she'd thought she'd befriended all those years ago. The boy whose absence she'd once mourned. She had thought it impossible to find herself in a colder situation than the one she had grown up in. But it seemed that she had.

Perhaps that wasn't fair to her father.

He had kept her fed and clothed. He had not sent her away. He had not struck her. She was lonely. But loneliness was not fatal.

'Are you spiriting me off to Scotland to be married right away?' She lifted her chin, trying not to appear frightened.

But she was frightened.

Still, she knew a bit about dealing with feral dogs and showing fear was a certain way to get bitten.

She had no desire to be bitten.

Not only that, she didn't want him to have the satisfaction of her fear. He hated her father. How much more joy would he get from his revenge if she cowered? If she wept?

The only control she had was in what she chose to keep hidden and what she chose to show.

Still, fear wound itself around her in cold coils like a viper.

Marriage, and all that it entailed, was a mystery to her in many ways. She could vaguely remember her mother and father speaking to each other. Her mother had always seemed pale and drawn. The sort of lonely Penny often felt. She could not remember her parents together. Many girls could take cues from the way their parents acted together—good or bad—and try to ascertain some of the mysteries therein. But she had not even had *that*.

She had felt confident that the Duke would make it right. That he would treat her with patience and that he would help her understand not only her duties as a duchess, but as a wife.

She had no such confidence in a man like Lachlan Bain.

What would he want from her? And how quickly?

Her entire body trembled at the thought.

She had such vague ideas of what passed between a man and a woman. She was a voracious reader and it was a topic she found quite curious. Her father's study was mostly absent of books that contained such topics, but she had a skill for finding mentions of copulation. Between horses. Chickens. Every so often hints at it between men and women.

She knew just enough to be mortified by the thought and little enough to feel as if she might as well know nothing at all.

'No, that is not what I have in mind. I have no patience for the reading of the banns, but I will purchase for us a special licence. We can get married immediately.'

'What is the purpose of that?'

'A wedding in a church. Legal in England. Gossiped about in England.'

'I think you're underestimating the power of an elopement.' She didn't know why she'd said that. She didn't *want* to elope.

'Not at all. But I take great joy in forcing your father to witness the event. At the same church where you might have married His Grace.' Somehow the Duke's honorific sounded like an insult on his tongue, the slight twist his accent making the word sound a vile curse.

She frowned deeply. 'You're playing a game.'

'Perhaps. One of logic. Chess, I think.'

'I don't fancy being a chess piece.'

'I don't think a chess piece gets to choose which game it's a part of. And that is all you are. A pawn.'

She had thought it impossible to be dismissed any more thoroughly than she often was by her father on a given day. Lachlan Bain proved it was in fact possible to make her feel yet more insignificant. Not a skill she would have listed as a high priority in a husband.

'Will I be given a chance to speak to him?'

'Your father?'

'The Duke.'

'I don't own your time yet, lass. If you've a desire to go and speak to him, that's your decision.'

'How very generous of you.'

Her toast was now rebelling in her stomach.

Did they eat toast in Scotland? She didn't know. In all her reading she hadn't studied the food of Scotland. She hadn't thought it would be relevant to her. It turned out it was desperately relevant.

'Do you eat toast?' The question came out quite a bit more plaintively than she had intended. Of course, of all the things she could have asked about, the presence of toast should perhaps have fallen to a lower priority.

It seemed imperative at the moment, however.

That granite face contorted into an expression of shock, if only for a fleeting moment. And were she not half so distressed she might take it as a victory.

'Toast?'

'I don't know very much about Scotland. My father's library is thin on the subject.'

'Oh, no,' he said. 'No toast. Nothing but haggis and porridge.'

She felt ill.

She suddenly wished she had been able to enjoy that toast more, if toast was about to become a rare commodity in her life.

'Well, I'm certain there will be many things to adjust to.'

'I see you've met.'

Penny turned and saw her father standing in the doorway. He looked a stranger to her. They had never been close and his gaze had never held any great affection for her, but even that sense of familiarity that she'd had from living within the same walls for so many years was absent now.

This man was selling her to pay his debts.

This man had put her in an impossible situation, where her life would only be given value if it saved his.

It hadn't been any different, of course. Her marrying the Duke of Kendal. In her father's eyes, it had been his accomplishment. The value in her existence.

But at least she had wanted that.

She did not want this. Not at all.

But the big Scottish brute was correct. If she refused, she wouldn't be marrying the Duke of Kendal anyway. The Duke was utterly and completely above reproach. His reputation was spotless, not just because he was insulated as a man of high position, but because he was a man of the greatest of integrity.

There had never been rumours of improper behaviour, secret children, gambling or any of the other vices that often gripped the peerage.

If she were to be disgraced, her family name and reputation damaged, the Duke would want nothing to do with her.

No matter what, there would be no saving that relationship.

So she had to swallow hard, had to lower her eyes to avoid allowing her father or Lachlan to see the distress in them. And she had to give the consent that Lachlan had been so confident she would give.

It burned at the last remaining vestiges of her pride to do so.

She was her father's property. Pretending otherwise was a luxury of the past. Remembering Lachlan's words about chess pieces, she had to reluctantly acknowledge to herself that she had been a far happier chess piece when she had been in a different game.

But when you were a chess piece, you did not get to choose. And any illusion of freedom had been just that. An illusion.

All that was left was her pride. The walls of that shiny jewellery box she'd built to hold all her pain.

She would not allow it to break now.

There was no point weeping. When she had been a bereaved five-year-old there had been no point to it. She'd wept and wailed and gained only her father's ire. She doubted she'd get anything more at twenty-two.

Penny had had, for a few sweet months, hope in a softer future at Bybee House. A life that had seemed too beautiful to be hers. And lo, it had turned out that it was.

But that hope had only existed inside her for such a short time, by comparison to what she knew best. Grim acceptance.

She knew how to protect herself. She knew how to find worlds of information in books, a salve for her soul in one-sided conversations. A sense of accomplishment in saving animals about the estate.

She knew how to move in limited quarters with grace and skill.

In short, she knew how to survive.

She would survive Lachlan Bain as she had survived everything else.

'Everything is settled then,' she said softly. 'I accept your very generous offer of marriage.'

Chapter Three

Her father had told her expressly that he would speak to the Duke, but she felt that she had to speak to him. She felt that she owed him some sort of explanation. It occurred to her as she approached the house that the Duke might not care at all for her explanation. But something had driven her here, far too late in the day and without a chaperon, which she knew would have been a death knell to her reputation were it not already to be killed at the hands of a Highlander.

She ached.

She felt as if she were dying. She had planned a life here. Over the past space of time the Duke had been courting her she had easily slipped into imagining what it would be like to call this place home.

It was the grandest residence she'd ever beheld. Nestled into rolling green hills, surrounded by lakes which provided fresh fish and backed by a forest filled with stags and boars, ensconced by great gardens that provided fresh herbs and vegetables, as well as cheerful English blooms, and orchards filled with apples, the estate was well able to sustain not only itself, but nearly all of the homes in the vicinity.

The limestone façade was stately without being imposing, the great white pillars that flanked the doors giving it the gravity of a Grecian temple. And indeed, the man the residence contained had the quality of a god.

It was warm inside, always. So much more comfortable than the manor house in Avondale could ever be. Adjacent to the great hall was a great, sweeping staircase with frescos of heavenly bodies painted along the walls and looming overhead. She'd always found it to be slightly intimidating. As if the man were really a god and was thus surrounded by angels.

There were many parties given at Bybee House, though she'd always had the sense the Duke was not the driving force behind them. Or rather, his desire for parties was not. They were something he did, rather, to please his family and to continue maintaining appearances fitting for a man of his status.

The Duke's father was long dead. Hugh Ashforth had assumed the title at twenty and had set about restoring the dignity to his family name that his father had destroyed with a life of debauchery, or so Penny had heard the servants whisper. The Duke's mother remained in residence, along with his much younger sister and his ward.

Penny had grown close to them all. She had never been surrounded by women in such a way. And it was that which had given her such a strong sense of home. Of family.

For the first time in her life she had felt as though she would be part of one in a true sense. But not now.

She shrugged off the brief fear that she might cause a scandal by turning up alone after dark. What did it matter? She was hurtling headlong into a scandal and there was no stopping it.

Lachlan was right.

That she would abandon the engagement of marrying the Duke to marry a soldier—a Scottish soldier—was going to create waves that would roll throughout all of London, if not all of England.

None of it would have mattered had it only been her. But she was betrothed to the Duke of Kendal. That would ensure that the scandal was far-reaching. She was sorry that it would touch him. It would. There was no avoiding it.

And she could not offer a full explanation, not without dragging unsavoury aspects of her father's character into the foreground, and a good portion of the reason she was marrying Lachlan in the first place was to avoid such a thing.

But she wanted to say goodbye. To this man who had never as much as touched her ungloved hand. This man who had made her feel as though she might, on some small level, matter even a little bit.

A man who had given her hope for a future that was softer, more civilised, and warmer than any reality she had yet inhabited.

She blinked back tears. Her throat had felt raw the entire day, as though she was coming down with an illness, though she suspected it was simply despair.

After she knocked on the door, she was ushered inside immediately, her arrival announced promptly.

The Duke was in residence, which was a blessing, she supposed. He could have easily been in London, seeing to business.

She had to wonder if part of her hoped that he might've been, if what she truly wanted was a chance to say goodbye to her friends, his sister and his ward.

Her heart thudded a dull rhythm, echoing in her ears, as she stood in the entry of the home that would have been hers. She gazed at her surroundings with longing.

The lovely marble floors, the walls the colour

of a robin's egg. It was beautiful. Though she ignored those frescoes, because she felt now as if the angels judged her.

But it didn't matter now. It wouldn't be hers. And neither would he.

It wasn't long before the Duke appeared in the entry. He was a tall man, his fine clothing perfectly tailored to suit his athletic figure. A navy coat over a white shirt, buckskin breeches and the finest boots she had ever seen. He was impeccable, even at home.

Though, she supposed she should expect nothing less of him. He was ever mindful of his image. A man in his position never did know when company might arrive.

There was a hardness to his handsome face though, a severity and sternness in his eyes she had never had directed at her before.

She understood at once.

Her father had been here already.

'I needed to speak to you...'

'Without a chaperon?' The note of judgment in his voice was unmistakable.

With the angels looming overhead, he made a thunderous picture. He was the sort of man she'd found it difficult to look at when she'd been on good terms with him. Now, having earned his displeasure, it was nearly impossible.

She took a breath and pushed her fear down

deep. Locked it away. 'I didn't want to rouse Mrs. McCready from her bed, so, no. I felt this was important and it could not wait.'

'And I find propriety to be important. As ever. Regardless of the situation we find ourselves in.' He turned his head slightly. 'Beatrice, perhaps you would like to formally bear witness to this interaction, as a female relative who is lurking in the shadows to eavesdrop on the conversation anyway.'

She heard timid footsteps, and then Lady Beatrice Ashforth appeared from an alcove, her hands clasped in front of her, her expression sheepish. Knowing Beatrice as she did, Penny didn't believe her friend was sheepish at all.

She had first met Beatrice covered in mud and distraught in a field, out exploring without her brother's permission. The Duke of Kendal disliked it when anything moved without his say so.

A sickly child, Beatrice had spent her life being cosseted and overly protected. Prodded by doctors and barred from playing outdoors, exerting herself or upsetting herself. Beatrice did not like to do as she was told.

Beatrice was also loyal to her brother with all that she was.

'I have spoken with the Earl.' His tone was dark and forbidding and she would have never ascribed those words to him before. He had always been polite. Solicitous.

A man who had never taken a liberty beyond taking her gloved hand in his to help her down from a carriage.

Now, she did not know where that man had gone.

'I assume he explained—'

'About your affair with a Scottish soldier?' The words were clipped, short and shocking. 'Yes.'

'My...*what*?'

He had done it. Her father had taken a burning arrow and fired it directly into the fortress of her reputation, not caring at all that it would reduce her to ash. Destroying his reputation would have taken hers along with it, but it was only her... Yes, he was keeping his own hands clean by making it her sin.

She had never thought him cruel, but this was cruel. Or the act of a truly desperate man. But she had never thought he would sacrifice her like this.

She had always felt as though he'd protected her at least.

But it was only ever physically.

He had locked her in that room with her grief when her mother had died, willing to let her sob until she was ill, alone.

This was much the same.

'Do not worry,' he said. 'I have no desire to see

your reputation in tatters. Your upcoming marriage will do that for me.'

And he would not have to sully himself with base gossip. He didn't say it, but it hung there in the air. All of the men involved would manage to stay above it.

The closest he'd come to debasing himself was saying the word *affair* at all. A word that touched on dark, illicit acts that Penny couldn't even form imagery for in her mind.

And he believed she had done it.

That's what happens when you're a chess piece...

'I bid you goodnight,' he said, turning and leaving her.

She could only stare after him, the sound of his footfalls on the marble floor, along with the air of disdain lingering behind long after he was gone.

A piece of her heart withered as he left.

Hope. Extinguished.

The life she'd dreamed of vanishing around her.

If the very walls of the manor dissolved she would not have been surprised in the least.

But they remained. And worse still, so did her friend.

Her friend, who she knew would be...perhaps not her friend now.

Penny turned to Beatrice, who was still standing there, looking pale, large eyed and filled with confusion, hurt. Anger. Beatrice had been her friend these past months, but any kinship they might have shared was gone now. Stolen by Penny's father's lies. And she would have to be content to let the Duke believe them, as contradicting them might cost her father his very life.

Surely Beatrice should know the truth. Beatrice, who had scarcely ever had a Season due to the overprotective nature of her mother and older brother. A childhood spent in ill health had caused all of them to treat her as a rare and fragile flower. Penny knew that Beatrice resented it and yearned for a more normal existence, hence her wanderings in the forest. Penny understood that. The wildness that was deep inside her.

She had thought they recognised it in each other, though they had not brought themselves to speak of it. Penny had been afraid to. If she gave away too much of what she was before her marriage to the Duke...well, she'd been sure he'd find her lacking.

It didn't matter now.

And what she needed in the moment was not the Duke of Kendal. She needed Beatrice's friendship. For she found as she stood there, the thing she grieved the most was the loss of her friend. Beatrice was the first woman she'd ever befriended. She'd been so lonely and having someone else her age to speak to had only ever been a dream until they'd met.

'I had to speak to him,' Penny said softly.

'You don't deserve to speak with him,' Beatrice said, her voice like ice. 'Not ever again. I will never forgive the blow you have dealt my brother's pride.'

'It's not as it seems,' Penny said. 'My father has put me in an impossible position.'

'And I'm certain that your affair with a Scotsman has nothing to do with the impossible position you're in.' She had never known her friend to speak with such acidity.

'Affair?' The truth didn't offer up less humiliation, for her father had left her exposed. Even if she absolved herself of immorality, her friend would know how callous her father had been in this. But she could not let her believe she would have betrayed the Duke. 'Never. I was sold. To pay my father's debt. But my father clearly wishes to put my own reputation on the altar and not his own.'

There was a pause. Beatrice looked at her sceptically. 'Is that the truth, Penelope?'

'I have no reason to lie. The end result is the same either way. And I could not tell your brother. Lachlan Bain...the secrets he knows about my father, the debts my father carries, they could cost him his life. At the very least his home, every last vestige of respectability. And my reputation would go down with it as well.' She felt as if she were on the edge of a void. 'There you have it. I doubt your brother could have truly married me after all. Pieces of the truth would have come forward no matter what. If not from Lachlan, than from somewhere else. Your brother would never marry a woman connected to scandal. There was never any protecting me, I suppose.'

'Isn't it a father's job to protect his children?' Beatrice whispered.

'I don't know.'

'Neither would I. But Hugh has certainly always protected us.'

She nodded, her throat tightening. She wondered when the Duke would have given her permission to call him by his Christian name.

She wouldn't know now. She would never say it.

Hugh.

His name burned bright inside her and it hurt.

'No one has ever protected me,' Penny said.

Not even the Duke, because he had to protect his family, his reputation. But she had loved him and he had not defended her. He had believed the lie because it was easy.

She'd been so certain this was love. But how could it be when it had been bound up in the way she'd felt safe and protected by him? By the way he'd brought her into his family? Now he had removed his protection. All of it.

Every man around her cared for his own ends and never hers.

'Will he hurt you?' Beatrice asked. 'Because if so then your father's reputation can go to the devil. He won't allow it.' She meant her brother and Penny thought it lovely Beatrice believed that. But after seeing the coldness in his eyes... Penny did not. 'He will not allow you to be carried off by a barbarian.'

'I... He's not a stranger to me. As a boy he worked on my father's estate. He's as a stranger now, but I don't believe he would harm me.'

She didn't know. Not for certain.

She thought of the way he had filled the entry hall, all broadness and power, with a sword strapped to his hip and his tartan proclaiming that he was a foreigner in this land. Foreign to her in every way.

She could not say for certain if *that* man might harm her.

But the boy who had helped her with the bird... He would not have harmed her. And perhaps, even if it were buried deep inside him, that boy still existed. She could only pray it was so.

'Please tell Eleanor goodbye. And...explain to her? I couldn't bear the thought of either of you hating me. And that's why I needed you to know.

I have never had friends. The two of you have been the dearest to me. And of all the things that I mourn because of the dissolution of this engagement, that friendship was of the highest value.'

She found herself being pulled into Beatrice's embrace. 'I wish there was something I could do. I could always appeal to Briggs.'

The Duke of Brigham, Hugh's friend, who Penny understood was like a brother to him. He was a notorious rake and every time Penny had been in his company he'd made her smile. But these men…they were second only to the Prince Regent.

They could not understand what it meant to be in her position. Even her father's. They would be shielded by rank. As evidenced by the Duke of Brigham's reputation. That it was spoken of with laughter, not with cruel disdain.

'There's nothing left for me,' she said, feeling pressure gathering behind her eyes. 'My reputation is destroyed. Where would I go?'

Emotion was a knot in her chest and she would not let it unravel. She would not let herself sink into melancholy.

'We could find something…'

She let out a hard breath, though it did nothing to loosen that pressure in her chest. 'At the cost of your reputation, perhaps Eleanor's. I won't allow you to take such a risk.'

She wished she could ask it. But she could not. Not in any good conscience. Finding that centre, that bit of purpose.

'It is enough,' Penny said, 'to know that you would. To know that I had such a friend.'

'Write to me,' Beatrice said. 'Promise.'

'Assuming that a letter can be sent from where I'm going.'

Her friend squeezed her hand and Penny tried not to think about the fact that she knew nothing of where she was headed. If she would just descend back into loneliness the way she had before. She'd had so much hope bound up in her marriage to the Duke. In joining his household and being part of something.

Now her entire future rested in the hands of a man who might as well be a stranger.

A man who was either intent on harming her or bedding her.

And, truth be told, she could not decide which prospect frightened her most.

Obtaining a special licence had been easy enough. Money, that was all it took.

As a boy he'd had wealth. He hadn't realised it was being stolen from the clan. But it hadn't taken the same shape in the Highlands as it did here in England. Or perhaps that was simply a boy's perspective. He'd wanted for nothing. If his stomach growled, food appeared. If he needed clothes, he had them. Warmth, shelter, all of it was there.

It was only as he got older and his father was in the castle less and less, spending money away from their homeland and on drinks and whores in Edinburgh, that he began to realise.

But that didn't matter now. Now, he had the money he needed and in this instance it made the process much shorter and simpler. The reading of the banns could be avoided completely. Which suited Lachlan's purposes. He wanted to publicly humiliate the Earl of Avondale, but he also felt the urge to get back home.

Home.

He had sailed the world over these past years. Had fought on foreign battlefields. His fortune had been earned both in valour there, and in trade on the seas, but he had not gone back to the Highlands.

After the death of his mother there had seemed little point.

He knew that his father would continue on his path. Destroying the once-proud name of their clan, a name that had belonged to Lachlan's mother and was badly used by his father, who had come by his position as chief through marriage. He had squandered any of the wealth the clan had ever possessed, that which was not taken from them already in the uprising.

The rent he had charged the farmers, who were responsible for feeding their people, had been nothing short of criminal. And all so that he could rub elbows with English aristocracy. Lachlan was well aware there were those within his clan who would consider him no less of a traitor, not simply for bearing his father's blood, but because he had fought with England against Napoleon. Because he had worn the uniform of a British soldier.

The uprising had been before Lachlan's time, but there were those who remembered and remembered it well. Lachlan's father was clearly not one of them, as he had taken to the excess of the English peerage with much enthusiasm.

Lachlan's aim was to restore that which had been damaged. He did not know if it were possible.

But when he returned, it would be with money and it would be with a bride.

Not for the first time he wondered if an English bride would cause difficulty, but he had to lay some hope in the idea his clan might see merit in him bringing a Sassenach back to a Scottish castle to live *their* way. For wasn't an English wife evidence that he might just as easily have stayed in England? Particularly one of aristocratic blood.

But she was his trophy. He saw it clearly. He would make his people see it, too.

And he had no intention of carrying on a bloodline. Not with her. Not with *anyone*.

There would be no bairns.

He would fix that which had been damaged. And he would return leadership of the clan to his mother's family when he went to the dirt. His cousin, Callum, had kept the clan going in his absence, even before his father's death. Callum, his children and their descendants, they could rule.

The problem now was resources, so depleted had they become.

He had learned all that he needed about managing industry as he had built his merchant fleet and he had capital enough to invest in his homeland. And his people.

But after that...

It was best if the name Bain died with him.

He was the only surviving child of his parents' union.

That in and of itself seemed a sign.

All of his brothers, dead at infancy, both before and after him. But he had survived.

He had survived childhood and he had survived war, he assumed for this purpose.

So, he would see it done.

It gave him deep satisfaction to go into this English church wearing his tartan. It was true that sentiments had changed regarding Scottish dress and custom, but he still bore the scars of a time when it had not been so readily accepted. His land bore the scars of war he had not seen with his eyes, but had lived through the consequences of all his life.

His loyalty could never entirely be to England. His blood flowed from the Highlands.

He ascended the stairs of the church and pushed the doors to the sanctuary open.

The priest was already in residence.

'And where is the bride?' Lachlan asked.

'She has yet to arrive,' the priest said. 'And when she does, I will want to be sure she is entering into the marriage of her own accord.'

'What a complicated concept,' Lachlan said. 'Do we do anything of our own accord, Father, or is it all some higher power?'

Lachlan himself knew what the highest power was. Money. Greed. In his case perhaps his motivations were honourable, but he did not think it was because he was a superior manner of man to his father.

Rather, just an angry one.

Angry that his mother had been so disgraced she had taken her own life. Angry that the Earl of Avondale had failed to give to him the compensation that was promised and therefore had prevented Lachlan from returning home in time to keep that tragedy from happening.

It was anger that drove him. And a strong sense

of how powerful, wealthy men destroyed the lives of those around them on a whim.

No, Lachlan was not a better man. He was just angry at men like his father. And that did colour his actions.

It was then the doors to the church did open again and his bride appeared. She wore a gown in blue silk, the colour like china making his little bride seem yet more fragile than she had when last he'd seen her. Her hair was tied back simply, something about the style drawing his eye to the elegant line of her neck. To the curves lower still.

It took him a moment to remember the Earl was even there. He was next to her, the distance between the two of them palpable.

'So, you've come,' he said.

'Yes,' she said. 'You made it quite clear that there was no other choice.'

The priest began to speak, as if to object. 'You consent to the marriage now, don't you, lass?'

'I *am* here. I didn't come to attend a service.' He did not know why he was pleased that her sharpness remained.

'There you have it,' Lachlan said to the priest. 'From her own mouth.'

Her father said nothing. Lachlan had thought he couldn't despise the man more, but in that he was proven wrong. The only opposition the Earl had voiced to Lachlan marrying his daughter related to the loss of the connection with the Duke of Kendal. It had nothing to do with Penelope. Her happiness. Her safety.

His own father had not cared a wit for his own either, but Lachlan was a son. He had been born to be hard, born to be a warrior.

A man should offer more protection for his daughter.

He deserved to wonder about her well-being. If he ever would.

He deserved to fear for her.

There were no words of reservation from the Earl. And the priest seemed placated as well, beginning the wedding invocation at once.

Lachlan had attended weddings in the Highlands, as a boy, but he'd never been to one in England. As with all things, he'd made a study of it. Often he found the expectation was that he would be an uneducated brute. He took great pride in proving to Englishmen that he was, in fact, an *educated* brute.

Lady Penelope spoke her vows with a clear voice that verged on defiant. As if she refused to show any sort of weakness. He had to respect her for that.

He had purchased a simple ring. When the time came, he slid it on to her finger. He was surprised by how very soft her hands were. By how fragile she felt.

Such a strong little thing, she was. And yet…

So easily breakable.

'With this ring I thee wed, with my body I thee worship and with all my worldly goods I thee endow.'

There was something in her eyes when he said that. A fleeting shock followed by something akin to fear. Perhaps it was the moment settling over her. The realisation that it was done. For all her bravery could not withstand this moment.

He should not be looking at her face. He should be looking at the Earl. For it was not his bride's fear and loathing that he craved. No. It was her father's. But he found he could not look away from her, from the very real consequence of his revenge.

But he would treat her well and he knew that. He'd given her no indication that he might, but he would.

He was not an abuser of women. No matter how deep his anger, that was something that would not change. And perhaps life in a castle in the Highlands was not the same as life for a duchess in London might be, but she would want for nothing.

Except bairns.

But her hand was still resting in his and her skin was soft, and he had not anticipated being affected by such.

He was a man. He had physical needs and he

dealt with those the way he dealt with all things. As a transaction. Money changed hands and pleasure was shared by both. But he was not looking for softness when he bedded a prostitute. He was looking for the basest, lowest form of release and he found it.

It had nothing to do with soft, delicate hands.

And certainly nothing to do with large eyes that seemed to offer a window to his past life.

The marriage bed was about duty and he would see the marriage consummated as it must be. But a young virgin would have no knowledge of how to please a man. However pretty she might be, she'd hold no candle to the trained whores he was accustomed to.

He had no doubt he would have to seek his pleasure outside of the union. But it was nothing to him. Vows easily spoken that didn't reach his heart.

As he thought of the hollowness of those vows, the marriage was done. Legal before God and, more importantly, recognised by the church.

Which meant it would have to be recognised by all of England.

Avondale's daughter officially belonged to him.

He looked at the man, his face drawn with sorrow and defeat, and a surge of triumph rocked through his chest. She was his.

No longer a pawn to be used by the Earl, Lady

Penelope Hastings belonged to Clan MacKenzie now. Whatever the people thought of his Sassenach bride was no concern of his. He would command their acceptance. For she was his, owed to him by a man and a country that had tried to strip him of his pride. Of all that he was.

She was his token.

His token of fifteen years spent in exile while he earned his way back to his home.

She was his payment.

He could think of nothing more upsetting for the Earl, a man who prized his lineage, a man who had secured such a boon of a marriage, a near miracle really considering his financial status.

And Lachlan had stolen it from him.

And now, he would steal the man's daughter physically as well.

'It is a long journey to the Highlands,' he said.

'What about my…my things, my…?'

'I've had new things purchased for you. Anything you will need is already in the carriage.' Because he would damn well see her taken off from the church in a near-parade that would rival anything the Duke could have provided for her.

He was not a boy any more. Avondale didn't own him. England didn't own him.

His bride didn't move. It was as if she were rooted to the spot. She didn't cling to her father. Her father would have offered her no comfort and he knew she wasn't fool enough to think he might.

'Your carriage waits, Wife,' he said.

Still she did not move.

'Your carriage might wait, but I will not.' He picked her up then, her weight insubstantial. And still he could not quite get over the softness.

She made a noise halfway between a squeak and growl, clinging for a moment to his shirt before releasing her hold on him and going limp, her hands dangling at her sides, her expression one of fury. 'I can walk,' she said, as he began to stride towards the church doors.

'But you weren't.'

'I would have!'

'I was tired of waiting,' he growled, pushing the doors open, early morning sunlight washing over them both.

The carriage was just outside, two shiny black horses, a driver and footman. When he saw Lachlan approaching, the footman scrambled down the side of the carriage and held the door for them. Lachlan deposited Penelope inside and she moved to the far corner, putting as much space between the two of them as possible. 'You were waiting for all of ten seconds,' she said.

'No,' he said, his voice like a stranger's. 'I've been waiting for fifteen years. I will wait no longer.'

Chapter Four

Penny curled deep into the corner of the closed carriage. And she looked across the space—not quite enough space for her peace of mind—at the man who was now her husband.

This man who was a stranger.

She was alone with him. She had never been alone with a man who was not a relative in her entire life. And yet, she was ensconced in this carriage, with this man. Panic clawed at the walls of her chest and she did her best to suppress it.

Fought to envision that little jewellery box. To find a way to lock her panic in there.

It was the vastness of the unknown.

Of what lay ahead with the wedding night itself and…how that was changed by him being the groom.

He was untamed. So very male. Foreign and large and utterly savage.

Everything that lay ahead of her now was unknown.

And that was when it occurred to her. 'Did you bring anything from my father's house?'

He looked at her, his green eyes cool and filled with disdain. 'It is unnecessary,' he said. 'Anything you need will be provided for you.'

'But my... My mother's jewellery box. I want to bring it with me.'

'It is not my concern, lass. I'm hardly going to make a journey back to your father's house for a trinket.'

'That trinket is the only thing I have of hers,' she said, squeezing her eyes shut for a moment. She wasn't afraid she would cry. There was no purpose in crying. It would accomplish nothing. She had trained herself to keep tears back long ago.

But her eyes burned and she felt awash in helplessness.

There was nothing she could do. Nothing to be done, as her father was so fond of saying.

She was being carried away from everything she had ever known and there was absolutely nothing she could do to fight against it. She couldn't fight him. And even if she did, there would be nothing left for her to return to. The Duke of Kendal would offer her no shelter. Her father... Her father had been willing to let her reputation burn. She couldn't go back to him. Her pride prevented it.

Her fate was tied to Lachlan Bain. He was her only protection now. He was all she had.

She did not even have her mother's jewellery box, after all.

'Where are we going?'

'To the Highlands,' he said, as if the question was the most foolish thing he'd ever heard.

'I didn't mean in the long term. I meant to-night.'

Tonight.

The word echoed inside her and she pushed her feelings of disquiet away.

How long would he torture her? How long would he draw all this out?

'We'll head to a coaching inn. I hope you find the carriage to your liking. Because it's a rather long trip to Scotland.'

'I know,' she said. 'What I mean to say is, I am aware that it is quite the trip. I've never been.'

'I thought your father's library was sparse on the subject of Scotland.'

'It is. But there is quite a lot of information on carriage routes.'

'How very interesting.'

'It's not really. But I had exhausted everything else.'

At least now she had some idea of the road they

would travel, the dangers it held and the distance they would traverse. Cold comfort, perhaps, but given all the rest of the unknown that was laid out before her, knowledge of the road felt like no small thing.

She could feel a gap between them and she had to decide what frightened her more. Being near him, or the sheer scope of all that wasn't known.

It was the unknown, she decided. And there was only one way to solve that.

Questions.

'Do you really not have toast? Because it's a very simple thing to make. Only you put the bread on a fork and—'

'I'm not confused as to how to warm bread on a fire,' he said.

'Well. You said you didn't have it.'

'Yes, and somehow I've spent a fair amount of time discussing it.'

'I don't feel this is an unreasonable amount of time given to the subject.'

'I do.'

And with that, the subject ended. She was beginning to think he was lying to her about the food.

'There's no need to be mean,' she said.

'There's no need to be nice either.'

Her lips twitched. Making conversation with him was like trying to talk to a stone. Fortunately, she had quite a bit of practice conversing with stones. Small animals, household staff. A great many things that were not inclined to answer her back.

'I don't know about that,' she said. 'It might make the journey more pleasant.'

He didn't respond to that at all. And she found herself gazing out the window, allowing herself to sink into the rhythm of the carriage. It was quite soothing, as long as she didn't think about where it was carrying her to, and it didn't take long for her to begin to drift off.

When she awoke, the dark was drawing low outside and the carriage had stopped.

There was a large, white-stone building bearing a sign that said Old Crown Coaching Inn, but it might as well have simply read: doom. And perhaps that might be seen as a bit dramatic, but Penny's heart was in her throat and she didn't feel one could be overly dramatic in such a situation.

The door to the carriage opened and the footman reached out as if to help her, but Lachlan moved quickly, exiting the carriage. As Lachlan moved, the footman froze, as if he could tell by his master's bearing that his movements were disapproved of.

The man moved aside and it was Lachlan who reached his hand out to her.

She found it nearly impossible to reach her own hand out to meet his. And that was when she found herself gripped around the waist and lowered slowly down to the ground. His strength was overwhelming. She felt engulfed by it, even after such a brief touch. He was so large and broad, and lifting her seemed no more difficult than lifting that injured sparrow from all those years ago.

She felt a glimmer of hope yet again. And she was as terrified of it as she was in need of it.

Because perhaps, just perhaps, that boy wasn't gone after all.

Because in his strength there was gentleness. Because he had not crushed her in those large hands of his.

She looked up at him and he looked away.

She swallowed hard.

'Come, lass,' he said, making his way towards the door of the inn.

She followed.

He issued orders to the innkeeper as if he were still in the army and the man, small and stooped, obeyed as if it were his commission.

The inn itself was clean, with heavy dark wood tables, filled with people. The beams that ran overhead were the same colour, the darkness lowering the ceiling and giving the place a cosy feel.

'I've never stayed in a place like this before.'

'Never?'

'No. I travelled so infrequently. To London occasionally, yes, but it's only three hours in a carriage, so we never stayed overnight on the road. And when Father wishes to spend time in London we rent a town house.'

Likely the reason they had not been in a couple of years. Her father wouldn't have the funds to rent them a place any more.

The innkeeper led them up a narrow staircase, down the hall, and it was then that the walls began to close in around her. She was headed to a room, a small room, with this very large man and everything was beginning to seem as though it was tilting over on to its side.

The door to the room opened and against the back wall was a bed that seemed far too small, made of the same heavy wood as everything else in the place. There was also a chair and a small table.

'I will see to my men and the horses,' Lachlan said. 'And that you're brought some dinner.'

With that, he left the room and she could breathe again.

Maybe she would get a reprieve tonight.

Even as the thought entered her mind, she was certain it wasn't true. Lachlan had no reason to offer reprieve.

She understood it was the way of things. She'd had a brief, short conversation on the subject with the Duchess, but it hadn't satisfied her curiosities. Penny had asked her one afternoon. She'd been a bit nervous, but nerves always made words come easier for her.

The older woman had seemed taken aback for a moment, but then had sat her down and looked at her with kind, grey eyes.

'You were such a small thing when your mother died, weren't you?' she'd asked.

Penny had confirmed it with a mute nod of her head and a pit of disquiet in her stomach.

'She didn't have the chance to speak to you. To tell you what would be required of a wife.'

'I tried to find out, but the servants wouldn't answer my questions. There is precious little in books and I'm very curious about—'

'You'll be fine, my dear,' she'd said, squeezing Penny's hand tightly. 'It is the natural way of the world and while knowledge might do something to ease your nerves, it is not required.'

'Is it not?' she'd asked, feeling unsettled that the one person she might have been able to question didn't seem to think Penny needed much in the way of answers. 'Only I feel that there is so much to learn and I want to know so I can be better prepared.'

Penny liked to hoard knowledge. It was her one source of power. She felt quite cross at her father for not keeping books on the subject.

The Duchess had patted Penny's hand, her expression cool, but the colour in her cheeks had mounted, betraying a small bit of discomfort. 'Men, well, you know, my dear, men are physical creatures and of course they come to the marriage bed with the benefit of experience.'

Penny had found that to be a source of deep irritation. But she'd said nothing.

'He will know what to do,' Her Grace whispered. 'If you find yourself in distress, simply think of something pleasant to pass the time. You are doing your duty as a wife and that's a thing to be pleased over. You might think of ways you can rearrange the household, as it will be yours.'

Penny had not found that at all reassuring.

She found it even less reassuring now because she could not think of anything pleasant in the presence of Lachlan Bain. There was no household to ponder rearranging. Even if there were, it wouldn't be enough to blot out his strength and outrageous maleness.

She hated not having a plan.

She nearly laughed. What plan could she possibly have? She'd been married off to a man she'd known only as a child. A stranger. She was going to Scotland when she'd been meant to go to the estate down the lane from the one she'd spent her life in.

She was supposed to be a duchess.

And now she'd been married off to a…to a barbarian.

He would claim his husbandly rights and she didn't know what it would entail. She didn't know how to manoeuvre herself into an active position in this situation.

He had all the power. And while enduring was a particular talent of Penny's…

She was still utterly terrified.

She felt vulnerable in a way she hadn't since childhood. Of all the things she resented, she perhaps resented that most of all.

She wrung her hands, pacing the room. But then a maid from the kitchen appeared, spiced wine and stew on a tray, which she set down on the table and left with a curtsy.

Penny found that though she was distressed, she was ravenous, and the stew, which was accompanied by a thick slice of bread, was very welcome indeed.

But when she was finished eating, it settled in her stomach like lead. She paced around for a moment, not sure what to do, then it occurred to her that she should probably get ready for bed while he was not in the room.

Of course, she didn't have anything to sleep in.

She didn't have a nightdress and was meant to be sharing a room with a man, and she felt as if she might actually expire from concern.

She stood there, rooted to the spot. The idea of taking off her dress, of stripping herself down to her chemise and letting her hair loose, knowing he would see her...

He would see more than that.

The heavy door to the room opened, this time with no knock, and Lachlan stood there, his massive frame dominating the doorway. On his shoulder, he carried a trunk.

'Tired?' he asked.

'Just a bit,' she said, her voice more of a croak.

She felt as though her feet had been cursed. Transformed into iron weights that kept her fixed to that exact space in the centre of the room.

When Lachlan entered, she wanted to move away from him, but found she could not.

'I told you, I had some things sent ahead.' He set the trunk down near her. 'Clothes for the journey. A nightdress. I assume you'll be wanting one.'

'I'm quite comfortable at the moment,' she said, curling her fingers into fists.

Her dress suddenly felt heavy and ill-fitting, her skin itchy. She was not comfortable in the least. But there was no nightdress, no matter how soft, that would fix her current situation.

He nodded once. 'As you wish.'

With heavy steps he crossed the room and went to stand by the bed, his back to her. Then he began to remove his clothes. The flame from the oil lamp nearest to him flickered, the light touching his muscles as he stripped the white shirt from his body.

She couldn't look away.

She knew that she should. Except…should she? They were married. And this was marriage. That he would remove her dress and he would… He would cover her, the way that she had seen animals do. She shivered, fighting against fear.

No matter that she had told herself it might not occur, she had known that it would. This bed was a marriage bed by virtue of the fact that they had said vows today. There was no getting around that. She was not a child and she knew the way of things. The way of this.

She knew the mechanics and purpose, as it applied to animals, and she knew it was much the same way for humans. Though her mind couldn't make sense of how those things shifted between man and woman, rather than stallion and mare.

She knew it was a woman's duty to produce children in a marriage. To be available to her husband in the ways he demanded. She might not know the specifics of those demands, but she knew that much.

The truth was, a woman in her position was required to be innocent in order to be desirable. In order to be the sort of woman who would be deemed worthy of marrying a man and bearing his children. A woman in her position's entire life centred on this act. If anyone thought she might have done it without the proper vows being spoken, then her entire life would be ruined. If she failed to secure a husband, then her body would be the currency by which she secured her protector.

And it was considered inappropriate for her to know the details of the act itself.

It suddenly seemed desperately and wholly unfair. Had her mother been alive, she would have asked her why it was the way of the world.

But her mother was dead. And as her father was so fond of saying: there was nothing to be done.

This man was her protector. And this was the cost of that protection.

But she found she couldn't simply think her way through this. She couldn't push her feelings away or lock them up tight.

Worse than the fear, she found she was transfixed by him. By all the unknown that he represented. By this wild and unyielding bend in her life's road that she had never seen coming.

She would have been a wife in only a month's time, but to another man. These were mysteries that would have been answered for her soon, but she had a feeling it would have been different than what was about to transpire with Lachlan.

But she didn't know enough about it, enough about men to know how.

Except she had felt the safety with the Duke that she did not feel here.

Because Lachlan had a wildness that radiated from the very centre of all that he was.

A wildness that stood in stark contrast to that cloistered upbringing of hers.

He was everything that she had learned to turn away from. Everything that she had spent her life repressing. For she had learned to spend her life walking an invisible, narrow cobbled street and if she took a turn off it, it was only when she was away from the sight of her father.

Whenever she felt an emotion that was too large, she shut it away. Whenever she had a burst of energy that would be too loud, she pushed it down.

She had the feeling that Lachlan Bain never pushed down a thing.

He turned then, not moving his hands to the kilt that he wore over the lower half of his body. She could see his whole chest, those broad shoulders, muscles that spoke of hard labour. A strange thing, how fascinating such a thing could be.

A simple physical feature like muscles.

He was a man and therefore physically stronger than she. He did labour, therefore, he had developed that strength.

These were easy lines to draw, yet there was a response that it created inside her body that had absolutely nothing to do with these facts. It was all simple appreciation for his form that made her stomach feel warm and her limbs feel languid.

How could she feel that and fear at the same time?

And she was still unable to move.

'Do you need help preparing for bed?' His voice was much softer than she had heard it before.

'I…'

'You've a lady's maid at home, have you not?'

'Yes,' she said.

'And usually she helps you get ready for bed?'

'Of course.' Her gown had tiny buttons down the back. Getting out of it on her own would be a graceless pursuit.

'I'll be assisting you, lass.'

He crossed the small space, coming perilously close to her as he bent and opened the trunk. From it he produced a simple, white night shift and a beautiful ivory hairbrush, far finer than anything she'd ever owned before.

'Sit,' he said, gesturing to the vanity that was shoved against the back wall.

And for some reason, now, her feet were capable of movement. And slowly carried her to that vanity, where she sat as he'd commanded.

She could see him behind her, large and impossibly broad. And she could see the reflection of her own fear looking back at her. Her eyes wide, dark half-moons beneath them as though someone had bruised them.

When he touched her, she jumped. Her lips parted and she despised the woman in the mirror. The woman who looked so fragile, so upset by the moment.

But his touch was gentle and it was clear he did not want her fear.

Something about that realisation made her shoulders relax. He said nothing as he began to remove the pins from her hair, curling locks falling down over her shoulders in golden waves.

'Aye,' he said, the word full of rough approval. 'I thought your hair would be a glory.'

He said the words as if to himself and not to her. They did not seem to require a response, so she did not give one. He lifted his hand, the ivory brush clutched tightly, looking far too delicate in a fist that she knew could easily wield a broadsword. Brute strength, leashed, as he began to comb her golden curls.

Her heart fluttered uncontrollably and she felt pain. Real, undeniable pain radiated through her.

For when had someone last been tender with her? She'd had a lovely governess for a while.

And she'd had a calm, soothing voice. She didn't like to think of her, because losing her had hurt.

She'd gone away because the money had gone away.

All the care she'd experienced since the death of her mother had been bought and paid for.

And now her father had…he'd paid a debt with her and it was as though the floor had become the ceiling, to experience this, from him.

She had expected him to be rough. Callous. Uncaring.

He was such a large man. He could easily kill her with a firm press of his thumb to her throat. He had made it no secret he was angry. That he hated her father.

This was not what she had expected. And more than that, she had not expected her own response to it. A deep ache that made her chest feel as if it was being torn in two.

He was compromising every wall she'd built up inside herself. She was stronger than this. She'd had to be. She'd cried all the tears out of her body when her mother had died.

And then there was him.

She hadn't cried when Lachlan had gone. She'd already let go of tears then. But he had given her a sense of friendship she hadn't experienced before she'd met him, and at nine his departure had left her devastated.

That he'd come back into her life only to destroy it, only to break barriers she'd built in part because of him, made her want to lash out.

She didn't want his care.

His care had mattered when she'd been a girl. And he'd left.

It didn't matter why. He didn't care for her, why should she care at all for him?

'I loved him,' she said, the words tumbling out of her mouth. 'Just so you know.'

Thinking of the Duke made her feel calm for a moment. Safe.

Until she forgot he was no longer her ally.

His home was no longer her haven.

His family would no longer be hers.

'No concern of mine,' he said. 'It's not your love that I'll be wanting tonight.'

'And you don't mind if my affections are with another man?'

'I have a hard time believing it's him you'll be thinking of. And it's not love that will make you cry out with pleasure.'

His words sent an arrow of sensation down low in her stomach. She didn't understand what her pleasure had to do with anything. She only knew enough about male jealousy and possession to know that it might bother him if she loved the Duke. 'My heart is with Hugh,' she said, his name feeling a strange impertinence on her lips.

'Aye,' he said. 'But your body's with me.'

The words felt a betrayal of the tender act of him combing her hair. Yet he kept on, his movements not coming any more hurried, not shifting into anything rougher.

She hated it. She wanted him to be angry.

It was easier to stand strong against anger.

'Beautiful,' he murmured as he parted her hair and shifted it over her shoulders so that it hung long and curling below her breasts. Then he began working on the small buttons on the back of her gown, letting the fabric go slack, then fall to her waist. It revealed her stays. Left one less barrier between them.

Her heart pounded a thick and heavy rhythm in her throat.

She fought to hang on to her anger, but fear… and something that felt closer to curiosity, rolled through her, beginning to eclipse it.

'Do you know of what happens between a man and a woman?' he asked, his voice rough.

'I know everything,' she said, keeping her chin tilted upward, her eyes steady with the mirror. She would not look at him.

And she would not give in to weakness.

'*Everything?*' His words held a hint of mockery. 'That is quite a lot.'

'I told you,' she said, the words wooden. 'I love another man.'

Perhaps if he believed she was ruined he would send her away. Ruined was the worst thing a woman could be, after all. Ruined was one thing you must never be, as then a man would not want you.

Lachlan did not react.

'I see,' he said. 'Then I shall expect you to teach me a few tricks. I have been to some of the finer whores that England has to offer, but I dare say not even they know everything.'

She shivered, disquiet moving down her spine like a wave.

His hands moved to the front of her body, where he unlaced her stays with steady hands and threw the small garment aside, leaving her in nothing but her chemise.

Rough hands went to her shoulders and the garment went down, only her hair covering her breasts. Her entire back was bare and she could feel the heat of him against her skin like a roaring fire.

'I will make a bargain with you,' he said. 'I'll not punish you for your lies. And I'll not treat you as you're asking to be treated. Because it's clear to me that you are nothing more than a frightened virgin and you don't know what it is you're tempting.'

'And what is my portion of the bargain?' she asked, the words barely a whisper.

'Your body.'

It felt an impossible ask.

'We're strangers,' she said.

But that was as close as she could bring herself to ask that he postpone the act. She knew the duties of a wife. She knew what was expected of her. He might not be the husband that she had anticipated, but he was the husband she had.

She knew there were no negotiations to be had. Not here.

Rough hands went to her bare waist and she waged a battle within herself against the desire to run. Against the desire to lean into his touch. She fought to remain still.

'We are not,' he said. 'I helped you save a bird.'

She had nothing to say to that.

No man had ever touched her like this. No man had laid his hands upon her bare skin.

And now these rough warrior's hands were resting against such an intimate part of her. She felt dizzy with it.

With those strong hands, he guided her upwards so that she was standing. Then he pushed her gown down her body, letting all of it fall to the floor.

He did something very unexpected after that.

He growled.

The sound rumbling in his chest, vibrating through her.

Her entire body went cold, then hot. Shame rioting through her.

She felt exposed and terribly afraid.

She was afraid to look at her reflection in the mirror because the woman there would be naked. While her hair might be concealing her breasts, the rest of her was terribly exposed. She didn't want to look at his reflection either. Didn't want to see him impossibly tall and ferocious behind her.

He moved closer to her and she could feel the heat and strength of his body. One hand was still on her waist and it moved, making its way around to her stomach, where he spread his fingers wide and pulled her back against him.

He was solid and hot like a furnace. He bent his head down and pressed a kiss to the back of her neck.

A shocked sound escaped her lips and heat radiated from where his mouth had touched, like the spark from a fire had landed on her skin.

She felt strange. Lightheaded. And then those rough hands moved over her skin, his calluses brushing over her stomach as he shifted and pressed another kiss against her, this time below the first.

Pinpricks of sensation broke out over her body.

His words echoed inside her. Pleasure.

She had never heard pleasure connected with

this act. Not for women. She knew that men were not supposed to be held responsible for their desires. But even then, it wasn't presented as pleasure as much as a natural instinct that could not be denied.

But he spoke of pleasure as if that was something she could expect. As if it were something that mattered.

And it didn't feel bad, the press of his hands on her. His mouth to her skin.

It didn't feel bad at all.

She could feel her nipples grow tight and a restless ache began to build between her legs. She looked up at the mirror and her eyes caught his. There was a black flame in those green depths and it startled her. She looked away, but it was no better, because she caught her own reflection in the mirror then. Golden hair cascading over her breasts, her slim exposed midsection with his large, dark hand resting there possessively. The pale thatch of curls just below.

Her heart was thundering wildly, threatening to gallop right out of her chest.

'Perhaps you don't know everything?' he asked.

She said nothing to that. She found strong arms wrapping themselves around her body, her bare skin against his naked chest. Then he lifted her off the ground as if she weighed nothing. 'You are my wife,' he said, the word filled with an intent sort of possessiveness.

She found herself being carried over to the bed, deposited in the centre of it. This was it. It would be it. That part that came with roughness and heaving, which she had of course witnessed between horses.

But he did not cover her. Instead, he stood back and looked down on her.

She fought the urge to cover herself, because again, she despised that fear. She didn't want to show him that she felt vulnerable. She wanted to find a way to go inside herself. To think of something pleasant. To remain passive and to keep herself from reacting. It seemed a better thing than weeping, which was what she truly wanted to do.

With methodical hands he divested himself of the kilt. There was nothing beneath it.

His male member stood out from his body, large and thick, and she knew that was meant to go inside her body and she had no idea how she was supposed to accommodate such a thing.

It didn't seem possible. Couldn't be possible.

But hadn't Her Grace said all a woman had to do was lie back?

That *he* would know what to do?

She had never heard of a woman being torn asunder on her wedding night, so she supposed she was in no more danger of it than anyone else.

Though, he was Scottish. And it was entirely possible he was simply larger than most men. Entirely possible that an Englishwoman was not made to accommodate such…vast maleness.

But when he came down on to the bed, he was beside her and reached out, taking a strand of her hair between his thumb and forefinger. It was not what she had expected. He looked at her, those eyes intense, and she felt she would have rather he'd simply done what he needed to and got it over with.

It seemed preferable to this. This long stretch of time, this suspended moment of agony where her innocence remained and her questions were only half-answered, taking her closer to truths that were hidden from her, without revealing them entirely.

'Put your hands on me,' he said.

'I…'

He wrapped one large hand around her wrist and brought it to his chest. His skin was hot, his heart raging beneath. He had hair on his body. She could feel her own heart thundering the same rhythm in response. But he wasn't nervous, surely. So why was his heart working in time with hers?

He made that same growling sound he'd done before, then he lowered his head.

His lips had never touched hers. Her lips had never touched anyone's.

His mouth was firm and masterful, slow, coaxing movements instructing her where words would have failed. He angled his head and then he did the strangest thing of all. He slipped his tongue between her lips.

She gasped and drew back. 'I don't think that's a done thing.'

He chuckled, the sound strained. 'It is. Believe me, it is.'

'But *why*?'

'You have to let me show you.' He brought his mouth back to hers again and this time, when his tongue parted her lips, she did not pull away. This time, she allowed him to lead with a slick, startling rhythm. Like a waltz. And she was lost.

Her skin felt hot, her body flushed as if she was sick.

But she didn't have time to think about it too long, because then he brought his hand to her breast, his calloused thumb moving over the tightened bud there.

It created a restless ache in her that no one had told her about. Was this what he meant? Was this the pleasure?

'I was told…' She tried to catch her breath. 'I was told that I was supposed to think of household chores during this act.'

'I thought you were going to think of your man?'

Her man? It took her a broad space of time to

remember who he was speaking of, because the only man in her mind was the one in this room. The one whose hands were creating dark magic inside her.

'His mother said I should think of duty.'

'I'll have you think of me,' he said.

His mouth went down over hers again, this time rougher. Harder. Deeper.

Everything he was doing, everything he made her feel, didn't seem as though it should be possible. Ladies did their duty and that was all.

It was men who had appetites.

Yet he made her feel hungry.

That's what it was like. Hunger pangs. But in low, intimate spaces.

Then he moved his hand, settled it between her thighs and she arched her hips up off the bed, trying to escape him. But he was too strong. He moved his fingers between her feminine crease, with startling ease. She was slick there. Wet.

It made her feel a blooming sense of heat and shame and she didn't even know why.

He felt no shame. His hands were sure and he began to move his thumb in slow, decisive circles. And she was lost. Lost in the pagan rhythm that he created there. She could no longer resist, could no longer find shame in the fact that he was a stranger and the fact that her body was responding in ways she hadn't known were possible. Somewhere, in the gauzy, confused mists of her mind, she realised that everything she'd ever been told about being a woman was a lie.

This was why women fell.

This was why there was such concern about ruination. It wasn't about a simple, accidental step into a darkened alcove. No. It was about the temptation that might wait there. She hadn't realised that. Because the way it had all sounded, it seemed a woman could not be tempted.

But his hands were temptation. His wicked mouth was temptation.

His muscles were a temptation. They were not simply a physicality. They were magic.

A sort of magic of masculinity that called to the feminine in her.

It went so much deeper than societal roles. So much deeper than body parts.

She felt something building inside her, foreign and delicious, and she found herself moving her hips in time with his fingers, chasing that nameless sensation inside her.

It was like a bowstring, pulled taut. And it stretched and stretched until she was certain it could go on no longer.

And that was when the release came. And she soared.

There was a great, gasping sound in the room and it took ages for her to figure out that it was coming from her own mouth. That *she* was the desperate, whimpering creature she could hear as if from a distance. That she was clinging to him as though he might anchor her to earth. She was shattered. And she didn't know if she would ever be able to be put back together.

He said nothing. He only regarded her with those eyes. Then he shifted his touch between her legs and breached her, one finger sliding deep inside. The invasion was strange, but not painful. Until he added a second finger to the first and she found herself gasping for breath.

'Best to make sure you're as ready as you can be,' he said, his voice rough.

She felt a flutter of terror in her breast, but then he had moved and was over her, the blunt head of that most masculine part of him where his fingers had been only a moment before. She nearly cried out in protest, but then his hips surged forward and she cried out in pain as he entered her.

This was what she had expected. And everything that had come before had been a cruel trick. This was why a woman needed to lie back and think of housekeeping. Because nothing could have prepared her for the pain she felt at his invasion.

Her eyes stung with tears.

Tears.

She fought to hold them back because she would not give this man her tears. But he had invaded her.

Why did any woman *ever* fall?

Was it because of the promises made with masculine hands that were not kept with masculine members? She wiggled against him, fighting it. Fighting against him. Because it was better than crying. She would not cry.

He made a low sound, comforting, as if he were trying to steady the horse. And she bucked against him in anger because she was not a horse and refused to be soothed.

'It will get better,' he said.

It wouldn't. He was lying. But he didn't move, his body resting heavily atop her, his hands pinning her wrists down to the mattress. She began to settle, the tears that had been threatening to spill from her eyes receding. And along with it, the pain.

She slowly began to grow accustomed to the size of him inside her.

And then, inexplicably, as she grew accustomed to him, she felt something more.

Not pleasure, not like before, but a strange sensation of being bonded.

She could not remember the last time she'd been held by another person. Not until he had lifted her in those strong arms and brought her to the bed. And now he was surrounding her. Now he was in her.

She had been lonely. So lonely for so long. And the only end to that loneliness that she had seen was through her marriage to the Duke. She had ached so much to belong to that household filled with wonderful women she could talk to. Whom she could confide in. Women who might understand her, who would not make her keep all that she was locked away in a box inside her heart.

But how could she be lonely like this?

There was no way to be closer to another human. Nothing separated them. Nothing. Even their breath mingled together as he stared down at her.

And he would give her children.

The thought made her heart lift.

The thought of having the Duke's children had made her happy. Of having a family. But he'd come with family and so part of that need had been fulfilled with them. Lachlan…

She'd been certain she'd been facing a future of unimaginable loneliness, but she had not thought of children.

She could still have that. That connection. She could be a mother.

The idea made her ache.

She'd lost her mother when she'd been a girl

and she could never have a mother's arms hold her again.

But she could hold a child.

Could offer comfort. Care. Love.

Could give all those soft, painful emotions that had spent years building inside her, locked away.

For the first time she thought perhaps this was not the prison sentence she had first imagined it to be.

Then he cupped her face and kissed her.

It was sweet. It was sweet and deep and tender, and she relaxed into it. Into him. It was wonderful. Those kisses.

Only moments before she hadn't understood. But she did now. This restless, deep need to be as close as possible.

And when he began to move inside her, she found it didn't hurt.

Rather it built a slow, aching rhythm somewhere deeper than the one that had come before.

He gripped her face, kissing her deeply, before pressing his forehead hard against hers, his movements becoming unrestrained. Gone was the tenderness of only a moment before. And somehow... Somehow it seemed right.

Because this wasn't sweet or tender. It was primal and it was quite the most intimate thing two people could share. She found herself arch-

ing to meet his every thrust, found herself moving against him, shamelessly.

Shameless.

Had she ever been shameless in all her life?

No.

She had always fought against her nature.
Against all that she was.

She had spent so much of her youth wanting to
disappear. And everything in her was wrong for
the life she'd been forced to lead. The daughter of
a man who wished her invisible...who wished her
gone instead of his wife, that much was certain.

Everything she was. Everything within her
was shame.

But not now. Not with *him*.

And when the cry of pleasure rose up in her
chest, she did not push it down. She did nothing
to silence it. She let herself shudder gloriously
and held nothing back.

He pulled away from her and she clung to his
shoulders. He shuddered against her, his breath
hot against her neck, as he seemed to find a release similar to her own, culminating in a feeling
of warmth on her skin. And then he pulled her
against his body for a brief moment, dropping a
kiss to her forehead, the moment unexpectedly
tender, but all too brief. Before she could revel in
the simple touch, he released her.

'Sleep,' he said, getting out of bed.

His departure felt abrupt and a personal insult, somehow.

'What?' She felt shattered and dishevelled and had no earthly idea what had just happened.

'I need to be sure everything is prepared for tomorrow. We leave early. Sleep.'

'You won't stay?'

'You don't need me.'

He began to collect his clothes and she could only lie there on the bed, watching as he did.

Now the shame was back. She felt small and wrong somehow, because certainly had she done right he would want to stay with her.

Then she felt angry that she would care at all. Why did she want him to stay? She didn't know him or care about him in any way. And what had happened between them wasn't...

It wasn't knowing someone.

And it was certainly nothing large enough to take away a lifetime of shame and loneliness. She had been foolish to think otherwise. Even for a moment.

He left her there and she curled in on herself, doing her very best to try to press her shattered pieces back together.

She hadn't known.

She hadn't known that the physical act between a husband and wife could take you up to the stars and then—back down to the rocks just as quickly.

That a moment of deep connectedness could leave you feeling lonelier than you ever had before.

It made her despise him. More than she had before.

Because he had shown her pleasure.

And then he had taken this new, fragile thing he had built inside her and broken off pieces of it. He had stolen her protection. Stripped her bare and made her vulnerable. Nearly brought her to tears.

She was strong and knew how to protect herself against all manner of things.

But he was a storm. And against him she had no defence.

She would have rather he'd been cruel.

She would have rather he'd made it harsh and painful, and nothing more.

He had made her feel.

Sensations that were too big to be contained. That could not be shoved down inside her.

And it was then she realised that he had withdrawn from her in such a way that pregnancy would be prevented.

The darkness and a sense of isolation crushed down on her.

He had taken something from her. And he had given the possibility of nothing back.

She lay there with her eyes dry and her heart thudding a full, defeated rhythm.

And her last thought before going to sleep was that he had compromised her ability to lock her emotions down inside herself. And if that were true, she had no idea how she would survive her marriage to Lachlan.

No idea at all.

Chapter Five

He'd thought his conscience long destroyed, but the woman had made him feel like a brute. And his intentions to simply claim the wedding night quickly had been dissolved by that wide-eyed, delicate look. He had walked into the room and she had been standing there, like a woman lost to herself, and sensation he had not known he possessed the power to feel had turned inside him.

She was an instrument in his revenge and nothing more. But she seemed much more a woman, a person, separated from her father and all he represented, and he took no joy in her fear.

Grown men had trembled in his presence and he'd taken lives on the battlefield. He was not so small a man he needed to find strength in the fear of a woman.

He felt much more inclined towards giving her pleasure.

And why not? he'd asked himself. She was his wife. He had been long without a woman, between his last voyage, and his determination to take himself straight to Penny's father once he had decided his course. Why not take his pleasure with her as he chose and not simply dispense her of her virginity as quickly as possible?

He might be accustomed to treating sex as a transaction between a man and a woman, but in that sense he had always felt the transaction should be equal. Women were capable of feeling desire and satisfaction in the same way he was. He had always found it unsatisfying to leave them without it. It was true some whores were jaded and didn't wish to release themselves in that way, but then he felt that was a choice.

Still, he'd found many were happy to make it an indulgence and he was always more satisfied for it.

So why should he not afford the same courtesy to his wife? Why should she not feel pleasure? It was clear to him that the idea of physical pleasure between a man and a woman was foreign to her. That it was something she had not considered to be possible.

It was the shifting in his chest that had occurred after they'd come together that had sent him to the stables. Pacing around in the cold might do him some good.

One of his men, William, was sleeping on the floor, a blanket tugged up under his arms, his head lolled to the side. Lachlan nudged him with the toe of his boot.

'Captain?' the man asked, waking quickly.

They had been soldiers together. Neither of them slept very deeply. Wakefulness was instantaneous for those who had spent years on frozen battlefields littered with enemies and bodies.

'I need you to go back to the lass's house. You must collect some things for me. Meet us at the next inn.'

William stood, nodding grimly, and if he were exhausted or resentful of the order, he did not show it.

Lachlan had earned the loyalty of his men in battle, and, to those who had no home or family, he had offered them work after. Some remained on the ships, some were returning to Scotland with him.

They would be welcomed into the clan. He would make sure of it. It was an oath he'd sworn to those who had left the Highlands, as he had. Some of those men no longer had clans to return to, poverty and skirmishes destroying all that was left behind.

He would not leave them in England. They had become his men on the battlefield, united in fighting for a country they had no allegiance to. He would bring them back to where they belonged.

'Yes, Captain.'

'When we are back home,' he said to the other man, 'I will be Laird to you. Not captain.'

'Yes, Laird,' the other man said, inclining his head.

Lachlan gave his instructions, then spent more time than was strictly necessary evaluating his horse, the one who would carry him from here to Scotland. The carriage team they would change out at every coaching inn, but not his horse.

Perhaps his disquiet came from the fact he had never been with a woman who was innocent.

He preferred jaded women. Their souls matched.

Women who had experienced little good in the world, who had been given nothing in the way of comfort. And for a time, together, they could find a bit of warmth. A bit of pleasure.

Penny needed something more from him and he did not know quite what it was. Even more, he wasn't certain why he felt compelled to give it.

She was not a weeping, delicate female. She surprised him. Through all of this, she had never once dissolved.

But there had been something in the way she had responded to his touch. Her shock, her shame. She hadn't known her body could feel such things, that much had been apparent by the way she had responded.

It had done something to him. Had made something inside him feel as though it might be new, too. He didn't want that.

He hadn't asked for any of it.

He hadn't asked to pity his little wife.

Or care at all about her bird.

Or her box.

He busied himself with plans and strategies he did not require until he was ready to collapse from lack of sleep. Only then did he return to the room upstairs. Only then did he allow himself to lie on the bed beside her, staying atop the blankets rather than joining her beneath them.

She looked small and vulnerable. And one thing he determined then.

He would protect her. With his sword, if need be. He would protect her from any enemy that she might face. What he did not know was if he possessed the power to protect her from himself.

Penny awoke the next morning, feeling more exhausted than when she'd fallen asleep. Her body ached in strange places and, when the maid brought a bowl with warm water and a pitcher into the room, her face burned with shame. As if the other woman knew why she might feel the need to cleanse. Naturally, she likely would.

The burning in her face persisted as she washed herself—intimately—before she dressed.

There was a bit of blood on the cloth she used. Which led her to go and look at the sheets. A bit of blood there as well.

Emotion pushed against her throat. She felt very alone. And Lachlan wasn't there. She knew that he'd come back. She had felt him lie upon the bed and had waited for him to put his hands on her again, but he had not.

She had drifted in and out of sleep. When she had finally awoken when the sun pierced through the small window of the room, he wasn't there.

She went through the trunk he had brought up and found a blue dress, new stays and a new chemise as well.

With no small amount of contortion she managed to get herself buttoned into the garment. There was also a bonnet, with a navy ribbon that matched the dress, and a rich wool overcoat of the same shade.

She arranged her hair simply, reusing the pins he had removed last night, and she examined herself, trying to see if she looked as different as she felt. She could see no mark of what had passed between them last night, but her soul felt branded.

Scalded.

As if he had been attuned to her movements, the door opened then.

He appeared, large and intimidating as ever, and ready for the day.

If he was affected by last night's intimacy, he did not show it. She had no idea how she was meant to ride in a carriage with him having been close to his body the way she'd been. It was as if she could feel him now. Pressed against her. Even with all the space between them.

She felt the building pressure between her thighs and had never been angrier at her own body than she was now, for the way it responded to him. She reminded herself, grimly, of that pain and loneliness that had accompanied the act.

Her body could remember only the pleasure.

She was forced again to grudgingly admit that this was why women allowed themselves to be ruined.

She had been told of the innocence of women. That they bore children, that they were the fairer sex in all ways. That they possessed an innate purity that men never would. It was women's job to steady their urges.

What tripe. How could she steady his urges when she couldn't master her own?

'We should be on our way,' he said, the first words spoken to her since he had left her last night. She didn't know what she expected from him. She had no right to expect anything. She didn't know why she felt gravely disappointed, why she felt restless and lonely and empty. She had never been told to expect more from marriage and her dreams regarding her union with the Duke of Kendal had centred around the female companionship she might find in his house. It was such a strange thing, because she had thought the Duke so beautiful. Because her heart had ached, but not after *him*, she realised now. After all that had come with him.

After what he had represented.

A softness and comfort she had never known. A warm house that was filled with people who cared for each other, rather than an old manor house that was always cold, containing two family members who did not know how to speak to each other.

Her sense of what her future might hold had been heavily influenced by those surrounding fantasies, but she had not known to dream of what her marriage itself might contain. A life living in that household, but not a life knowing a man as deeply as she realised one did know a husband.

Except, she didn't know him. She knew little about him, yet he had seen her in a state that no one else ever had. She knew next to nothing about him, yet she had touched his body in a fashion she couldn't fathom touching another. In a fashion she wouldn't have been able to fathom touching him had it not occurred.

It was disorientating to say the least.

When all her things were packed away she found herself being bundled into the carriage. He did not join her.

'What are you doing?' she asked, sticking her head out the window.

'I'm riding,' he said. 'Have no patience for sitting in a carriage that many hours.'

'I'm going to be alone for the duration?'

'You may occupy yourself with whatever you like.'

'I haven't got anything to occupy myself, if you will recall. I did not bring any of my things. I haven't a book.'

'I believe the woman who helped assemble your trunk included needlepoint.'

She quite liked needlepoint, but she didn't want to give him the satisfaction of knowing that. 'I would prefer nature writings on the flora and fauna of Scotland.'

'You won't be needing a book. I can instruct you.'

'But you won't be in the carriage with me.'

'And we'll not be in Scotland today.'

With that, the conversation ended.

* * *

They pushed themselves further that day than they had the first and, by the time they arrived at the inn, she was exhausted and her nerves were frayed. He did not help her get ready for bed, rather he sent a maid up to assist her, though Penny knew she could have done without.

She lowered all the lamps, save one by the door, and got into bed.

She couldn't sleep. She wondered if he would come to bed. She was angry, because she was so tired, but she found herself on edge, waiting for the man.

How could she sleep knowing that she might have an experience like she had the night before? Not being certain?

It had been altering and much as though someone had taken small scissors to the places where she was stitched together, snipped them all out and she was waiting to be made anew.

She didn't know if a reprieve was the answer, or if his touch might be.

She was resentful that he had suddenly become the largest thought in her head.

She hadn't chosen this. She hadn't chosen him.

And he consumed her all the same. Had burst through her defences in a way that she hadn't foreseen and she hated it. She needed to find a way to remake herself.

And silence had only ever been her enemy.

The door opened then and there he was. She shivered. She couldn't help but react.

He began to strip off his clothes, the dim light from the single lantern playing tricks with light and shadow over that warrior's body.

She had been so overwhelmed by him last night that, while she had looked, she felt as if she hadn't been able to fully get a grasp of how he truly appeared. It had been like staring into the sun.

He had scars. Ridges of flesh that spoke of wounds sustained in battle. His chest was broad, his waist narrow, his thighs well muscled. And then there was… Well, the rest of him. Now that she didn't feel quite so intimidated she could see that he was, in totality, beautiful.

She had seen paintings of naked men, but their members were small and wilted. Not his. It was… In full bloom, by contrast to wilted, she supposed.

She wanted to ask him the words. For everything. That was what she really wanted. She needed a book, an encyclopaedia of his body, one that might come with labels and terms for each illustrated figure.

It was how she learned.

How she had learned everything that she knew so far. It seemed reasonable enough to wish that she might have a book for him. For this. For them.

He said nothing to her, came over to the bed and settled on top of it. Then she waited.

He didn't move. He didn't get beneath the blankets. She stole a glance at him and could see that he was lying on his back with his arm thrown up over his face.

He lay there brazen, uncovered, clearly not at all ashamed of his exposed form. She began to feel restless, for she could not sleep with such a great awareness of his presence. With him right there, not knowing what he intended to do. With that strange pressure building between her legs and creating a restlessness in the pit of her stomach.

'Lachlan,' she said.

'Don't,' was his response, clipped and short and angry.

'Don't what?'

'I'm not in the mood to be gentle tonight, lass. Just sleep.'

'I don't know what that means,' she said, feeling frustrated.

He growled and, suddenly, he was over her, his green eyes blazing into hers.

'You do that quite a lot,' she whispered. 'Growling like a beast.'

'You tempt me to it.'

'I don't know what that means either.'

'All the more reason you should have let me sleep.'

'I *can't* sleep,' she confessed.

He kissed her then and she wanted to weep. Because finally, finally she felt something. A surge of strength and power. She had felt so hollow and miserable and lonely all day, ever since he had left her bed last night. But now he was kissing her and every possibility he had raised the night before was there again. It was a magical thing, the way that his kiss burned away the anger she had felt. Her fear. Her trepidation.

He pushed the bedding down with no small amount of violence in his movement and pushed her nightdress up, settling himself between her legs, pressing his hardness to the cleft between her thighs and shifting his hips slowly. She was wet there again and the glide of his heat was smooth, stoking that desire inside her that she had felt the last time they were together.

He entered her much more quickly this time, but it didn't hurt. She felt slightly tender for a moment, but it receded quickly. His strokes were hard and fast, his grip bruising on her hips, and when his teeth closed down on her lower lip, the shock sent an arrow of even deeper pleasure through her body.

She was like spun glass and knew that he would shatter her soon. But this was so different than how she'd felt all day in the silence. There was a power in this because, as fragile as she was, he was right there with her. She tried to hold back, because she knew how undone it made her feel and it frightened her more than a little. But soon, she couldn't. His breath, his body, his kiss. The way his heart raged in his chest, the deep, masculine sounds of pleasure that were foreign and mystical to her ears, all combined to stoke the flame of her desire.

'Penny,' he said and, the moment his name fell from her lips, a plea she didn't quite understand, she broke.

She gasped her pleasure, clinging to his shoulders, and that was when he withdrew, spending his own pleasure on to the sheets.

She wanted to ask him why, but her thoughts and words were tangled, and he didn't leave tonight. Instead he settled himself on the blankets, keeping distance between them, and slept.

How…how could he? How could he sleep with all of this between them?

It forced her to conclude that he felt nothing. That somehow this had changed nothing in him.

That she was alone in feeling altered. That created a terrible loneliness indeed.

In the morning, he was gone again, just as he been the night before. Once again, he bundled her into the carriage and rode on his horse. And again, any closeness that she had felt evaporated.

Of all the concerns she had about marriage, she realised now that they were foolish. She hadn't even known what concerns to have.

Right now, the deepest was all the feelings she had no names for. And a husband who made her feel both more whole than she'd ever felt in her life and lonelier, too.

This was not the life she had dreamed of.

'You're a fool for thinking you could have dreams in the first place.' And since she was alone in the carriage, she could say it out loud.

But then she rebelled against herself. No, she was not a fool. She was only a fool if she allowed it to stand.

If she wanted change, she would have to make it.

Chapter Six

She never turned him away. Over the next three nights she allowed him to lift her nightdress and take his pleasure in her.

Just looking at her filled him with a strange heaviness and he was grateful for the distance he could keep from her during the days they travelled. Her in the carriage, he on his horse. He did not understand the sense of growing connection to this wide-eyed Englishwoman.

By the time they were in their room at night, he was half-wild with a thing he couldn't name that made his body hard—but stranger still—made his heart beat too quickly.

As if somehow she had begun to set the pace for the blood in his veins.

He did not allow it.

He set the pace. He did not allow her to touch him. He kept control, at all times. But part of him ached to strip her completely bare and explore her body at length.

But she was a wife, not a prostitute. And the things he wanted to do to her were not indignities a man visited upon his wife. His education on carnal acts had been conducted in brothels. He had been a young soldier and it was the way of things. He'd been warned by one of the women there very early on that those who made a business of pleasure were different from delicate society women.

Especially if they were English.

And this he'd confirmed over the years listening to the men in his company talk. Even men who had wives at home, who found solace between battles in the arms of whores.

He'd thought of his own father and his reputation. The way he treated women. And how fragile his mother had been.

The only conclusion he could draw was that this was true. The line between wives and whores.

He gritted his teeth against his own hypocrisy. Because hadn't he only thought that if he were taking pleasure, the woman deserved it as well?

She had her pleasure. Every time he had his.

But there were certain acts that one did not sully a lady with.

A lady you forced into marriage.

Forced marriage was common enough. If not

forced then arranged, based on little more than mutual need.

He had no reason to feel guilt for that.

On the morning of the fourth day, he set his delicate wife in the carriage and mounted his horse as he always did.

'I'm tired of the carriage,' she announced, her delicate face appearing in the window.

'You've a few more days of it yet,' he responded.

'I wish to ride today.'

'I haven't an extra horse for you.'

'I shall ride with you,' she persisted.

'You will be wanting the comfort of the carriage,' he said through gritted teeth.

'Then you can put me back in the carriage when you've tired of me. Or when I've tired of you. Whichever comes first.'

They had managed to exchange a few words since that first day they'd ridden in the carriage together. Since then, only their bodies had shared communication. But he knew full well that if he put the woman on the front of his horse he would be forced to listen to her talk about toast or birds or any number of inane things.

That he found he could not deny her enraged him.

'Be quick about it,' he said, dismounting to help her alight from the carriage. He opened the door, lifted her out, then propelled her up on to the horse, nestling her in front of him, her round, glorious backside fitting snugly against his cock.

So it was to be torture for the next several hours.

She fit perfectly against him. He had never had occasion to put a woman on the front of his horse before and he had not appreciated the situation it might create.

And he had been correct about the chatter. For she did chatter.

'I do believe that is a Scots pine,' she said, the fifth tree she had named in as many minutes.

'Do you?'

'Yes,' she said. 'At least, it's what I recall reading in one of Gilbert White's papers.'

'You've truly spent that much of your time educating yourself on pines?'

'My father didn't have fiction in his library. So, I've spent a good deal of time collecting all types of information. On plants. Animals. Aqueducts.'

'An impressive array of subjects.'

'The Greek pantheon. Religion in general. But there was one area of my father's library that was sadly lacking.'

'Other than Scotland, you mean?'

'Yes,' she said. 'Other than Scotland.' She made a small sound that he couldn't quite interpret. A hum, as if she was considering whether or not she would carry on. Or pretending to consider it. In the short time he'd known Penny he'd never once got the sense she'd held back something she truly wanted to say. 'It was alarmingly lacking in the subject of human anatomy. As well as other… practicalities. I have some questions.'

The way she wiggled against him created a pull of desire in his body. 'Do you now?'

She paused for a moment, then turned her head to the side. He could see her elegant profile, her rosy cheeks partly concealed by the rounded curve of her bonnet. 'What do you call it?'

'My apologies, lass, I'm not sure what you mean.' He had a feeling he did know what she meant and that the intended target was stirring against her backside even as she manoeuvred around the topic like a battle strategist.

'Your…that is… I am actually aware of the biological…that is to say the Latin…'

'A cock,' he said, opting for bluntness.

Her shoulders twitched.

'Really?' she asked, her head whipping to the side again, the blue ribbon on her bonnet moving with her. 'Like a rooster?'

'Aye,' he returned.

He had the strangest urge to laugh. Not at her, so much as the situation itself. He could not remember the last time he'd laughed from humour. At least when not in his cups.

'Fascinating indeed.' It wasn't his imagination. She arched her back against him just then. 'A cock.' She tested the word and it was far too enticing, that sweet voice and the innocence wound through it, saying such a provoking thing.

'Be careful wielding that,' he said. 'That word on a woman's lips could cause the downfall of mankind. Or cause a scandal at the very least.'

'Is it? It's very difficult to know what's scandalous when you haven't the context. I've been so protected from scandal that I fear I'm not as shocked by some things as I ought to be. Ruination is such a broad term, don't you think? And, as far as I'm aware, a woman can be ruined by going into a closed carriage with a man, or a darkened path in a garden, as easily as she can be ruined by the actual... Well, by copulation.'

'Is that so?'

'Yes.' She paused for a moment. Then made that same humming noise she had before. 'What do you call *that*? Is it the same as it is with animals?'

Then he would have laughed if she wasn't sitting so close to him. Were he not pressed against her temptation of a backside. 'There are many things you can call it.'

'Tell me.' She sounded eager and bright and he wanted—badly—to drag her down from the horse, tell his men to occupy themselves, take her into the nearest copse of trees and spend his time naming the act while performing it with her in a variety of fashions.

It was the strength of the need that stopped him.

For where there was no control, there was chaos.

And Lachlan was not a man who indulged in chaos.

He shifted. 'Tup. *Screwing*. But then neither is a term you would use in polite company.'

She made a noise as if considering it.

'Don't go saying that,' he said.

'Why not?'

'Not fitting for a lady.'

'But the act is? For a married lady, at least. So why can't I say it?'

'You're not such an innocent, surely.' He knew fine ladies were sheltered from the world and he'd known she was untouched, but how could she know so little, yet respond to his touch so beautifully?

'I don't know. I feel as though I have gaps in my knowledge of the world. Of life. I didn't know that the act between a man and a woman would feel quite so good. Or quite so terrible.'

He stiffened. 'It's terrible?'

'Oh, it feels wonderful while you do it. But I don't understand why you won't…' She twitched her shoulders and for some reason he had the deep sense that she was frowning, though he couldn't see her face. 'I don't know the word for that either.'

'Orgasm,' he said. 'That's what the peak is called. The little death.'

'Oh,' she said. 'It does feel like that. As though your whole body might shutter to a stop at any moment. As if you're shattered and crushed back together all at once.'

He had nothing to say to that. He shouldn't feel…pleased.

He had never imagined that he might have such a forthright talk about such subjects with his wife. Not that he wasn't accustomed to speaking of it. The men of his acquaintance were quite bold about such things and whores certainly had no cause to blush about the subject.

He had not imagined that a woman of her breeding would engage in the discussion, but she seemed fascinated.

He remembered well the way that she had tackled saving the small bird. The tenacity of her. It was the same now.

'I know how one—or rather two—creates a child,' she said. 'I've read a great many books about farm animals. And I figure, as it is the same with all animals, it is the same with people. Also, I had a governess who presented quite a few stern warnings about men and their predation. Why do you not wish to create a child with me?'

'I'll not carry on my line,' he said. 'A decision I made long before I chose you as a wife.'

He didn't see the point in manoeuvring around the truth. He owed her nothing, it was true. He had married her only to take something from her father, not to give anything to her. It cost him nothing to tell her why he had no interest in fathering a child. 'My father was chief of the clan. By marriage to my mother. MacKenzie is her name. *Was* her name. My father earned his position through the trust of her father. The trust of the people. But he was weak. While the clan was diminished my father went to Edinburgh, and he spent his money, the money of the people, on frivolous things. On women, on houses about the city. He wanted to buy his way into being like them. Like a Sassenach.'

'What is that?'

'An outsider. English. That was what he became. He forsook his clan. The Highlands. After everything the English did to us.'

'But you fought for England. In the war.'

'Aye,' he said. 'I did. I would do it again, because the world has no place for bloodthirsty madmen and I would stand against that even if it meant standing with an enemy. Don't mistake me, my relationship with your country is complicated. But my allegiance first and foremost is to Scotland. Is to the clan. My father traded his al-

legiance for his own comfort. Charged outland-
ish rents to the farmers and spent their money.
He used them poorly. I would see everything returned to the people. I will not carry on a weak
bloodline.'

'You think your bloodline is weak because of
your father's actions? If we're doomed to be our
parents, then I'm fated to die very soon. Or become like my father, which I feel is only slightly
preferable to early death.'

'My mother had many children,' he said. 'All
of them are dead.'

'All of them?' she asked, her voice hushed.
'You lost all of your brothers and sisters?'

He dismissed the tenderness in her voice. 'I
don't remember most of them.'

Only James had lived long enough to be given
a name. Only he had lived long enough for Lachlan to remember his cries, his ruddy little face.
His small, angry fists that he'd waved in the air
as he wailed. Fever had taken him. And quickly.

'That's tragic, Lachlan. I'm very sorry.'

'The world is a harsh place. Life and happiness
are guaranteed to no one. I survived. There must
be a purpose to that.'

'And you don't think that that purpose is to
have more children?'

'My purpose is to get the land back to the clan.
To make sure that balance is restored.'

'So you've taken me from…from marriage to a duke, a household full of people and a life where I would have children to…to taking me up to a foreign land where I will have no one.'

No one but him.

But she didn't say that.

'Babies die, lass,' he said, his voice flat. 'If I remember anything from my youth, it's that.'

'I don't understand,' she said softly, 'why you would do this to me?'

'It's nothing to do with you.'

He felt her shrink against him. 'Of course it's not. Nothing is. I'm a pawn, aren't I? I don't get toast or my jewellery box. And none of it matters, because you are getting your revenge. And you're going to restore the Highlands the way that you see fit. You don't much care if I could marry the man that I loved. You don't much care if I wish you would…say something to me after you use my body. You don't care if I want to hold a baby in my arms some day. That is…a wife and mother is something I should be. It's… the way of things.'

'I don't have pity in my heart, Penny,' he said, feeling a strange tenderness there all the same. 'It's a wasted speech on me, bonnie girl.'

'What good is being beautiful? My father thought that beauty was my triumph. That it was what had got me into marriage with the Duke.

But my beauty doesn't mean anything, because you would have married me even if I looked like a toadstool. All you wanted was his suffering.'

'Yes, but had you been ugly my marrying you would've been a favour. Instead, it was an insult. That his beautiful daughter would be wasted on a barbarian.'

'So glad I could help with that,' she said, each word bitten off at its end.

'How is it you have such a tongue in your head? Such a sheltered girl, yet you don't seem to fear me.'

'Why should I? What else can you possibly take from me?'

The words scraped against something he hadn't known existed inside him.

'You will have a castle.'

'A castle?'

'Yes. The clan has a proper castle and it is no medieval fortress. My father used his money to make it quite modern. I think you'll appreciate it. All the comforts of home behind fortified stone walls.'

'Without a friend. Without children. I can go from one mausoleum to the other. A monument to sins that were not mine. I am truly a fortunate *lass*.'

He urged his horse forward, at a faster pace. 'There are always children running about the castle. I'm sure you'll find a bairn if it's what you desire.'

She said nothing to that and absurdly he found he wanted to go back to naming body parts and ecstasy for her education. For anything would be better than this. Knowing he had disappointed her and caring even the slightest bit.

What was it about this creature that called forth *feelings* in him? He knew drive. He knew how to chart a course and sail his ship to that destiny. He knew how to plan and wait and execute. He did not feel.

But she shifted things in his chest, like the rising and falling of a tide rearranged even the heaviest of boulders, and he could not see the reason for it.

'I swear to you this,' he said. 'Your life will not be a misery.'

Then he knew, for he was thinking of his mother. His mother, who had been so badly disgraced by his father, who had lost all of her children but one. And though he knew his father deserved the largest share of the blame, he could not shake the guilt. It had followed him through life, following him on to the battlefield. All the women he'd failed to save. He might have married Penny for revenge, but he would never treat her cruelly. 'You will not fade away to misery. My mother took her own life, Penny. That was where her misery took her. That was where my father took her. I have seen things on a battlefield that would tear you right in two. I have seen what it does to men, the madness that overtakes them. Rather than protecting the vulnerable they…use their strength against them. They forget they are men and become like animals. I have seen men lose all hope and decide death is preferable to the life around them. The despair that takes you to get to that point is a tremendous pit. The pit my mother fell prey to. You may not understand my reasons, but you can take me at my word. That will not be your fate. But trust that my decisions are for the best.'

He had partly expected a quick rejoinder, but she said nothing. Not for a while.

'I'm sorry about your mother. I'm sorry if what my father did made it worse. Made it harder.'

'It did,' he said.

'Of course it did. If it hadn't, you wouldn't have been so bent on revenge, would you?'

'And what can you take from a man who has nothing?'

'His daughter,' she said, softly. 'And his chance to have a relation to a duke by marriage.'

'So you see that I had no choice.'

'You always have a choice,' she said. 'It's just that you might not like the results of some of those choices. And so you chose the one that suits you best. I could've run away from our marriage. I had a choice. Society would have made it very difficult for me to find a way to survive. The Duke's sister offered me help, but I couldn't in good conscience risk Beatrice's reputation. Or even the Duke of Kendal's. A duke he might be, but he is still beholden to society and they love nothing more than to watch a man of quality fall. He prizes his integrity and reputation. How could I be the one to damage all that he's built?'

'And so you fell on your sword for the sake of their reputation, then complained to me about my revenge?'

'And you have twisted my words and used them against me.' She sounded grudgingly impressed.

'I have experience in war. I'm trained to fight.'

'And I am trained to do needlepoint. So I am outmatched.'

'Somehow, I doubt it.'

For there was something about the woman that got beneath his skin and he could not figure out the where or why.

The road went on, wide and smooth, the fields on either side of them rolling and green, sharp rocks rising from the grass out in the distance, creating a shoddy patchwork that extended to the horizon line.

'What did you dream your life would look like?'

'Must you talk?'

'It's the reason that I'm riding on the horse with you,' she said. 'I don't like the quiet. It's heavy. I was tired of being alone.'

'I was not.'

'Was that your dream, then?' she asked. 'To be alone? In which case, choosing a wife as a pawn in your revenge game was poor planning.'

'Many men do not often see their wives.'

'Of course,' she said.

'Your dreams,' he said. 'Tell me of your dreams, Lady Penelope. If you want to know mine, surely you should tell me yours first.'

'When? My dreams recently consisted of a duke and his beautiful country home.'

'Somehow, I can't imagine you wished to marry him for his rank and title.'

He didn't know why he was so certain of that. Any person would be tempted by a title so lofty. Why should she be any different? Yet he sensed that she was. He sensed that it was not his title that had appealed to her at all.

'I'm tired of being alone,' she said. 'That's why I used to wander the estate the way that I did. Looking for small animals. I used to dream of being like the birds. I used to dream of flying away.'

He was not looking to fulfil this woman's dreams. He was not the husband she'd chosen. But her sadness bothered him and it made him want to offer her something.

'Well. The horse doesn't have wings, but it is carrying you away to Scotland.'

She took a sharp breath, her shoulders pitching upward. 'I suppose that's true. But I had been to Bybee House. I've spent so much time there. And I know the Duke's mother. His sister. She was one of my dearest friends, before her brother was told that I betrayed him. And his ward. Such lovely girls, and… They were the first real friends that I've ever had. I want to not hurt. To not have to… feel fear or grief.'

Her words, her face, mingled with images from the past. With a woman he couldn't save, whose last moment he knew had been spent in fear and despair.

'Aye, lass, wouldn't we all.'

'You can't tell me you feel fear.'

'I fought in a war for ten years and, no matter how grimly I told myself death was to be accepted, greeted like a friend, I fought to preserve myself as well as those around me. Death was commonplace, but one thing you learn is how strong the will to survive is.' A strange sensation tightened his chest. 'The very worst thing of all is to see that will stolen from another person. You must have some sense of the future. For me…it was restoring the clan.'

'And revenge,' she said, her tone filled with mock cheer.

'Aye.'

'I thought I knew what my life would be, then the Duke proposed. Suddenly I could dream of a whole new future. You took that from me.'

'Dreams, perhaps. But there is always adventure. Adventure often lies just far enough in front of us that we cannot see the destination,' he said. 'You cannot know to dream of what's on the other side of that.'

'Is that what you've had these last years? An adventure?'

He nodded slowly. 'Adventure is also not always good. I came to England to make my fortune and I did. But it was a circuitous route that took me over battlefields and brings me to a home where none of my clan may remember or accept me as chief. But make my fortune I did.'

'Was making your fortune your dream?'

'I was born with fortune. I did not need to dream of it.'

'Then what was your dream?'

'Nothing,' he said. 'I had everything until I had nothing. And then there was no purpose to dreams.'

'Only revenge?'

'A dream is nothing more than a wish. Revenge takes planning.'

'Well, then I suppose you planned well.'

'That I did.'

Yet, as he sat atop his horse with his wife clutched tightly against him and the carriage rolling behind them, he had the sense that his plan might not be going quite as he had expected.

It didn't matter. She didn't matter and neither did the feelings that she roused in his soul. What mattered was getting back to Scotland, not concerning himself with her feelings of loneliness or her thoughts of her own shattered dreams. Or giving names to the mysteries in her universe.

She was not a bland, English miss and he should have given her more credit than that. But her failure to be boring hardly meant that he needed to recalibrate the way that he saw his life moving forward.

He was the husband, after all.

His wife was his property.

He protected what was his, kept it safe. He was not his father and he would not treat ill that which was his to protect. But she was his none the less.

He was returning home to the Highlands with much more property than he had when he left and that was a triumph.

It was all that mattered. He would concern himself with nothing else.

'That's an oak,' Penny said, though it lacked the spirit of her earlier proclamations.

For the rest of the day he contented himself with listening to her name the obvious, while the press of her arse kept him hard with wanting.

When they arrived at the next inn, he had his way with her as he had done every night before and, when he was finished, he did not concern himself with her loneliness.

Chapter Seven

The further north they'd gone, the more the landscape had changed. The greens became ethereal and she could easily imagine fairies hiding out behind the rocks, which grew to enormous proportions, jagged and sheer faced.

She wouldn't have known when they passed into Scotland, except that Lachlan told her.

She hadn't tried to talk to him again, not like that one day on the horse. She had kept things light.

She hadn't used the new vocabulary he'd given her either, but she had locked it away inside herself, for later use, because knowledge was power, after all, and she could use whatever she could lay hands on.

He had not changed his actions towards her at night. Still she found ecstasy in his arms, only to crash back down to earth when it was all finished.

Maybe that was just the way of things.

Maybe there was no answer. Maybe the intimacy between a husband and a wife created only questions, at least in the wife.

She felt startlingly vulnerable and didn't like it. She had spent her life working at ways to not be weak, to not be a potential victim to those around her. Her father was so volatile. Though he had not used his fists on her, his words had often cut deep grooves inside her soul. The games he played with isolation had tested her fortitude. If she had not found ways to layer protection over herself, if she had not found ways to please herself, ways to insulate herself, she would have been destroyed by now.

Lachlan had asked her how she had such a tongue in her head. She could only attribute it to her ability to protect herself, so why then did she find it so difficult to control that tongue around Lachlan and also to shield herself against the feelings that he created inside her?

It was distressing.

Today, they would arrive on the land of Clan MacKenzie. He had warned her that their reception might not be warm. He had sent his men ahead and, had the reception been deadly, he had assured her that he would have received word from a survivor. Unless there were none.

He'd given her a grim smile after that and she had not been able to discern if he were teasing.

She was not entirely sure if Scottish warriors engaged in teasing.

She found her husband extremely difficult to divine.

But then, she didn't find her own feelings any more clear.

Today, though, she kept her focus on what was ahead. She was seeing her new home. Her new home.

The words radiated inside her and she did not know what they meant. Not truly. For how could she make sense of calling this strange place home?

It was beautifully alien.

She could feel Lachlan's tension increase the closer they got to his home. The green went deeper as they went, the mountains higher, craggier. Penny felt like exactly what he'd told her she was.

An outsider.

They weren't the same. And this was not where she was from.

She understood now what he had meant. Understood now that this wasn't just a place a bit further to the north, but a stark, unforgiving landscape. Looking at Lachlan's face over her shoulder as they rode reminded her that he was from here. But he had lived in England for a great many years. If she found him uncompromising and forbidding…how much more so were the people who had been here all this time?

Some hours on, the path curved and she could see it. A great, great castle that stood against the sharp blue of the sky, the deep green fields rolling down below. It was high on a hill, overlooking a lake. There were houses dotting the landscape, rolling down to flatter green.

'Here it is, lass,' he said. 'These are the lands of Clan MacKenzie.'

'What are you doing?'

He stopped the horse and dismounted, taking her down to the ground with him. 'Get in the carriage,' he said.

'Why?' she asked.

'In case we are met with a volley of arrows.'

Fear gripped her. 'You don't think that will happen?'

His expression was grave. 'I don't know what will happen.'

She could see that it cost him to make such an admission, for her husband was a man who wanted to anticipate everything.

And if not even Lachlan Bain knew what might befall them here, then…

She was filled with disquiet and for the first time obeyed him without argument.

As they drew closer, she could see that there was a line of men in tartan standing in front of the castle. They had swords and all other manner of weapons strapped to their bodies and held in their hands. They looked grim and forbidding, and not at all welcoming.

But no shots were fired.

That was a small comfort, at least.

'I'm Lachlan Bain,' he said. 'Son of Angus Bain. I've returned as promised. I have come to restore the land and make repayment for that which my father stole. I am here to take my rightful place as chief.'

A shiver went through Penny's body and something that felt a lot like pride. For he was the biggest, strongest man in a whole group of them, and his bearing was that of a leader. His words, his vows were true.

And in that moment…she trusted him. Trusted he was everything he'd said. It mattered to her. It was silly, maybe, that it mattered, that there was some measure of honour in what he'd done to her, even if she were a pawn.

He was driven by the need to protect his clan. To avenge the indignity visited on his family.

She might not have asked to be caught up in it but, looking at him now, she could see the full measure of the man he was and she found him… beautiful.

The line of men remained impassive, then one man stepped forward. 'Laird,' he said, inclining his head.

Penny didn't understand the protocol here, but she knew enough to understand the weight in that word. That at least one man was ready to acknowledge Lachlan's place.

'My father has ill used these lands and these people,' Lachlan continued. 'And you have my word that I will make right what he has done wrong.'

'With due respect,' the man who'd stepped forward said. He was tall, older than Lachlan, but it was impossible to tell by how many years for his face was brutally scarred. 'How do we know you will keep your word?'

'Execute me if I don't,' Lachlan said. 'You might remember me from when I was a boy. I went away to try to make my fortune and I have done so. My time in England was not what I planned for it to be. But I made more than I could have imagined. And I'm still learning. I have merchant ships and have left men in charge of my business in London. I am an asset to the clan.'

'Aye,' the man said. 'I swear that I will be the one to kill you if you don't keep your word. Laird.'

'I would expect nothing less. But I am not on trial. I am Laird here. And my word will be obeyed.' He tilted his head upwards and she could easily imagine the look on his face. Iron. Uncompromising. 'There can be no question. A house without a head will not know which way to turn. It will not stand. I will have no dissension in the ranks.'

She could see two men, on the end of the line, exchange a look, and her stomach went tight. Lachlan was hard and he was terrifying, but she could see loyalty would not be easily won, not even for him.

'It has been years, Cousin.' The man on the end moved forward and, as he spoke, Penny could see the resemblance between the two men, though this man was not as tall or broad or fearsome as Lachlan. 'I have been taking care in your stead.'

'And for that I am grateful, Callum,' Lachlan said. 'Your work here will never be forgotten. For I honour blood. I honour that which is mine. My family. My clan.'

He dismounted his horse and went back to the carriage, opening the door. Green eyes met hers and he extended his hand. She took it, trembling slightly as she exited the carriage. The dress she wore today was much finer than the one she had adorned herself in for the other days of travel. But she had known that they would arrive today. Had known she would stand before his people and it had seemed important that she looked the part of wife to the Highland chief.

Not that she had any idea what the appropriate dress was for that role. But her yellow dress with its gauzy white fichu would have to do.

She accepted Lachlan's hand, and allowed him to lift her down from the carriage. 'My wife,' he said. 'Lady Penelope Bain. She is to be treated with respect.'

Something swelled in her breast, joining the pride that was growing there. That he was presenting her in this way. That they were…together. United. The satisfaction she felt went deep beneath the surface of her skin.

She felt part of him. Bonded to him.

'You bring us a Sassenach wife and demand respect?' The tall man spoke.

'I demand the respect owed me by my birthright,' Lachlan said.

'Are you not just an Englishman?' the man spat. 'You have been away these many years. You fought for their army.'

'I'm not like my father. I've no love of the English aristocracy, nor do I feel the need to make merry with them. This woman is my payment. When I went to England I took work with her father, who promised me a ship. He lied. He sent me off with no wages, nowhere to go. And that delayed my return home. I became a war hero. A captain in the British Army.' His laugh was hollow. 'And with that I purchased my freedom. Our freedom. And when I had the money, when I had the power, I returned and took what was dearest to him. She is not evidence that England has conquered me, but that I have conquered England.'

Penelope felt stricken, as if her husband had reached out and slapped her. Presenting her as a token of war. She had no idea he'd intended to do so. She kept her head high, though her heart was hammering heavily.

'You'll find the castle ready for you,' said the first man who'd spoken. 'We began to discuss this when your coin first arrived, and made our final decision when your men arrived ahead of you.'

'An honour,' Lachlan said, inclining his head.

There was no emotion on his face. He betrayed nothing of what he felt.

Penny wondered if he felt anything.

It was the strangest thing she'd ever borne witness to. One moment they were standing opposite those men guarding the front of the castle like rabid dogs, the next they were moving to do Lachlan's bidding.

Lachlan barked orders, as if his position weren't new, as if there was nothing tenuous about it, as if there had been no doubt a few moments ago if the people would accept or kill him. Orders to have things arranged, to have rooms prepared. To have the horses put away. He took Penelope by the arm and led her towards the door of the castle.

It was so large, stone and imposing and mighty in its magnitude. A manifestation of her husband in many ways. Because there were castles in England and it was not demonstrably different from those that stood there, but there was a wildness to it all that made it feel like something separate altogether.

There were men in England. Warriors. Strong, brave men with height and breadth and strength. But they were still not Lachlan.

They entered the grand doors and she was struck by how different it was inside to what she had expected. For there was wallpaper, like in the great manor homes of England, and large, plush carpets. And it was nothing quite so cold or medieval as it had looked from the outside.

'I think you will feel at home. My father had a fascination with the English.' He said it with his lip curled, obvious disgust filling his being.

'I gathered as much,' she said.

The great hall was massive, most of the original stone intact, with grand dining tables and other pieces of magnificence about the room. Grand portraiture hanging there, pictures of Lachlan's ancestors. Grand tributes to the clan. And at the head of a massive table hung a coat of arms.

As if she could forget that these were a different people. Their own nation in essence. The pride and fierceness seemed to reach from within the rocks. And she could feel injustice here.

Injustice that these people had been taken by England.

A proud people with a history that stretched back further than modern memory. They had been diminished by greed. The greed of Lachlan's father, yes. But more than that, the greed of England.

Penny couldn't blame them for being distrustful of her, not for one moment.

For they had been conquered and enslaved, their kilts outlawed for a time. Pieces of their national pride that made them what they were.

And it was only in fighting for a nation that had betrayed them and stolen from them that they had been given some of their national identity back.

She felt ashamed then, standing there, an Englishwoman in the centre of a Scottish hall.

Still, she didn't relish her husband presenting her as a prize.

There was unfairness in the world, but she didn't have enough power to cause it and her humiliation certainly wasn't going to diminish it.

Just a pawn...

All that hope that had been preparing to take flight in her chest had its wings ripped clean away. They were not one. She was little better than a prisoner. Him feeling loyalty to a clan, a castle, his family, had nothing to do with how he felt about her. She'd been an idiot to think it did.

She waited for him to make introductions of her to the household staff, but he didn't. Rather, he ushered her up the stairs and down a long corridor. It was true that much of the castle had been modernised, but there were great portions that remained part of the Middle Ages. Cold and grey and stone.

'Our rooms,' he said. There were two doors, side by side. He pushed one open. 'I imagine you're tired from the journey. I will send a maid up to help you bathe.'

'Thank you,' she said, her voice sounding detached and not quite like her own. 'I... I could certainly use one.'

'The door there leads to my chamber. If you need anything. But it is likely that anyone on the staff can meet your needs should need arise.'

She nodded. 'All right.'

'I'm going down to the village.'

'Yes,' she said, as if she understood and agreed, but mostly she said it because she didn't think there was another option available to her.

Then he turned and left her there, standing in the chamber, quite alone.

She moved into the room cautiously. It was, as he promised, outfitted with every convenience she might have expected. Just as grand as the room she might have had in the Duke's country home. An intricately carved bed with swathes of fabric draped around the top of the wooden frame. The bedclothes were rich and velvet, plush and glorious looking.

The room possessed a grand fireplace that would ensure she was never cold. There was a *chaise*, a small table with chairs. Bookcases.

A large armoire and, when she opened it to look inside, she found dresses. More even than had been in the trunk for the journey. More than she ever owned in her life. He'd said he had things sent ahead. And he had not lied. But none of them were her things. Everything in the room was beautiful, rich and lovely, but none of it was familiar and it only added to that sense of being outside herself.

If she were to dissolve, there would be no one to see it.

She had no purpose or reasoning to push her fear or sadness or loneliness down into that place inside her, because there was no one to put a brave face on for.

She walked over to a vanity at the far end of the room, looked at the lovely, velvet-covered bench, then at the beautiful, marble-topped vanity to see something very familiar. That simple wooden jewellery box. The one left to her by her mother. The one that contained nothing more than pebbles collected at the estate, feathers. Things that mattered only to her. Things her father had not been able to sell. Things that were dear to her heart and only hers.

He had retrieved it. He'd said he wouldn't.

Lachlan had made sure she had her jewellery box.

If she were nothing more than a conquest, nothing more than a prisoner of war he had been fighting in his own heart for all these years, would he have done such a thing?

She didn't know.

She sat down at the vanity and wished she could cry. Her eyes hurt, pressure building behind them and growing in her chest. But she couldn't because she'd spent so long training herself to stay in one piece and, even when she was desperate to shatter, she didn't know how.

She hated this. In the moment, she hated him.

No. It wasn't his touch she feared, but the desperation it left behind. The need for something she could not put a name to. The desperate desire for something she had never expected her life would contain.

She sat in silence, her eyes filled with grit. And then she made a decision. She was not simply going to sit here and wait for a maid to come and bathe her. She was not simply going to be installed in a room.

It was up to her whether or not she was seen as a conquest.

It was her decision to make what her life became now.

Too long, men had controlled all that she was and all that she could be.

Yes, Lachlan was her husband. And, yes, there were decisions he had made for her life and her future that she could not control. But she was a woman and the household belonged to the wife. She would have been the Duchess at Bybee House and she would have made it her own. She would have had the responsibilities of running a household and she would have them here as well.

He would not simply relegate her to a bedroom and leave her here.

Something about that jewellery box, about its presence on the vanity, gave her the confidence that he would not wish that.

That he perhaps cared a small amount more than he pretended.

He could not possibly care to pretend less.

It was true. The only time she felt connected to him was when he came to her at night.

But this place was his. Part of him. And she had felt that the moment she had entered. The history in the stones. If she became part of this house, then she would be part of the history of Clan MacKenzie. Part of the history of Lachlan.

She was determined to see it so.

And one thing that was true of Penny was that once she made a determination towards something, then she would not be deterred.

And this would be no different.

Lachlan had stopped at every farm. His people were proud and they did not necessarily trust the new Laird. When he had presented the gifts of coin, he had to be careful to make sure he called it what it was: restitution. Not charity. Not mites being given to beggars, but property being returned, for the rents his father had charged during his life. For the cost it had had for the people.

By the time he was finished, his exhaustion was bone deep. They had travelled for hours today, then he'd had to make sure this bit of business was done and done right. He was a soldier and it was rare that anything took a physical toll on him. It was being back here. This place.

It was so familiar, yet he could not stop staring at it as if he had never seen it before. And he realised, as he stood there by the loch, the shadow of the castle looming over him, that he had never truly believed he would come back here.

He'd have thought it a dream misremembered by a desperate fourteen-year-old boy who wanted to believe there was a home that belonged to him somewhere in the world.

He had many homes. Had the money to instal himself wherever he chose in London. But it was not the same. For his blood flowed from here. The clan was his blood. His breath. His life.

For all the hatred he carried in his heart towards his father all these years since he'd been away, it was only intensified now. For how could he give allegiance to anything other than this place?

How could anything matter but the sacred earth that was enriched by the bones of their ancestors, down beneath the surface? How could anything bear more weight than the land? Their pride. Their strength. Their people. For you could purchase the title and you could dine in Edinburgh with the esteemed, make a play for being part of the peerage, but it would not change blood. Money could not purchase a home. A place of belonging.

It came from blood. The blood of his mother's family. Clan MacKenzie. And even if his mother's body was not in consecrated ground, she was here.

She was part of this earth.

He had brought his men with him—the men who had fought with him in the war—and a few of the men who had set themselves up as protectors of the clan, the gentry and chieftains who had been holding the clan steady since the death of his father and prior to his return.

Though he did not have an easy camaraderie with the men, they'd all pledged their loyalty to him.

It was all that mattered.

They rode their horses down to the cottages that sat in the outlying areas. They were in disrepair here. The poverty pronounced. The fields around them fallow.

The door to one of the homes opened and a man came out, staggering. 'What is it ye're after?' he slurred.

'This is the Laird, McLaren,' a chieftain of the clan, Glenn, shouted at the drunk. 'Mind yourself.'

'Laird?' he said, his lip curled. 'Oh, we've all heard about you.'

'Then you've heard I've come to restore the clan.'

'Can't restore what's dead,' the man said. 'It's too late for us.' He swept his hand to the side, indicating the fields. 'While you were making merry in England your father destroyed us. Bankrupted us.' He spat on the ground. 'I'll have nothing from you. You and your Sassenach bitch.'

Lachlan drew his sword and got off his horse. The man stumbled back, fell to the ground. A woman appeared in the doorway behind him and screamed, 'Ye can't kill him!'

But Lachlan's vision was a red haze. He would not have his wife questioned. Would have no words spoken against her. Her honour, her safety, would be protected.

'I will have your allegiance,' Lachlan said. 'I am Laird here. My wife is the lady of the castle and you owe her respect.'

'Cut my throat,' the man said. 'I owe you nothing.'

'No!' the woman shouted. 'Ye cannae take him from me. We'll all die.'

He saw a child in the doorway then, staring up at him as if he were a devil.

'You will pledge your fealty to me,' Lachlan said. The man paled as Lachlan took a step closer. 'I am your Laird.'

'You have my allegiance.' The man's lip curled and it was clear in every line of his body he hadn't wanted to pledge it, but it was of no matter to Lachlan. The inhabitants of every house within sight were watching now.

He was a conqueror. This was what he knew. There was only one way to take respect and he would do it at the point of his sword if he had to.

'Are there any others who wish to voice dissent?' he asked, looking around at those who were gaping at the scene before them.

No one spoke.

'I have come to make restitution,' he said. 'But make no mistake. I am The MacKenzie. There is only one voice that matters here. Mine.'

There was nothing more to say than that.

They finished afterwards and, if his men disapproved of what had happened, they said nothing. He'd made it clear what he thought of those who questioned him.

He would not afford dissention in the ranks. Many clans had been destroyed. Farms abandoned. Castles left crumbling. He was fighting against a tide that would not turn unless he did it with his own hands.

He had to be in charge and unquestionably. One drunken fool would not undermine what he was. And he would not issue threats, however veiled, to Lachlan's wife. He would not call her honour into question. Lachlan would not allow it.

He made his way back into the castle, ravenous. He went back to his bedchamber and changed clothes, ignoring the hunger that flared inside him as he looked at the door that connected his room to his wife's.

When he went down the stairs and into the dining room, he was surprised to hear an English voice rising above the familiar cadence of all the Scottish burrs around it. 'And what does the daily routine generally consist of?'

'You needn't worry about it.'

'Quite to the contrary,' Penny said. 'I do believe it is my position to worry about it.'

His wife was standing next to the dining table

with the housekeeper and both women were regarding each other with deep suspicion.

'I'm hungry,' Lachlan said.

'Of course,' the housekeeper said, casting Penny a frosty glare before turning and making her way towards the kitchen.

'What is it you've got up to?'

'I need to know my duties,' Penny said.

She had bathed.

She had exchanged the heavier dress she had worn for travel for one that was white, light and ethereal and put him in the mind of the dress she had worn on their wedding day.

She wore a fichu which covered the swell of her glorious bosom, a pity, he thought, and her hair was arranged in an artful fashion, low on her neck, not quite to the English style.

He preferred it.

'You don't have duties.'

'I do. The duty of a wife is to see to the running of the household.'

'You're an outsider. You don't know our ways.'

'And I'm determined to learn them. You have not lived here as a man. I wouldn't imagine you know much more about the running of a household than I do.'

He went to issue a denial, then found that he couldn't. For, in many ways, she was correct. He had lived here until the household had become somewhat derelict. Ignored by his father. Only then had he even begun to consider what went into the maintaining of a household when the lack of it had become apparent.

'It is my job to organise the servants and oversee the menus.'

'The menu is my only concern at the moment. I'm ravenous.'

She looked up at him, her expression sharp. 'I did note that there is a bit more available than haggis and blood pudding.'

'Am I to look forward to a dinner of toast, then?'

Her lips twitched. 'It would serve you right.'

But when the meal appeared, it was rich and fast, with a great amount of variety. Pheasant and eggs and sturgeon. Root vegetables and a stew.

Fresh bread—he was extraordinarily thankful for the fresh bread. And the ale. The food felt like home. He felt home.

'You brought me my jewellery box?' she asked, looking up at him, something shining in her blue eyes that he couldn't read.

'I sent a man for it, aye.'

'You… After I asked you to?'

'Aye.'

'You said you wouldn't.'

Her gaze made something shift in his chest,

made him feel as though he was reaching for something he couldn't put a name to. 'What is it you're asking for, lass?'

'Why did you do it?'

There was a feeling for it, but no words. He didn't like it. Didn't like the sense that there was something in him he couldn't identify.

He did not believe in such things. A man in his position had to know. There was no space for uncertainty.

But he could not put words to it and, more to the point, he did not want to. For there was a softness to the feeling and he could not allow for softness.

'It's not a matter of consequence,' he said, ignoring the itch beneath the surface of his skin.

'It is to me.'

'But not to me,' he said, his tone hard. 'And if it is of no consequence to me, it is of no consequence to anyone.'

'Of all the arrogant...'

'I am Laird of this castle. Chief of Clan MacKenzie. A lack of arrogance would not engender faith.'

'You didn't fetch the box to make me happy? Or to...be kind or...?'

'I wished to shut you up, even if just for a time, but it appears it hasn't worked.'

Colour flared in her cheeks and she looked

away from him. He had done wrong by her. And that…he felt regret for that.

But to do right by his people meant he could not put her first. He had to guard against anything that might put the clan at risk.

He turned his focus back to his meal.

He didn't speak as he ate. And it took him a while to notice that she was sitting there quietly, much of her food untouched.

'You're not hungry?' he asked.

'I think I'm a bit more tired than I realised. I have lived a lifetime in less than a fortnight.'

He stared at her, quite unable to make sense of her words. This moment was the culmination of an actual lifetime for him.

These last days on the road had been simply that. Days. The woman knew nothing of the passage of time.

'You make no sense.'

'I fear we don't make sense to each other,' she said. 'For there is nothing terribly different about all of this for you, is there? You make a decisive move, claim what it is you want. And that's the way of it. It's nothing for you to use my body, because it could be myself or a woman who takes coin for such an act. It is nothing for you to travel, for you've been all around the Continent and I have never left England. I've scarcely been away from the estate. No man had ever put his hands

on me, his mouth on me, until you. And you...
You just say how it is, how it will be, and trust
that it will be done. You don't worry at all what
that means for me. What it feels like for me. I
lost the future I had planned. The hope of children. And you can't understand why it feels I've
lived a lifetime in this span of days? You couldn't
even give me a lie about my jewellery box. Some
indication that you have a heart. I've had to replace any thoughts of what I had to what my lifetime might be with new ones. With yours. I'm
glad it feels inconsequential to you.' She stood
and moved away from the table. 'I'm tired. Don't
come to my room.'

And with that she made a very decisive choice.
She left him there with a full belly and less of a
sense of triumph than he felt he ought to have.

He didn't know why in hell he'd felt he had to
fight her about the damn box. Except it shouldn't
matter.

And neither should the feelings of a woman
who had been a small piece of what he'd planned
to accomplish. His revenge was done and she was
his. He had the clan to concern himself with now.

Yet he found himself concerned with her. And
he did not know a way to banish those feelings
now that they'd taken hold.

Chapter Eight

There was, Penny found, a strange sort of pleasure to be had in barring him from her room. For the first two nights, she was drunk on it. She'd ordered him not to come the first night. She'd locked the door the second. He'd tried it. Once.

She could practically feel his outraged pride through the heavy wood and she'd gloried in it. She didn't lock it the next night because she'd been hoping he might come through that door and she'd have an excuse to turn him away directly again.

Because all those nights he had come to her room while they had been traveling to the Highlands she had surrendered herself. All the pleasure that he had added to her body he had taken away again when he left.

When he finished and simply fell asleep.

Then it cost her when he took that small gesture, that beacon of hope represented in her jewellery box, and crushed it so callously.

The distance felt like a reclamation.

It was difficult for her to get the women in the household to warm up to her. She did not experience open hostility, but the frosty nature of her interactions with Rona, the housekeeper, made it clear that she was not welcome as the lady of the house.

The kitchen maids, Margaret and Flora, were marginally better. Her personal maid, Isla, was quiet, but didn't seem to have any ill will towards her.

But she had heard whispers about Lachlan. The staff might ignore her, but there was an advantage to that. They often didn't notice when she was around and she was accomplished at listening in on other people's conversations. It was the only method of gleaning information that was as good as asking.

They said it was suspected he was no different than his father and that his English bride was evidence of this. Of his obsession with their oppressors.

Penny knew that wasn't true. Her husband was far from obsessed with her. In fact, he seemed quite happy to ignore her.

But she had concerns about the fact that his marriage to her was causing him trouble.

She gritted her teeth. She shouldn't care.

Except... This was her home. This was her home, whether she had chosen it or not. And she didn't want to spend her years here as an outsider. She could understand why they hated her. Her people had disrupted their way of life. While Lachlan might have a hope of restoring his clan, so much of the Highlands had been scarred beyond repair. The way of the clans was becoming near extinct and she did not expect that they would welcome her with open arms easily.

She had also heard that Lachlan had brought terror into the village. That a man had expressed his concerns about his return and Lachlan had drawn his sword.

She knew that he wasn't going to be violent without cause, but the fact he was trying to rule with iron over a people who were already inclined to distrust him... It wasn't going to work.

She had been victim of his remoteness. She already knew the way those green eyes could make a person feel.

Small.

He was not going to earn allegiance by terrifying everybody, by turning this place into an army, where he acted as captain as he had done during the war.

She was forming an idea, a plan. But she was going to need help.

It was not enough to simply plan menus. She was the lady of the castle and she was going to make that matter. But she had reached her limit here within the castle walls. She needed to get out. She hated the silence, the stillness.

She'd already taken a large chunk out of the library. She'd walked every bit of the gardens contained within the castle grounds. She'd retrieved her needlepoint supplies and had worked at stitching little flowers for hours on end. She'd begun inserting herself into the kitchen, learning to cook certain meals even though the maid protested. Gradually, in those things, she'd been reminded of who she was. It was like coming up out of a fog.

This life was still hers, even if Lachlan had put himself in position as Laird over her.

She could make the connections she craved. She could create a life she enjoyed out of what she had here. Lachlan didn't get to decide.

'Isla,' she said to her maid one day. 'I think I should like to meet more of the people. Lachlan spends his days working the land, working to restore his relationship to the people. It seems that as his wife I should do something.'

'The MacKenzie hasn't left any orders for you.'

The MacKenzie, she had learned, was what a

man in his position was called. Like the King, but the highest of his clan. The most singular.

'I don't await his orders for everything,' she said. 'He thinks that he has full control, but he does not.'

'He must not be a cruel man, then.' Penny was surprised when Isla continued the conversation. Surprised and pleased. Her interactions with her maid had grown more cordial recently, but they still hadn't had much conversation. She was eager to get to know her better. They spent so much time near each other...why couldn't they be friends?

Penny frowned. 'No. Why do you say that, though?'

'Because it sounds to me that he hasn't got control of you simply because he won't exercise the right. And that means something stops him. A limit to his cruelty.'

Penny leaned towards Isla. 'Did the previous chief... The MacKenzie...did he not have a limit to his cruelty?'

'No. He wanted land. And he wanted money. He wanted to be part of the English peerage. It was a gift when he began spending so much time away from the Highlands.'

'I know as much from my husband.'

'His temper was a beast and one all the more

easily roused when he was in his cups. He had many mistresses and beat them all.'

'He beat them?' Not even her father had ever sunk so low.

'Aye,' she said. 'One so badly she died.'

'He killed a woman?' She tried to imagine Lachlan losing his temper, tried to imagine him raging on her with his fists. She couldn't. And she had felt supremely wounded by the fact he had not fetched that jewellery box for her out of the kindness of his heart.

But he had been raised by a man who truly would harm a woman if he was of a mind to do so.

She had never felt protected. She had been sheltered in many ways. The cruelty she'd been exposed to had been a particular kind of neglect. It had shielded her from many of the other atrocities in the world. That a man could beat his lover to death…

'That's why he thinks there is something wrong with his blood,' she whispered.

'It's a silly thing,' Isla said. 'He's not a bad man.'

'You don't think so? I have… I've heard some of the household whispering. They think what he did in the village was a sign he might be violent.'

Isla shook her head. 'He didn't kill anyone.'

'That is a low standard for behaviour.' She paused. 'They also think…they also think his marrying me shows he's like his father. That he likes…English things. I don't know if they'll ever accept me.'

Isla made a tsking sound. 'You didn't personally slaughter our people. I understand the distrust. I don't fear you.'

'Well, I'm not very frightening. Lachlan, though…'

'If he were a bad man, you would know already. They would know already. Evil men don't take long to show it.'

'Don't they?'

'It's not been my experience. A drink or two and the alcohol ignites the temper on some brutes.'

Her maid could not be any older than she was. To think that she already had such experiences made Penny's heart squeeze.

'I hope you have a good man now,' Penny said.

Isla blushed. 'Aye. Though I know I shouldn't speak of it.'

'I don't mind,' Penny said. 'I've been very lonely. For…for ever. And I would like a friend.'

'I don't know if that's allowed.'

'Aren't I the lady of the manor?'

'I suppose you are.'

'Then it seems that I should get to make some rules. And I say that we should be allowed to be friends. But that isn't an order,' Penny said. 'You can't order someone to be your friend.'

'I will be your friend,' Isla said. 'It can be lonely in this house.'

'Then you'll come down to the village with me?'

'Yes,' Isla said. 'What is it you wish to do?'

'We can bring bread.' Penny brightened. 'We can bring bread and we can meet everyone. And you can show me who I should speak to.'

'I can do that.'

'Good.'

Perhaps she could help Lachlan find his place here. If she could balance his hardness with some of her softness.

As silly as it was, Penny felt triumphant because she truly felt that if she could make a difference here, if she could carve out a space for herself, then perhaps it might feel more like her life. And not simply a sentence that had been handed down to her by her father and his failures.

How strange. She had not thought of her father for some time. She didn't miss him or regret leaving home in the least.

For so many years her life had been consumed with him. And he hadn't loved her. He might not have used his fists on her the way that Lachlan's father used his fists, but his coldness had been an arrow through the heart.

The way that she had spent her life cut off, the way that she had spent it so lonely...

It ended here.

Her life was not where she had planned for it to be.

But she had been set on being a duchess. And there would've been responsibilities that went with that. There would've been this. This community of people that she bore responsibility for, and that she could have. She could make a full life.

With a heavy cloak settled over her shoulders, she and Isla ventured out into the village. Round rock houses were surrounded on all sides by sweeping mountains with sharp angles and curves that protected the dwellings from the harsh, cold winds. Grey stone broke through the blankets of green lichen, the only contrast to the deep colour, so vivid it nearly overwhelmed her vision.

It was wild, this place. The sky somehow higher here than in England. But great clouds reached down to touch the earth, wreath the mountains in mist.

Great meadows unfolded and rolled down towards the loch, while behind the village was a dark, imposing forest.

It was so vast it nearly overwhelmed her. This was adventure. Lachlan had spoken of adventure. And it was here. In this great monster of a place that felt as though it could consume her as easily as it could bring her to freedom.

She turned her focus back to the houses. Some were well kept, others in shambles.

Some had crops growing nearby, others looked as though they had a blight. When Penny knocked and offered food, some were kind. Some welcomed her and spoke of their hope for the future.

Others treated her with disdain.

Still more treated her less with open hostility and more with wary distrust. She was a reminder to them of why they struggled, of why they suffered.

But Penny was certain that kindness, softness, would help win the day here.

The path continued on down the hill and Penny charged in that direction, while Isla slowed.

'What's wrong?'

'It's bad down there,' Isla said.

'What do you mean?'

'Dugan McLaren and his wife. Their children… He's a drunk, and he spends all they have on alcohol.'

'Oh,' she said. 'Well, don't you think they'll need bread?'

'He's mean.' She hesitated. 'He's the man who spoke openly against The MacKenzie.'

A ripple of disquiet moved through Penny. 'Oh.'

'He will not welcome you.'

'Perhaps not,' Penny said, taking a sharp

breath, 'but my husband is strong. Not cruel, as you said, and I don't think Lachlan would take kindly to knowing that there was a man in his clan buying drink rather than caring for his family.'

'It won't matter what The MacKenzie thinks if McLaren takes his fists to you now.'

'If he takes his fists to me, my husband will have him... Well, I don't know, but it would be something violent. I assume this man is well aware of that.'

She felt determined now. She carried on the path and then came to the most ramshackle of homes that she had encountered on this journey. The smell that emanated from it was rotted food, despair and drink. Filth.

She steeled herself, grateful they had quite a bit of bread left because she had a feeling that the children in this place would need it most of all.

Lachlan's father had been cruel. Her own father neglectful. And while it might not be the same as it was in this place, she knew what it was to have your life and your future dictated by the shortcomings of the man who had fathered you.

It wasn't fair. Not in any of those circumstances.

She went to the door and knocked. It opened a crack and a woman's face appeared. She was drawn and pale, exhausted looking. 'Hello,' Penny said. 'I'm Lady Penelope Bain. I'm the wife of the…The MacKenzie.'

'You're his fancy English lady?' The woman asked.

'Not fancy. But regrettably English.' She tried to smile, but the woman did not return it. 'I brought bread.'

'We are not beggars,' the woman said. 'And your husband has already terrorised my house.'

A high-pitched wail came from inside the house and she heard a chorus of small voices after.

'But maybe the children are hungry?' she asked.

A flash of something, not softness but not quite so brittle, came over the woman's face. 'If you have to force your charity on us, do it quickly and then be gone.'

The woman was stooped before her time, the house itself a hovel. The smell inside was nearly overwhelming.

'How many children are there?' Penny asked.

'Twelve living,' the woman said, her tone bitter.

'Oh, my,' Penny responded. 'Well, I doubt this will be enough bread.'

'They aren't all here. The Father knows where my whore of a daughter has gone off to.'

Penny drew back, shocked by the woman's words.

'If she's going to spread her legs so freely she

ought to do it for pay. At least then we might eat better.'

'I...' Penny could not think past the intimacy of what the woman had said. She knew how overwhelming the act was. How wrecked she felt after. The other woman spoke of her daughter doing it as easily as breathing. 'There is bread.'

'Don't think we allow it,' the woman said. 'But if her father ever discovered it... He'd beat her to death.'

For the first time, Penny realised that the woman's face wasn't just haggard with lines of exhaustion. There were scars there.

'And does he...? Would he lay his hands on you?'

'I've made my bed. But if your Laird is anything like his father, you'll know the bite of his fists soon enough. Don't think your pretty manners will save you from it. Men are the beasts, they are.'

Penny didn't see the point in arguing with the woman. She didn't see the point of much of anything in the face of so much despair.

She had never seen anything like this. There were so many children. So much squalor, so little of anything that might help.

Yet again she was struck by how she had been protected even in her loneliness.

For her virtue had been shielded. She had always been full. Her father had never beaten her.

The world was such a harsh and unyielding place. And she had felt so hard done by in it.

But this… This was hardship.

She was angry about being lonely. Angry about the way her father had isolated her. But there wasn't a space to turn around in this house that didn't contain another person. At least back at her father's house she had had a place to escape. At least she had been safe.

'If ever you find yourself in danger…' Penny said. 'If you are ever in danger…come to the castle. He will not turn you away. If he knew of your husband's cruelty…'

'He's just a husband,' the woman said.

'Surely it doesn't have to be like this,' Penny said.

'Aye,' the woman said. 'But it does. I'm sure that women like yourself are treated like fine pieces. And in England I'm sure your rank and title protected you from all manner of things. But don't make the mistake of thinking it will be like that here in the Highlands. He is The MacKenzie and what he says is the law. If he decides to take his liquor and his rage out on you, then he will. And there will be nothing to stop him.'

Penny couldn't imagine why a woman she was bringing kindness to would speak to her in such a fashion. But that was when she realised: shame. Because nobody wanted to be in a position of pity.

And this woman was surely to be pitied. Penny spent some quiet moments talking to the children, and Isla joined in. They broke pieces of bread off and gave it to the *wee bairns*, as Isla called them.

When they left, her maid looked grim.

'It's a hell growing up that way.'

'You know?'

'It was a blessing to get work at the castle,' Isla said. 'Being in my father's house… But he drank himself to death.' Isla didn't sound regretful.

'A gift, surely,' Penny agreed.

'Aye,' Isla said. 'Until there wasn't money any more. Until my mother had to sell her own body to try to feed all the bairns. My wages weren't enough.'

'Where is your mother now?'

'Long dead,' Isla said. 'Women like her… women like my mother…they're not afforded a long life.'

'Your brothers and sisters?'

'Went to other family. Went to find work.'

They rounded to the back of the old house and there was a figure, cloaked in muddy brown, just walking up through the fields. She was a young girl. Maybe thirteen.

And when she shifted, moving the cloak to the side, something became very clear to Penny.

'She's got one in the basket,' Isla said, horror in her tone.

'Is that Mrs McLaren's daughter?' The girl was with child. It was clear from a distance. 'It must be. How she's hiding it... Her father must be more than a bit drunk to not have noticed.'

'She probably stays away. Stays hidden until he's too drunk to notice either way.'

'We will have to come and check on her,' Penny said.

She was suddenly overwhelmed by a strange sort of gratitude for life that she had never felt before.

She had long had the sense that her life was tragic. But it was nothing compared to a girl who was little more than a child herself, ready to bring a baby into the world, with no food, no money and a father who would no doubt harm her and the baby if he was in a black enough mood.

'That we will,' Isla said.

Chapter Nine

〜∽∽∽〜

It was becoming an interesting battle with his wife. This fight for who might break first when it came to giving in to the need between them. A need he knew was mutual.

He could see it in the pitch of her breathing, the way she looked at him. The way her eyes shone bright when they sparred. Which was often.

It was a strange thing, though, to have cut off physical contact. For all of their desire had to find relief in their conversation and that had sharpened something inside him in new and fascinating ways.

He found her vexing still, of course. But it surprised him how much he enjoyed dodging her barbs at the door between their rooms. If he could not have satisfaction in her arms, he at least enjoyed her wit.

'Not tonight, I have developed a sensitivity to arrogance.'

'Ah,' he said. 'It must be difficult being so near to yourself then.'

'I sally forth.'

And another night...

'Tonight I have important needlepointing to finish.'

'Lass, I think we could accomplish your needlepointing and marital duties.'

'Lachlan, my fears of where the needle might end up... I am thinking only of you.'

Of course, this was amusing, but beneath it all...she was hurt and he could see it. He also didn't know how to heal the wound.

Now though, he had found out she was planning a party. A party.

Rona, the head housekeeper, informed him of this with great umbrage. 'She has also been going out into the village with regularity,' she said.

Anger that felt particularly sharp-edged lodged itself in his chest. Penny? In the village? With no protection?

'And what do they think of her there?' he asked.

'She's an outsider,' the woman said. 'But the people are grateful for bread.'

He was...in awe of her. He had been focused on exerting his authority. It was important that the people knew that he was here to rule. His father had shirked his duties and Lachlan would do no such thing. In his mind, a leader had a steady, iron hand.

But he had not considered this. Basic needs and comfort. These gestures of care.

'And what is my outsider bride planning exactly?'

'She claims it will bring a sense of…goodwill.'

'Does she now.'

He walked away from Rona and made his way up the stairs to their rooms.

He opened the door to Penny's bedchamber. He did not knock.

When he opened the door, she gasped, and her little maid drew back along with her.

'What is this I hear about you planning a celebration?'

'It seems only logical,' she fired back at him as if she had not just recoiled at the sight of him.

'Go,' he said, addressing the maid.

She scuttled out of the room, her head low, closing the door behind her.

'Are you going to draw your sword and hold it against my throat?' She had a bit more frost to her tone than she often did when they sparred.

'When have I ever threatened you, lass?'

She looked away. 'You haven't. But I have heard rumours about you terrorising the villagers.'

'I defended your honour. The man spoke against you.'

It did not matter if he was barred from her bed. She was his wife.

'I know,' she said softly. 'I went to visit the household. I spoke to his wife.'

'Foolish,' Lachlan said, that sharp-edged fear he'd felt earlier expanding inside him. 'You put yourself in danger.'

She had no idea the resentment, the anger that existed here. She had no idea of any of it. She had tripped out about the village like an unsteady lamb who had no idea predators might be near.

She was planning a party as if a merry time might heal deep scars in an evening.

'I was never in danger,' she said.

She had no idea. 'That you believe this is exactly why you are no longer permitted to wander the grounds.'

'And how will you stop me?'

'I am not above locking you in here, lass.'

'And I'm certain that I would find a way to escape.'

'You do not understand what you're playing with. These people do not all trust me and they will not all trust you. Some of them may see to use you against me. This is not your clan. These are not your people.'

'It is the life I have been given,' she retorted fiercely. 'I will not stand down. Not again. I have lived quietly for far too long. Was it not enough that I paid my father's debt with my body?'

'Not as often as you might.'

'Will you take it, then?'

It was a challenge. She was facing him down, daring him to be the beast that his father was.

He knew well that his father would have thought nothing of it and he would've beaten her for her insolence.

And he knew how that ended.

With a woman stepping out a tower window, down to the rocks below. To her demise. He would never crush Penny in such a way. That large, unnamed thing that lived inside him, that roared to life when she was near…

It would not allow it.

He would never hurt her.

And if anyone ever tried to harm his bride… It would be the end of them.

'I can take what I need elsewhere. I do not need to force myself on an unwilling woman. There are many that are more than willing.'

She tilted her chin up. 'Good.'

She refused to show him any sort of deference. And she made his body feel like not quite his own. It enraged him.

'Men tremble before me,' he said. 'Do you have

any idea how many bodies I left littered on battle-fields in France?'

'I don't,' she said. 'But are you saying you would kill me? Because I don't believe that. You could have done that as soon as we got into Scot-land.'

'I've no wish to kill you.'

'A relief. You also have no wish to be a beloved leader to your people, do you?'

'Love is not the goal. Loyalty—that, I think you will find, is of greater importance.'

'They don't trust you.'

'Due to you, in part.'

'And I was a decision you made. In anger, I imagine. So, unless you decide to make a public spectacle of me, execute me in the courtyard, I expect I have work to do to prove to them that I am not simply evidence that you're like your fa-ther. Don't get angry with me for trying to fix what you might have broken with your revenge.'

He had nothing to say to that and was in a rage that she had struck him dumb. She had been a focus of his revenge. Repayment for years spent in England.

And she was correct. His marriage to her had only created more suspicion among the people.

'Tell me about your party,' he said.

'A celebration,' she said. 'Invite the other clans. Invite the people from the village. Fling open the doors. Food. So much food. Music, dancing. Make them happy. Yes, people want to know they are safe. They want to know that they have a leader who can protect them. No one who looks at you could be in any doubt that you could. That you could defend against any army. But life here has been bleak.' She let out a long, slow breath. 'And I know what it is to live a bleak life you cannot see any hope of having change.'

'You speak of your time with your father.'

'Yes. But my time here also if you don't allow me to find a place. And I believe that this will help. It is not enough to come in swinging a sword and making proclamations. There is pain here. They are wounded. The fields are scarred. So are their hearts. I've seen them. I've been talking to them.'

'I know,' he said.

'It is not enough to rule by making your subjects afraid of you.'

'I don't want them afraid. I want them to give me their respect. My father did nothing to earn it.'

'Terror is terror either way. You must show them something more.'

'I am not in need of the advice of a woman.'

Not even that caused her to back down. If anything, she bristled. 'You are. Very clearly you are. You are incapable of fixing this yourself. Rage at me if you want, but you know I'm right.'

He would admit no such thing. These sorts of things, this…this softness that she was talking about was outside his experience. He had never had a moment of softness. Not in his life.

He fought against images. Images of a woman long dead. Of babies who smelled sweet and felt so fragile, and died far too quickly.

'I don't understand,' he said.

'That's okay. You don't have to understand. But you could trust me on this.'

'And why would you know anything about this?'

'Because, as I said, I know what it is to live bleak. A moment of happiness can heal so many things. Just a glimmer of hope. An evening to dance, to have a full belly. Think of what it was like when you were at war. What would you have given for those things?'

He felt as if she had turned a key that was in a lock somewhere inside him. An understanding flooded him.

'It has been war here,' he said. 'Without violence, but no different.'

'Yes,' she said, the look of relief on her face doing something to that vulnerable place inside him that she had just discovered.

'If you see to the planning of this, then it will happen. I will… I will trust you.'

'Thank you.'

He moved towards her, but she shrank back. Rage filled him. He had the strongest desire to pull her against him anyway. To ignore her fear. Her reluctance.

But his father felt far too close to the surface of his veins and he'd meant what he said. There were many women who would have him. He'd no need to slake himself with her fear.

He did not know why it was different here. He didn't know why she had given herself to him willingly on the road, but in the castle she acted as if the idea disgusted her.

Perhaps she was afraid for her life, then?

He gritted his teeth. 'I don't want to be troubled with the details of this.'

'You have my word.'

'Good. At least there is some use for you.'

And with that, he left her as abruptly as he had come into the room. He raged down the hall, all the way out of the castle. He knew where he could find a lightskirt. That had, of course, been one of the first things his men had made sure to inform him of.

He could make merry with her. Give her that moment of hope that his wife was so entranced with.

But he thought of the way Penny had looked at him before she had shrunk back. When she had looked at him with hope that he might not disappoint her. That he might understand her. Do what she felt was right.

And he knew he was in no fit state to be with a woman.

'William,' he said, finding his man lounging in the courtyard. 'Pick up your sword.'

What he could not work out in the bedroom, he would work out on a created battlefield.

After a few hours of steel hitting steel, he felt exhausted.

But his desire was still not satisfied. There was only so much that talking could fix.

And he might feel a sense of pride that his wife had thought of dealing with the clan in a softer way...but he did not like having to participate in...levity.

Still, he would allow her to have her way here.

For whatever she thought, he had no wish to crush her. None at all.

If anything gave him hope for his grim soul, it might well be that.

Chapter Ten

The planning of the feast had been…interesting, to say the least. Mostly because it had forced her to lock horns with the indomitable Rona.

The other woman did not like her interfering with matters of the household, but Penny had a vision for what was to occur and she needed her help to accomplish it.

They had fought over the menu, over the acquisition of the food.

It had required sending men on a long journey to Edinburgh in order to acquire all that would be needed.

The land here would be restored, but as of now, anything that needed this sort of excess… There was no excess to be had. But her husband had money. A great deal of it.

When the men returned, they not only had what was required for the party, but had brought staples that they could store. So that there would be more bread, cakes even. There was flour and sugar, and butter.

And Rona'd had to admit that perhaps Penny wasn't so bad, as she had convinced the Laird to open his purse to this extent.

But the next order of business was to inform the people in the village. Yet again, Penny selected herself as ambassador. They were, of course, wary. There had been nothing like this for longer than many of them could remember. No celebrations, for there had been little to celebrate. Anything extra had gone to Lachlan's father. To the lavish lifestyle he was bent on living in town. Just the mention of a celebration had gone a long way in proving to people that Lachlan might be different.

If he was willing to spend his riches on the people here, then perhaps that was a sign that things would continue to improve.

It made her feel useful. It made her feel…

This was what she'd needed. Lachlan made chaos reign in her heart and body and she'd hated that. The sense her emotions were no longer in her control.

Sitting in silence had always been the enemy. Her own thoughts. Her own heart.

But she could make a difference here. She didn't have to sit around and wait and feel.

She could act.

And so she did.

When she and Isla approached the McLaren residence, they both paused. 'They will be invited, too,' Penny said, feeling determined. She was nearing the door when she caught sight of the girl again.

Her heart jumped and she moved forward.

'You,' Penny said.

The girl stopped and met her gaze, wide-eyed. 'What's your name?' Penny asked.

'Nothing of consequence,' the girl said.

'But I've asked. And I'm sorry, I didn't tell you mine.'

'I know who you are. The MacKenzie's fancy piece.'

'His wife.' Penny refused to allow a child to offend her. 'Lady Penelope Bain. We're here to invite you and your family to the castle for celebration.'

The girl contorted her face. 'Why would we ever go there?'

'There will be dancing. Food.'

'I don't think my father will go.'

'Does he have to? It seems to me you're well capable of sneaking off when you wish.'

'I don't do anything of the sort.' The girl scowled even deeper.

Penny looked down meaningfully at the girl's rounded belly. The girl shifted, moving her dress.

'Don't be afraid of me. I want to help you. I… Does he know?'

The girl's eyes widened. 'I don't know what you mean.'

'You're with child. It's not well hidden.'

'Hidden well enough.'

'But you won't be able to hide a baby so easily.'

'I have time.'

'The father?'

The girl looked away. 'Not from here.'

'And you don't know him?'

'Well, he just took what he wanted. Didn't ask me.'

Anger and horror twisted inside Penelope. 'You were forced?'

'I'm not an idiot. I know what happens to women who say yes to men. Look at my mother and her twelve children.'

'Does your mother know you were forced?'

'She doesn't believe me. And if she does, she doesn't care. It only makes me more foolish that I put myself in such a position. Men are men. You cannae keep them from their nature.'

Penny's whole heart rebelled against that. But this wasn't the time for lectures. It was the time for action. 'What's going to happen to you?'

'Can't say as I know. I couldn't get rid of it.'

The girl frowned. 'I tried. It didn't work. It's still there.'

Pity overwhelmed Penny. Along with fear. The girl was in danger. The baby was clearly in danger. And they had no one to protect them. And this, again, was something she could do. She was not helpless. She was Lady Bain.

She'd been a helpless girl locked in a room, once. And no one had possessed the authority to help her. No one but her father.

But this girl... Penny could help this girl.

'Listen to me. When the time comes, you can come to the castle. You'll be welcomed in. I'll bring a midwife to help you. We'll keep you safe.'

The girl looked shocked, then afraid. Penny could understand. Those closest to her were not offering help. Why wouldn't she be suspicious of a stranger offering it? 'I don't need help.'

'There's no shame in needing help.'

The sound of voices came from inside the house and the girl jumped slightly.

'Go,' she said.

'Will you tell your parents that they're invited?'

'Won't make a difference. You can't fix us. You can't fix me.'

The girl lowered her head and walked away, hunched over herself and the babe she carried.

'I'm beginning to recognise the expression on your face,' Isla said.

'What expression is that?' Penny asked, staring after the girl.

'That one that says you're ready to try to do the impossible.'

'Well, I've got Lachlan to agree to throw a party at the castle. I'd say I do quite well with the impossible.'

'Aye,' Isla said. 'I'd say that you do.'

Chapter Eleven

It was the day of the grand celebration and the amount of food was stunning. There were places to sit out in front of the castle. The door stood open. Tables and blankets were placed everywhere. There were musicians and dancers.

The great stone courtyard had a massive bonfire roaring at its centre. And food...there was such a feast laid out, for all. Not simply the chieftains and other gentry, but for the whole of the clan. Fish, game and fowl. Breads and cakes.

Everyone was dressed in their finest—whatever that might mean. From faded gowns that looked to have passed through several generations, to sweeping great kilts in different tartans.

It was quite unlike anything to ever grace the clan before. At least, not in Lachlan's memory.

And Penny was at the centre of the preparation. Her hair was a tangle, her eyes bright. She was wearing a dress that, if he was not mistaken, must've come from one of the maids.

She was working. And she looked...happy. Happier than he had ever seen her, certainly.

They had a few hours yet until the festivities began and she seemed bound and determined to have a hand in every last bit.

For his part, he had done nothing.

But this was her business. Her idea. He was still not convinced that it would have a bearing on anything. She was the one who seemed absolutely certain that it was necessary to the happiness of the clan.

The smell of meat roasting on spits was thick in the air, along with music, laughter and bawdy songs.

Inside the great hall, the setting was yet more grand. People filled the room, both from Clan MacKenzie and from other clans who had come from near and far. A mix of people and times. For this felt more like the stories of old, from when the clans had endless power and resources, and had not been touched by England.

The music was from an era gone by. The food—by virtue of the sheer, vast quantity—was as well.

This was the Highlands. The clan. Scotland. In a deep, essential way that stirred his blood.

One thing he had not considered was what

a great demonstration of strength and power this was.

Because excess like this did nothing to dent his wealth, yet it was far beyond anything his people would have seen in more than a generation.

'You've done well,' he said.

She paused, looking startled. 'Well. Thank you. A surprise coming from you, considering that you've had little to do with the process.'

'You didn't need me.'

Something flashed in her blue eyes and, somehow, he felt an echo of it in his chest. He couldn't name it or hold on to it. But he felt it all the same.

'Well. It doesn't matter. Everything is in hand.'

'The clans will see how powerful Clan Mac-Kenzie is. We are not on the brink of destruction. Not any more.'

'I did not have cakes made as an act of war. Please don't turn it into one.'

'Who said anything about war? But it is clear that we are the strongest.'

'That right there. Not everything has to be about strength.'

'It does. The reality of the world is that the winner will always be the strongest.'

'That's bleak. Why does there have to be a winner? Why can't people simply live and be happy?'

'Because there will always be a conqueror. Always. And if you are not a conqueror, you will be the conquered.'

'Truths learned in war?'

'Truth is learned here. In my whole life. Had I stayed here, this clan would have been conquered by my father's greed. I went to England to try to make my fortune. Your father bested me. I had to obtain power. I had to obtain strength. Had I not done so, these people would have fallen into ruin.'

'I can see that,' she said softly. 'But you're not at war any more.'

'There is always a war on the horizon. Even if it is not war as you think of it. You must always be prepared. You cannot show weakness.'

'What about kindness?'

He looked around. 'You have done that for the both of us.'

'They might like to see it from you.' Her words were soft, the touch of her fingertips on his arm softer still. But he felt it, like the blow from a weapon, so hard it radiated through him, settling low in his stomach.

'Do you intend to dance tonight? To show them that you have a bit of humour?'

'Why would I do that? I haven't got humour.'

'You don't think so? I thought sometimes it felt as though we found some together,' she said, looking sad. Why was she sad? She had got what she wanted. And as for the way things were between the two of them, it had been her decision.

If there was distance, it was not down to his choice.

The back of his teeth ached. She was lovely, even now, even in this scullery maid's costume. It was confounding. As was she.

'There has been no room for it in my life.'

'Well, show them that you're human tonight.'

'Why? I would show them that I am a king.'

'You don't have to struggle to show that, Lachlan. But you might have to work a bit to show them that you have a heart.'

'The people don't need to know their leader has a heart. They need to know I have a sword.'

And with that, he left her. But something about the conversation lingered with him. Made him feel disquiet.

He did prepare himself, putting on a great kilt, his sword at his hip. He was ready to make a display, both for his people and for the guests.

When it was time, he went between the connecting doors to his and Penny's room, again without knocking.

'It's time,' he said.

'You might knock,' she said.

'I don't have to do any such thing, lass,' he said. 'It is my castle. My domain.'

'How nice for you.'

She had transformed from when he had last seen her in the courtyard, overseeing the preparations.

And she was beautiful. Even angry at him. Her blonde hair was pinned low on her neck, her gown a delicate gold, the neckline low and wide revealing the creamy curves of breasts he had nearly forgotten the touch and taste of. She was a vixen, this woman.

She haunted his dreams and he couldn't pretend it wasn't so.

She had bewitched him in some manner. He had had no answer for her when she had asked him about the jewellery box and he was convinced it was somehow related to his exile. But the only answer that he'd been able to find, there beneath the discomfort of his skin, had been that he had cared. Had cared about whether or not she was happy. And that did not seem real or possible in any regard. He was a man driven by revenge. A man driven by duty, honour and a sense of what was right. A man determined to be the very opposite of his father, Who had been hot-blooded and driven by such weaker devices as his feelings.

She looked up at him, an air of defiance in her blue eyes.

He took hold of her arm and it lit him up like

the fire in the great hearth. 'It's time for us to meet our guests.'

'Of course,' she said. But her smile was cold. 'You must behave, Lachlan.'

'I am Laird here. I determine the behaviour.'

'Then don't turn this into a funeral. It is meant to be a happy occasion.'

'I will do my best not to frighten small children.'

'Please do.' She paused for a moment. 'That man…the one who challenged you. I invited his family to the celebration. He's consumed with drink and his wife and children live in fear of him. They don't have enough food…'

'There will be enough food,' he said, his voice grim. 'For everyone. As for the rest, it is a tragedy to be sure. And were I to ever witness a man harming his wife or children the consequence would be severe.'

'That isn't enough. We have to do something.'

'We are. This changes things. You have to have some trust in that. You cannot heal all the ills of the world, lass.'

'Isn't that what you're trying to do? Heal the ills of the world by pouring your money back into this clan? How is what I want any different?'

'There is a system here. A structure. The people here work the land and they should benefit from it. My father stole. Profited off the backs of his labourers in an unjust manner. That I can restore. That I can heal. The rest... That is up to them.'

That seemed to infuriate her, but she said no more because they were descending the stairs, and making their way towards the great hall. That was where they were announced by one of the chieftains. He as the Laird—and she as his lady.

The crowd of people let up a cheer as they made their way into the great hall. This was a hero's welcome.

This was the welcome Penny's actions had brought to him.

He had not truly understood what she was doing, planning this. But now that he stood here, surveying the people, the food, he understood. It was not only a demonstration for the people, but for him. Of what it meant to be here. Of what it truly was to be home.

And Penny was by his side.

She might not wish to take him into her bed, but she was here. And she was his.

The possessiveness he felt was strange. For while he understood the desire to possess, and to protect...

What he did not understand was his desire to see her smile. The pride he felt over this thing she had planned.

He took a seat at the head of the table, with

her at his left. And as he sat, he spoke to the men
there about the way the Highlands had been these
last years. The way that things had changed. And
the ways in which Lachlan was determined to see
them restored.

All the while, Penelope sat, bearing the coun-
tenance of a real wife. A proper wife.

A lie.

When dinner was finished, the music began
to play. And his men, deep in their cups by then,
all began to shout for the Laird and lady to give
them a dance.

Lachlan, for his part, hadn't danced without the
aid of alcohol and outside a pub for more years
than he could count. And before that, he did not
think he ever danced.

This was necessary. The show of strength and
unity. And if it was what the people wanted, he
could not deny them. If part of him relished the
idea that Penny would have to be close to his body
again, that was inconsequential.

He was simply human.

Simply a man. A man who wanted to dance
with his wife.

He pulled her to him, the dance much more at
home in a tavern than here, but he didn't much
care. The fiddle was moving fast and the other
dancers were already drunk. Penny clearly didn't

know how to dance a reel, but she followed as best she could.

When it was his turn to grab hold of his bride, he took her in his arms and didn't return her to the line, spinning her around with her crushed against his chest.

She laughed, her smile wide with her joy...

She was happy. Here with him.

In this moment she was happy.

It tangled itself around his heart, around his soul. He hadn't thought either of those things still existed inside him.

It was clear the display pleased his men, for they clapped along with the music, sending great shouts up into the air. And something shifted inside him. For this was what it meant to be home. This was what it meant to be in Scotland. To be in his clan. This hall. This castle. This music.

He was not an outsider here.

He was not an outsider for the first time in years. His accent was no different, his words not unique. The manners and dancing and food were familiar.

Penny smiled, her blonde hair twirling right along with her.

And he felt something...something he had not felt in years.

Happiness.

It was an ache that bloomed in his chest and

spread outward. And for a moment, he could not breathe past it.

She had been right. There was happiness here.

He thought it might be contained in her smile.

When the dance finished, his heart was thundering hard, his blood firing through his veins. And perhaps his head was a bit dizzy from drink, though he hadn't had overmuch, but he dragged her away from the dance floor, away from the party and into an alcove. He backed her against the wall then and finally did what he had wanted to do for days.

He crushed her mouth beneath his, claiming every stolen kiss that she'd taken from him. Every missed touch.

She wrapped her arms around him, her fingers spearing into his hair, kittenish sounds rising in her throat. Sounds of encouragement.

She had inflamed in him a desire that he did not understand. This creature who he had bedded in the most perfunctory of ways, but who had ignited in him a need that far surpassed any he had ever felt before.

He was not gentle. He did not give quarter to her innocence. He consumed her, his kisses deep and long and hard. He plundered her mouth with his tongue, taking all that she would give and then demanding yet more.

He was hard as steel and, if she were a whore,

he would have demanded she take herself down to her knees and pleasure him with her mouth. The very image of his darling angel taking his cock between her lips created a fire in his veins.

They were so close to the party that anyone could see them. But it didn't matter, for he was chief. He was The MacKenzie. And this was his home. This was Scotland. It wasn't England. She belonged to him here. Him and no other. And whatever he desired, it might be his. Whatever he wanted.

He was not in shackles any more. He was not enslaved.

He had spent so many years labouring to find himself a free man. Fighting for a country he didn't owe allegiance to. Earning what should have been his twice over.

He had earned it with bravery on the battle-field, had seen countless atrocities and more bloodshed then those who had not been to war could ever believe. He had toiled and clawed his way back to Scotland. And he had claimed her on his way. Payment for all those years of working for her father.

His payment.

Justification for his kisses, for risking her exposure, fuelled him.

He pulled the top of her dress down, exposing

the rosy crests of her breasts. She was lovely. Far beyond anything he could've possibly dreamed.

So changed from the little creature who had brought him the bird.

How would he have ever known that he would have found such satisfaction in her arms? There was no thought now. Only a roaring in his veins. In his head.

Mine.

For he was a conqueror, his bloodline that of warriors.

And what his body understood was staking a claim.

Not wedding vows spoken in a church and recognised by soft English society, but an earthy, physical alliance. One that she had denied him these many days.

He would be denied no longer.

He kissed her. Kissed her until her lips were the colour of crushed rose petals, until she trembled beneath his touch.

'To your knees, lass,' he said, his voice rough.

She looked up at him, with wide, wild blue eyes. 'I don't understand.'

Suddenly, the world came back into focus.

Suddenly, realisation overtook him. He was no better than his father acting out of the fire in his blood. Acting like a man possessed. Like a man owed the bodies of everyone and everything around him.

Yes, it might be the law that a man owned his wife, but he had seen what happened when a man took that to heart. The ways in which it could destroy a woman. A good woman. Of course she didn't understand. She was an innocent. Corrupted only by the few times he had taken her, quickly and without much finesse, in narrow, hard beds in coaching inns. And he was demanding she get on her knees like a seasoned piece in a near public alcove where anyone could walk in. This lady of a wife.

Wasn't that the point of her? To disgrace her? No.

He had only ever wanted to disgrace her father. But tonight he had come close to disgracing her and that meant he'd dishonoured himself.

It could not be borne. Because that made him his father. The truth of his blood borne out in front of him.

'Go back to the celebrations,' he said.

'Lachlan...' Her voice was breathy, stunned.

'Go back, lass,' he said, his voice hard. 'If you know what's good for you.'

She left, backing away from him, her eyes on his the whole time. An accusation, he felt.

Back here so little time and the corruption of

his own blood was beginning to seep through his veins.

He waited a moment. Waited until the evidence of his own arousal was no longer pressing against the front of his kilt.

When he rejoined the party, Penny was there, looking stunned.

But she didn't stay away from him. Rather, she crossed the space and joined him.

'Lachlan… Why did you tell me to leave?'

'You know perfectly well.'

'I don't.'

'There are things a man does not use his wife for, Penny.'

'What things?'

'I'm not going to speak to you of this.'

'Why not?'

'Enough,' he said, his voice hard.

'Why?' She pressed again. 'Why do you care how you use me?'

She asked the question without malice. And he had the feeling that she was asking it in much the same way she had asked why he had given her the jewellery box.

'It's nothing to do with you,' he said, keeping his tone deliberately uncompromising. 'It is simply the way of it.'

If he had failed the first time for answering

in such a manner, then he had deliberately failed this time.

All the better.

For here, with all the power in the world he could want, he did not feel any more able to protect the weak than he had out in the world.

For he could not protect Penny from himself.

And that was a failure deeper than he could face.

Chapter Twelve

Penny had been brooding since his kiss at the party.

He had...he had made demands of her she didn't understand, then pushed her away, and she had never been more confused.

The touch of his mouth to hers had brought everything she'd spent the past few days avoiding roaring back to life inside her.

She hadn't banished loneliness by barring him from her bed. She'd simply built a wall between her emotions and the manner he used to reach them. But it couldn't hold for ever.

Because the silence between them was swollen. Large and filled with all manner of things Penny didn't want to navigate. She had been doing well. She'd spent more time in the village, had started a sewing circle with some of the ladies and had become more than competent at cooking. And she had been able to set Lachlan to one side. Or at least see him as a project rather than a husband.

Then he had kissed her.

With that kiss he had stirred up every deep, longing thing inside her. There was that fire, that physical need. He aroused it in her so easily.

But there was more.

Deeper.

The way he'd danced with her in the great hall had felt like flying. His strength—whether quiet or on brute display—felt like a living force within her sometimes. As if his confidence and bravery had taken root inside her and grown, flourished and made her someone so different from what she'd been before.

She wanted to know him.

All those nights she'd refused him entry to her room and they talked. And in those quick moments he'd shown her so much. That humour he said he didn't have. Patience. Kindness.

She ached to be close to him in every way she could.

She hadn't allowed herself to think of it. But now she was consumed with it yet again. Along with his rejection.

It forced her to consider that he might not have pressed her, withholding because he didn't want her. That she hadn't ever had power over him as she'd imagined.

That second time they were together she'd felt his body tremble and she'd taken it to mean she could make him desperate, as he had made her.

But perhaps that wasn't so.

Because she was naive. Because apparently there were things men did not ask of wives. And he had wanted one of those things, but…but not from her.

And she didn't even have a clue what it might be.

It would have been better if she could hate him.

But the longer she saw him here, with his people, acting the part of chief, the more entranced she was by him. As she had been when she was a girl, trailing after him at the estate. How she hated that. That he seemed to have so much of a hold over her and she had none over him.

But he was so broad and brave, so willing to serve all of the people around him. Lachlan might not know how to show warmth, but she did. What he gave was strength, a steadiness that one could lean on. And while he had underestimated how much his people might need to have some joy… she thought she might not have understood how much they needed his strength.

As she talked to those who worked in the castle, it became clear just how badly scarred the clan was from the way his father had conducted his affairs.

Isla had told her horrible stories, worse even than about the mistress Lachlan's father had killed. Understanding more of where Lachlan came from, why he hated his father so much that he despised the blood in his own veins...

It made her care more for the strong, iron Highlander who didn't seem to have it in him to bend.

His uncompromising nature could be trying. And she'd seen it as an obstacle at first. Now she saw it as a gift.

She'd also discovered that Lachlan had been sending money back to his people from the moment he found out about his father's death. A great many things had been restored in the months it had taken him to gain order with his business and get himself back to the Highlands.

It was why the castle was so comfortable now. Why it was fully stocked with food and staff. It also led her to truly believe that what he'd said to her about his bloodline was a truth he held deep in his heart. Because if he felt it was the most honourable thing for him to produce an heir, then he would. She could not understand, though, because she did not know men who weren't utterly concerned with the carrying on of their line.

She had always assumed marriage would mean

children. And she hadn't realised how deeply comforting she'd found that certainty until it had been taken from her. How much she'd wanted that.

To be a mother. To have someone to love and care for. To find that connection.

But as much as many men were driven to further their bloodline, he was opposed.

His father had damaged him. Everything she'd heard about the previous MacKenzie convinced her of that.

She wanted to find a path to connect the ways in which she knew him. The way that they had been intimate in the bedroom. The way that they had talked on the back of his horse on their journey to Scotland. The commanding, forbidding man that she saw prowling around the castle, who had kissed her as though she was the feast, then ordered her to leave him. The man who said her jewellery box had meant nothing to him, but had seen it fetched all the same.

She even wanted to understand the man who presented her to his people as a prisoner of war, more than his wife, but who had presented her to all the clans as his lady. Because she felt that the truth of Lachlan Bain was somewhere at the centre of all those things, whether she was particularly fond of each and every piece of him or not.

She had a feeling that some of her problems with him stemmed from the fact that she was so horrendously ignorant of men and all there was to know about their physical desires. For she felt there was a key in that. To the things that bothered her now. She wished that she knew more.

But she had got to know a few of the women who worked in the castle. Most especially the maid who attended her.

She found it strange that Penny enjoyed making conversation and Penny knew that. But she couldn't help herself. She was lonely. And she finally lived in a house filled with people. She was intent on taking advantage of that.

The head of the household found Penny's intrusions somewhat irritating and Penny could tell. But then, one thing she was very good at was ignoring when people found her irritating.

It was a gift.

She was in the kitchen, poring over the weekly menu, Isla next to her eating a midday meal of bread and cheese, the young scullery maids rushing about the kitchen. 'What do you know of men?'

Isla looked up from her bread. 'I'm not sure I understand.' But she could see that Isla did understand, only that she was hoping she might not have.

'Men,' Penny said. 'I find that I'm woefully ignorant on the subject.'

One of the maids—Margaret—laughed. 'You're a married woman.'

'It hasn't seemed to help.'

She waved a hand. 'Fine ladies who are married often know less than kitchen maids who are not.'

'Why is that?' Penny asked.

It suddenly seemed deeply unfair to her.

'Your lot protect you from the way of the world,' Margaret said. 'It's not a bad thing, mind you. Men can be…'

'Right rubbish,' Flora, the other scullery maid, finished.

'True,' Margaret agreed.

'Well, Lachlan is not. That is to say… The MacKenzie…'

'Yes. I know what you mean.'

'It just seems as though there must be *more* to pleasing men.'

The maids exchanged looks.

'Do you know?'

'I know a fair bit,' Flora said, looking sly.

'I was able to convince him to give me some proper terms.'

'Which ones?' Margaret asked, looking amused.

Penny knew that she was being mildly teased,

but she didn't much care. 'Well, I know what a cock is.'

Margaret laughed, the sound a hoot, and Flora and Isla joined in. 'That is a good place to start. Men are fond of their cocks.'

'I'm not unfond of it myself.'

'Also a good thing,' Margaret said. 'Nothing worse than finding yourself in the position of having to please a man you don't find pleasing.'

'All I knew about men and women I had... pieced together from reading about nature. Then I was a wife. I expected to hate him. He stole me from my home, from an engagement to another man. I didn't know what to expect of a wedding night. But he can be so wonderful. And I find him beautiful.'

'That's a gift,' Flora said.

'It feels like a gift when we're together. But then it feels as though he's taken all the power away from me when it's over. And I just feel... I feel.'

Margaret just looked sad for her then. 'You have feelings for him.'

'Feelings?'

'Aye. I reckon you love him.'

Her words hit a strange place inside Penny. Love.

She had never expected to love the man she'd

married. She had felt, though, that she might love the Duke, and that had been such a wondrous and unexpected gift. With some distance she'd realised that it had never been him—she had not known him, how could she love him?—but the idea of him and all he represented.

Loving Lachlan could not be possible.

He had no softness. His manners were not lovely.

It wouldn't be easy to love him. And it made her feel as though the walls inside her heart were being stretched, stressed. In danger of crumbling.

'I don't. He kidnapped me. He forced me into marriage. I was supposed to marry a *duke*.'

'Lah,' Margaret said. 'But I still think you love him.'

She pushed that away. Firmly. 'I never expected love.'

So what then was all of this truly about? Why did she feel an ache in herself that wouldn't go away? Why did she feel a deep pull towards *more*?

She thought of those nights in the coaching inns. 'I don't want him to be in control like he is. He pushes me away and it makes me…sad. He has let me keep him from my bed for over a week and I…there must be more than just him lifting my skirts and…and having done with it.'

Flora frowned. 'He doesn't see to your pleasure?'

'Oh, he does,' Penny said. 'But I never… He doesn't allow me to touch him. Or truly see him. And I feel like the key to him, to this… I've been holding him back from my room, but I don't want that any more. Are there books?'

'I don't know about books,' Flora said. 'The real truths come from women and far too many men are charged with the actual recording of things.'

'Well, I've never had any women to tell me such things. I made friends with the Duke's sister and his ward, but they know no more of men than I do. And his mother told me to simply think of household chores if I found the act overwhelming.'

Margaret wrinkled her nose. 'If you can think of chores, you might as well be off baking bread.'

'I can't think of chores when I'm with him. I don't want to. But I want…something else.'

'These men,' Margaret said, 'they spend all their time turning their wives into little mice. Teaching you to be scared of a naked man. Why is that? Because a lady with some boldness is what truly tempts them. And they want all the control.'

'That's just it,' Penny said. 'He has all the control. He comes to me and I give him exactly what he wants, because he's made me want it. I have no fortitude. I absolutely give in. He makes my knees weak and he makes me…'

'He is a handsome man,' Isla said.

Penny felt a strange surge of possessiveness rise up inside her. He was her handsome man, infuriating though he was. 'He is. But I don't want him to have all the control. I want to have some.'

This, and the man himself, had become a problem she was desperate to solve. She didn't want to mope around being smothered by feelings.

'Then you need to take it,' Flora said.

'How?'

'Seduction.'

'I don't know how to seduce anything!' Penny said. 'I haven't any experience of men, I told you.'

'Well, what *do* you have experience with?' Margaret asked.

'I have nursed several small animals back to health.'

Flora coughed and Margaret smothered a fit of giggles with her hand. Isla, for her part, looked away.

'Right,' Flora said. 'That is not the same. And it won't help you.' She tapped her chin. 'You're very beautiful. Use your body.'

'How?'

'Go to him naked.'

'I couldn't do that.'

'Why not?'

'It's obscene.'

'It is,' Flora said. 'What you'll be doing with him is more obscene still.'

This was true. Everything that took place between them was shocking. And the fact of the matter was…she wanted to know more.

'There is a book,' Isla said. 'It's hidden. But I know it belonged to the previous Laird and it is… informative.'

'Where is it hidden?' she asked.

'There is a box in the library. It has a lock, but the key is in a tableside drawer by the chair at the far wall.'

'Well, that's…thorough.'

Isla looked very serious. 'The book is quite… thorough.'

'Take me to it.'

And that was how she ended up making her way to the library with a trail of housemaids giggling behind her. But Isla, true to her word, led her straight to the key and box, and placed the key in her palm. 'Use it well.'

Penny opened it slowly to find a slim volume with a nondescript cover. She opened it and her eyes widened at the sight.

The art was quite lavish and very detailed. On

some pages there was a man and a woman. On many…a man with several women.

She could not look away, the scenes so shocking and entrancing, the descriptions frank and bold.

It would seem that what she and Lachlan had engaged in was an incredibly basic version of all the various things a man and woman could do with each other's bodies.

She was not interested in the scenes containing a crowd, not in a personal sense. Though she did spend a good while turning the book in various different ways to try to fully grasp the mechanics of the situation.

She'd have thought she might be shocked to look at such graphic instruction. But the primary thing she felt was…hurt. She put her fingertips over a particularly salacious drawing of a woman using her mouth on a man's most intimate part. Did he not want these things from her? Or was this the same as him not wanting to give her a baby? The same as him treating her like a prisoner?

Was he doing all of these things with females elsewhere? Because if all of these things were possible, and surely a man like Lachlan would know about them, then he could not be satisfied with the brisk actions they committed under the cover of darkness. Those acts had been altering for her, but she had no experience. So of course it was the absolute heights for her. But for a man such as him? Would he want more?

She did not find herself disgusted, not by any of it. There was no reason to be, after all. Every touch that she had received from his hands had been pleasurable. And the idea of exploring him more only excited her.

Ruin.

The word whispered inside her and echoed off all the tender, hurt places in her heart, an excitement threading itself through her soul and making her feel renewed.

She was a married woman now and could not be ruined. She had been brought here and, as with the running of a household, her relationship with Lachlan was something she had to find a way to control.

Her heart thundered heavily and she took a large volume of Shakespeare off the shelf, held it against her chest, in front of that forbidden book, and made her way to her bedroom. The book bordered on vulgar in places, but it inflamed her imagination.

It seemed that there were very few borders when it came to relations. But this, she supposed, was the difference between copulation—in that reproductive sense that she knew from scientific texts in regards to roosters—and screwing.

He'd said she shouldn't say that word. But then, she felt that she didn't have the knowledge to understand what it had meant.

In the text, various activities were referred to as bed sport and she could see why. It looked all very athletic and like something quite sporting. A fox hunt. That took place in the nude.

And the fox might want to be caught, because the consequences seemed…delicious.

She closed the book and sat on the edge of the bed, feeling…bright. As though she had been lit up from the inside. All those possibilities swirled in her head. And there in the centre was her own pain. At the way he had treated her. At the fact he had not come to her.

And she wondered if he was going to, or if she was going to have to be the one to bridge the gap, with all of this. With her newfound knowledge on the subject of what was possible between a husband and a wife.

Part of her wanted to protect herself.

She crossed the room and went back over to her vanity, to the jewellery box.

Yes. Part of her wanted to protect herself and badly. But there was this jewellery box. Evidence that perhaps she was more than simply a prisoner to him. That she was more than simply the satisfaction of a decade-long quest for revenge. He might not understand the way that he had shaped her life. The way that he had changed it. But he never would as long as she didn't force him to reckon with who she was.

She could fade into the woodwork. She could become that prisoner.

Or she could continue to create the life that she wanted. To take the raw material that she had and build for herself something happy.

But she couldn't do it as long as the sadness existed inside her. This deep loneliness that she felt when she thought of the man.

She felt certain that there was happiness to be had here, but it was not apart from her relationship with her husband. How nice it would be if it were.

You have feelings for him.

He was the one who had rearranged her existence. How could she feel nothing? She felt a great many things for Lachlan Bain. It was impossible for her to not.

He had awakened her passion. Had inflamed her senses.

He had stolen her from the only life she had ever known.

The man had to reckon with her and her curiosity. Her feelings, whatever they were. Because who else would?

Determined, she pressed her fingers against the jewellery box. This time, when her emotions rose up inside her she did not push them down. This time, she held them close to her breast and let them burn into a flame of determination.

Lachlan Bain might be accustomed to being a conqueror. But tonight, he was going to learn what it meant to be claimed by his prisoner. And maybe, in the end, she would be free.

Chapter Thirteen

Lachlan was bone tired by the time he settled into his bed. And what he did not expect was for the door between the rooms to open.

He had not tried to go to her room since the party. And he had missed talking to her. As much as he missed the scent of her. The feel of her softness beneath his hands. He'd got another taste of her and it had been fire.

He'd done his best to ignore it.

But now the door was open. And there stood Penny, wearing nothing but her nightdress, her hair loose and curling, falling down over her shoulders in great golden waves.

Other than that first night, they'd made love in the dark, so he had not seen her in such a state of undress often enough to be immune to it. There was a determined glint in her blue eyes, her full mouth set into a firm line.

'What is it you're doing, lass?' The words came out rougher than he would've liked. 'I'm tired. I'm not in the mood to demonstrate restraint. And I'm certainly not in the frame of mind to talk.'

'I didn't come to talk,' she said.

And with a fluid motion she let her nightdress fall in a diaphanous puddle, away from her body. There she stood, naked, her body glowing in the candlelight. The flames licked and danced over her skin and he was transfixed.

'I told you,' he said, his voice rough, 'to leave me.'

'Yes. For the first time you came to me and then you sent me away when I faltered.'

'It is not you who faltered,' he said.

'It doesn't matter.' She licked her lips and he felt the action in his cock. 'I have spent some time in your father's library. And I've found something...that I believe was meant to be hidden.'

She made her way towards the bed, each step decisive, her hips swaying with the motion. She was like one of the fae folk. Otherworldly and magical. Potentially dangerous to a foolish mortal. She was nothing like the prim English miss she'd been that first time he'd seen her in her father's house. Except...

Even then, there had been a glint of something in her eyes. She'd always had spirit. The spirit that had carried her through their marriage, the trip to Scotland. That had seen her planning banquets for the entire village. Delivering bread to places she was not welcome.

She was a most unexpected woman. Certainly not the pale pawn he had imagined he was manoeuvring about the board when he had first met her.

She had proven herself to be not a pawn, but an ally. She saw manoeuvres he did not. She was quick and warm, and had an ease with people that he had certainly never had.

She was something quite a bit more than he'd anticipated.

She came to the foot of the bed and he went tense. It was against his every instinct to lie there still. He was naked beneath the bedclothes and what he wanted to do was reach out and take hold of her, bring her down over his body and impale her with his aching stiffness. He had been denied for far too long and for the life of him he couldn't say why he had allowed it.

Except something inside him whispered, *For this*.

Because it had been a challenge and one he had been determined not to lose.

He was not a slave to this Englishwoman whom he had brought with him to Scotland. He was not his father. And it would've been a blow to his pride to be unable to keep away from her when she was not willing.

Any man would have a woman who came naked into his bedchamber.

She did not control him.

So he lay still and allowed her to spin her plan out and see where it might take them both. 'I understand now,' she said softly. 'I understand what you intended me to do when you asked me to get down on my knees. I didn't.' She licked her lips again.

Provocative tart.

'I spent the afternoon looking at pictures. They made me feel so very strange.'

She was a lady. And he could imagine her feeling nothing beyond disgust for the kinds of things she would have found in a book of that nature.

'Here,' she said, pressing her hand low against her stomach. 'And lower still.' Her gaze was earnest and forthright, and he found himself wondering why it was he'd thought this lady would do anything but face the challenge head on.

This lady who had asked him what his cock was called. Who had asked for the frank names of all they'd done and who had dared to defy him whenever he laid out an expectation.

Her eager innocence meant that she did not play games when it came to matters of intimacy. Though, withholding had been a game in and of itself. But when it came to the actual act her curiosity overrode any sort of coquettishness.

'Often when I was alone at my father's house, there was only my imagination for company. And I realise now there was such a gap in my education that my imagination suffered. Realising what I could have occupied myself with... If I would've known to dream of a man's body... I would have. If I would have known to think of a kiss as deep and wonderful as the ones I've had from you... I would have thought of nothing more.' She reached out and drew back the blanket that was covering him at his waist. She revealed his aroused state and her eyes went round. 'If I would have known...'

'What?' he asked, his voice rough. 'Would you have lain in your bed and put your hand between your legs? Would you have tried to do something to satisfy the restless need that you found there?'

Colour flooded her cheeks. 'I'm sure that's a very wicked sin.'

'Aye. But I'm a wicked sinner. It's far too late for my soul. So I wouldn't have wanted you to abstain from such things on my account.'

'I would have,' she said, her voice soft.

'Have you done so at night? When you thought of me.'

He didn't know why it might matter, not in ways beyond the physical. But it did. For this moment brought together all that time spent talking at their bedroom doors, rather than screwing. And all the times he'd desired her, too. It all bled into this moment.

Made it sharper. Keener somehow.

'I didn't know you could do such a thing. I squeezed my thighs together tight when I felt restless.'

'A lesson to you, then. You can find pleasure from your own hand. But you can be sure it will never be as keen as the pleasure you find with me.'

'I see.'

She looked obscenely intrigued by the idea. She curled her fingers around his length. 'I did see that men could find satisfaction from a woman putting her hand on him.'

'Aye,' he said, his voice rough.

'You feel… You're so hot.'

'You put a fire in my blood,' he said.

'Good. Because there's a fire in mine as well.'

'And why have you not come to me these last nights? Why have you closed your door to me?'

'Why did you not walk through it?'

An impasse. Perhaps they were both too stubborn to allow the other to see any sort of weakness. Weakness in the form of wanting.

'There was one act in the book that I was curious about above all others,' she said.

But she didn't tell him. Rather she lowered herself over his body, pressing her lips lightly to his shaft.

His hips bucked upwards and she startled. He put his hand on the back of her head and urged her back to him.

'Take me in your mouth,' he growled.

He had thought this a bad idea only days ago, but he had lost sight of why with her naked and soft and glorious above him. With her on her knees ready to worship in this way, why should he stop her, why should he not take what she was offering?

He was a man of battle. A man who sought to control all that was around him. A man who'd failed to change the tide when it counted. A man who felt awash at times in those failures. And this…this was like a baptism.

He needed it. He could not turn her away.

Her pink lips parted and she took in the head of him slowly, working her mouth up and down over his shaft. He moved his fingers deep into that thick, silky hair and guided her as she tried to take him deeper, and deeper still.

This was far beyond what he had ever envisioned. An angel, fallen to her knees, fallen from heaven, taking part in pagan delights here in his bed.

And this was why he had not been able to bring

himself to lay down with a doxy. Because this was what he wanted. Penny. On her knees before him. Pleasuring him, not with skill, but with all the bright-eyed determination she put into everything that she did.

The slick heat of her mouth took him nearly to the brink. It had been far too long since he'd been inside her and his hold on his control was tenuous. She created magic with her tongue and set fire to his reason. There was nothing except for the wet, deep suction of her mouth. There was nothing but them. He had been a man of base needs for as long as he could remember. When he was hungry, he wanted food. When his lust was inflamed, he wanted sex. When his anger was stoked, he wanted satisfaction. When wrong was done to him, he wanted revenge.

He did not care about the manner in which he received those things. But she created in him an appetite that could only be filled by her.

And she created in him a yawning ache for more. But as quickly as she created that need, she fulfilled it, the glide of her tongue over his body a sort of witchcraft.

Pleasure built behind his eyes, his whole body tensed. While he wouldn't mind spending himself down her lovely throat, he felt that was a step too advanced in her education.

And he wanted to be inside her. Properly.

He pulled her away from him, then lay down on his back, bringing her over the top of him, her slick entrance resting against his hard shaft.

'Now, lass,' he said. 'You wanted control? It's your turn to ride me.'

Penny was trembling, both with arousal and with shock over what she was doing.

She had done it. She had steeled up her resolve and gone into his room. She had done exactly what Isla and the others had described.

And it had been wonderful. She had never, ever once thought that perhaps the act might disgust her. No. She had known that everything about his body was pleasing to her. Absolutely everything. And if it made her a wanton, then so be it.

Now, as she sat astride him, his big, hard body pulsing beneath hers, she had different thoughts about ruination.

She was not going to be ruined in this bed. She was being remade. Reclaimed.

Or perhaps claimed for the first time.

For all of her life she had been an oversight. A creature that no one much cared about except what she might do for them. Her isolation and her position in society as a gently bred lady meant that she was not only ignorant of the world around her, but of her own body. Of the magic that it contained. Of the true beauty of being a woman. Heat bloomed low in her belly and in that place where she was slick and hollow, waiting for him.

She had felt conquered by him on their wedding night, and every night after. But she saw it differently now all of a sudden. After the way that he had trembled as she taken him into her mouth. After the way that she had found her own power as she lavished pleasure upon him.

He was not taking from her by being inside her. Rather, he was demolishing walls built up high and thick inside her, around all that she was and all that she expected to be. She felt strong, because she knew these things now. Because she knew of her own power. And men—men like him, gentlemen, even—they already knew. They knew what it was to have the sort of passion between men and women, and they deliberately kept it from ladies. Deliberately kept secrets about their own bodies from them. And by laying with Lachlan, she had discovered truths. By being with a man who shared and shared freely, she had found that there could be more.

Not for wives, Lachlan had said. No, for some mythical class of woman, prostitutes, harlots. Women who were disdained in fine circles, but valued in the bedroom, by men who desired acts that they could never teach the women they married, because then they might understand, fully, the power that they wielded.

But she understood. She understood it now.

And she had meant to come back together with him so that she might find closeness with this man, but she had found a closeness with her own self that she had not anticipated.

She had been locked in a prison for weeping when she'd been a girl. She'd been locked in herself for years since. Expectation and carefully concealed knowledge, and the weight of the fact she had no true control over her destiny.

But here…

She felt free.

She manoeuvred herself so that the head of his cock was pressing against the entrance of her body, then she lowered herself over him, inch by tantalising inch. She looked down at him, at her brawny captive, who filled her with his hardness to the hilt. He was so handsome it made her ache. And that was the other side of this power.

She was not unaffected.

For he was utterly and incredibly captivating. The hard lines of his face, the sculpted angles and planes of his chest. The cords in his neck stood out, his biceps straining as he moved his hands to grip her hips and hold her down over his pulsing manhood.

She could feel how much he wanted her and that drove her on. Made her feel a power unlike anything else. But it also heightened her own need. Made her slick and desperate for satisfaction.

It had been so long for her.

She didn't know if it had been for him.

Her stomach soured at the thought of him laying with a prostitute.

And whatever other women there might have been, they weren't here now.

It was something that ladies were supposed to accept. That their husbands would seek entertainment elsewhere.

She did not share. And after tonight she would make that clear.

He had taught her what it was to feel pleasure in that first week of their marriage. And now she would teach him what it was to be hers.

She began to move, arching her hips up and down, shuddering with satisfaction as she felt the length of him sliding inside her.

She had missed him. She had missed this.

Yet it had never been like this. Because here, with the candles flickering over his face, she could see that he was in the grips of a pleasure that looked nearly like pain. That he was utterly hers. In this moment.

Inside her.

She rode him until waves of need made her internal muscles pulse, until ripples of desire radiated out from low in her stomach further down.

Until her head fell back and she cried out her pleasure, crashing down over her. In her. Then on a growl she found their positions reversed, found herself lying on her back, her great warrior looming over her.

He was fierce and he was strong, and was terrifying in the most thrilling of ways.

He had told her that a show of strength was always necessary. That it always benefited a man for those around him to know he was strong.

Tonight she thrilled in that. In his strength. And how very much a man he was.

It had been so foreign to her at first. But now suddenly she understood. She was soft. She was female. And her body had the power to make him shake. He was man. He had killed countless men in battle, hadn't he told her so?

He could easily kill her. With one large hand wrapped around her throat, he could end her before she ever had the chance to scream. But he chose instead to give pleasure with those hands. To hold her in all of that strength and not crush her with it. The strength of a woman. The tenderness in a man.

Though he was not tender now, his powerful thrusts pushing her back against the headboard, making her cry out in pleasure. The ridges of wood bit into her skull. She didn't care. She was so desperate for all that he could give her. For what she wanted. She was desperate for everything.

And suddenly she understood. She understood that great well of emptiness that had opened up inside her after the other times they had come together. For their bodies had connected, but this time their souls had entwined.

This was unleashed. And it was what she wanted. The warrior. The man. The one who was frightening and beautiful all at once.

She wanted to see not only what his lovers had seen, but what men on the battlefield had seen before them at the end of their life. She wanted every piece of Lachlan.

She didn't understand it. Didn't think she ever could.

But it didn't matter, because there was no room for thought now. She was a creature made entirely of sensation, when for most of her life she had been stitched together by too many thoughts and a great hollow pit of loneliness.

But not now.

Now, she was bursting with sensation. With pleasure like she had never known.

She had come to seduce him and had been thoroughly seduced in return.

And she was glad.

'Lachlan,' she whispered his name.

'Penny.'

Her name on his lips made her soar.

She hadn't imagined that she might find her peak again after she had already done that so quickly before. But when she did, it was earthy. Deeper. Her second climax shaking her, rocking the very centre of what she was. Then he growled and did not withdraw from her body. Instead, he poured himself into her as he shuddered out his own orgasm.

Little aftershocks of pleasure made her quake and she clung to those brawny shoulders.

When she fell asleep, she tangled her body around his. And she did not allow for distance.

In the morning, Penny was woken up by, not Isla, but Lachlan.

The night before came flooding back to her in great, colourful images.

Her face burned.

He was standing there at the centre of the room, gloriously naked. His broad chest bare, chiselled and covered with hair. His waist was lean, his hips narrow. And his manhood…was very definitely interested in exploring yet more pleasure between them.

It took her a moment to realise he was holding a tray. With a tea service, and a plate that seemed to have…

A piece of toast.

'I had thought you might wish to take breakfast in bed.'

He set the tray down in front of her.

'Did you fetch that naked?' She was trying to imagine the kitchen maids handling all that rampant virility in their midst.

And while she was only teasing, even in her own thoughts, she found that the idea made her burn with jealousy. Because she didn't want to share the glorious sight of Lachlan's body. It was hers. Hers alone.

She picked up the piece of toast and bit into it fiercely.

'I don't get thanks for that?'

'Oh, of course you do. But you didn't go into the kitchen naked, did you?'

'I did not. It might surprise you to learn that I do possess some manners.'

'Good. I feel that it has not been established between us, but I would like it very much if you did not go to see whores.'

She successfully shocked him into making a sound somewhere between a laugh and choking. 'You would appreciate that?'

'I find I don't relish the idea of sharing your body.'

'Well now, lass, you denied me your body.'

'I did,' she said. 'Though I sort of expected you to take your husbandly rights without my leave.'

'Is that what you would have preferred?'

'No,' she said, her face feeling hot, her throat scratchy.

'And so now you're concerned about my taste for doxies?'

'It is a concern.'

'There haven't been any,' he said.

She blinked. 'None?'

'Oh, no, lass, many. But all before you.'

'Oh.'

'I found I didn't have the taste for it.'

'Why not?'

'The hell if I know. All I know is that when craving the touch of my innocent wife, it did not appeal to me to go to a lightskirt to find my pleasure.'

'Well, I would like for that to be... I would like for you to not.'

'I promise,' he said. 'I vow. Only you.'

She hadn't expected that. She hadn't expected for him to promise, to vow. And he had. Easily.

'Good. And if there any more...tricks that you wish for me to learn that are not becoming of a lady... I find that I quite enjoyed learning those others.'

'Vixen.'

'Perhaps I am. I would've done quite well as a duke's wife. The peerage are notoriously unfaithful to one another. Perhaps I would've enjoyed exploring my many options.'

'You have one option.'

'And that is?'

'My cock. And with it, you may unveil the mysteries of the universe.'

'That is quite a lot of confidence in one cock.'

'Confidence has never been my issue.'

'Thank you,' she said finally. 'For the toast.'

'You're welcome.'

A warmth spread in her chest. This was what had been missing. This. He held her all night long, then he had brought her toast. In that, he had shown just a small bit of caring. And she found that she had desperately needed it. Just something to show that he was...changed.

Because she was changed. And there was no denying it.

'And thank you for the fidelity.'

'There is a cost to that,' he said.

'What is that?'

'You no longer have your own bedchamber.'

A delicious, forbidden shiver raced through her. 'If I can have toast, then it will be a small price to pay.'

'I believe you've just sold your body for toast.'

'And yet I find myself unashamed.'

It was true. With him, there was no shame.

She had made friends here and they were a

balm for her loneliness. But this was something more. The fulfilment of a need she hadn't realised she'd had.

Such a strange thing to have moved into a life so far away from the one she had imagined, only to find exactly what she had been searching for.

Chapter Fourteen

Lachlan's men had convened for a meeting. They had been issued an invitation to visit the Laird of Clan Darrach and he felt it only right to consult his men. Though he would decide how to proceed as he saw fit.

That was the easy part of the meeting. They would be gone at least three nights, between travel and the acceptance of hospitality. Some would remain behind to protect the people, but Lachlan and a select group would go.

He had been back for over a month now, and he felt it was time to get a sense for the way things had progressed.

Penny was the biggest surprise. Lachlan saw her strengths easily, but when he introduced her as a topic among his men he was surprised to see they saw them as well. That they gave full credit for her planning of the party, which had brought the clans together and felt like the start of a new era. That they saw her caring for the people in the village, building relationships and community.

Of course, not everyone was accepting of the Sassenach bride, but he felt that more were than were not.

Tensions remained, however, most disturbingly within the men who acted as warriors for the clan. The biggest opposition came from his cousin, Callum, and the men who served under him. But he was blood and Lachlan felt a particular loyalty to him out of that connection.

Callum was from Lachlan's mother's line. And he owed loyalty to that. To the MacKenzies.

'The feast was excessive,' Callum said. 'There is concern that, while you shared this time, your English wife will beckon you to behaviour more like that of the English aristocracy. Such unrestrained displays of craven wealth are not welcome here.'

'It was a gift,' Lachlan said, protective of his wife and of the celebration she had planned.

'Aye, and the people loved it.' Lachlan was surprised when Paden, one who was loyal to Callum, spoke out against him. 'Though there is unrest still regarding your wife.'

Rage ignited in Lachlan's gut. 'And many of the people love her. She has gone out daily into the village to share food. To offer aid. She is the one who brings back the needs of the people to me. I have no interest. Were it not for her, they would find their bellies much less full.'

'You must be firmer,' Callum said. 'What we need is a Laird with a fist of iron. We have no need for parties.'

'Yet it seemed as if the people *did* need a party.'

'This is not a London ballroom,' Callum said. 'This is Scotland. Clan MacKenzie is proud. We are warriors.'

'You need not speak to me of war,' Lachlan said. 'I know war. It was my world for nearly ten years. All of life cannot be a war. I fought tirelessly. And it was that fighting that gave me what I needed to return here. To restore our people and our land. I know war. Not the petty skirmishes that happen here, but devastation on muddy battlefields. Young men filled with lead. Their bodies destroyed by cannon fire. I have no desire to be at war for all of my lifetime. And perhaps the people of the clan deserve better.'

'Austerity with survival is better than luxury for a time, only to have it end in death,' Callum said.

'Where is death?' Lachlan asked. 'There is no enemy at the gate.'

'But there could be an enemy at the gate, any day. At any moment. And we must be prepared.'

'There is a difference between being prepared and living under siege when it is not necessary.'

'You would be better off divorcing your wife. Sending her back to England. Picking a Scottish girl from the village,' Paden said.

'I have married Penelope.' He thought of last night, of the brilliant fire that had burned between them. It had been like that ever since the night she had come to him a fortnight before.

The distance and coolness that had existed between them in those first weeks since their return to Scotland had melted away. Whatever reason she had for keeping her body back from him, she had banished it. She came to him joyfully. Freely.

And he received everything she gave. And took more.

There was disquiet, in the back of his mind, a concern that perhaps he was allowing himself to become far too consumed with her. It didn't help that one of these trusted warriors seemed to agree. But there was something far too English and foreign about her. He was in danger of being infected by it.

'I could've stayed in England. I have great wealth there. A thriving shipping company. But I'm Scottish. I am the clan. And I came here as quickly as I could because this is what kept me going when there was nothing else. Knowing that my responsibility lay here. An English wife should not concern the people. If I wanted to be English, I would've stayed there.'

'That's enough,' Graham said. 'Your wife is your wife. It is done. There is no reason to pretend it could be otherwise. Any mutterings from the people... They will be silent once they see the prosperity that's to come.'

'They had better.'

'A threat against your own people to protect a Sassenach?' Callum asked.

'To protect my wife.'

He had vowed that the day he'd taken her from England. He had always known that, physically, he would defend her. He was a man who did not tolerate the mistreatment of the vulnerable. And to him, women and children were vulnerable.

But that had been a vow in keeping with his sense of honour.

This wasn't about the vulnerable or the weak. This was about Penny.

She was good, better than he deserved. Better, he thought, than these men deserved and that was certain.

And as he stormed out of the great hall, he realised it was true. Protecting Penny had become important, for she had become more than a pawn. She had become more than he had ever intended.

She was his queen.

She was, like the rest of his clan, *his*.

And that meant he would protect her. With all that he was.

The weather was truly vile. Rain poured down, creating boggy soup out of the mud all around the castle. Penny felt as though she was going to go insane from being cooped up as she was. But when she had suggested going out, Isla had clucked her tongue and made proclamations about all the ways in which Penny might catch her death.

There was little movement outside. Those in the village who could hunkered down to escape the storm. Lachlan and most of his men had gone to a neighbouring clan and they weren't expected back before morning.

She could only hope that he was safe. It was such a strange thing, to worry about the man. He had survived years of war. Violence she couldn't fathom. And she was concerned about rain being his undoing.

But her worries were shoved aside when Rona came racing into Penny's bedchamber.

'There is a girl here,' she said. 'She said that you told her to come to you if she had a need to.'

'Yes,' Penny said, standing before she could even think of what she might be doing. She didn't need to know who it was. She didn't need to be told. She already knew.

The girl whose name she didn't even know.

And there she was, standing in the core door, looking wild eyed and frightened. 'It's too soon,' the girl said.

And to Penny, she truly looked like a child in that moment. Pale and frightened. Not a woman ready to give birth.

'How soon?'

'I don't know,' the girl said. 'I don't know enough about such things. But my mother... She's had twelve children, and I have some idea of... It's too soon.'

'We need a midwife,' Penny said.

'I'll fetch one,' Isla said. She turned to the girl. 'Do you want your mother?'

'She said she wouldn't help me,' the girl said, hysteria colouring her voice. 'She said I had to leave. She said my father would kill me and it was better if I died out in the rain than to force him to sin in such a way.'

'I'll have his head,' Penny said. 'I won't need Lachlan to do it. I'll take his sword and I'll have his head myself.'

Perhaps that was the influence of her brawny, Scottish husband, but she felt terribly bloodthirsty in this moment. She wanted to lay steel into all the men who had harmed this girl and into the woman who protected a man above her child.

What a deadly weapon, this thing that took place between men and women. What a horrendous way it could be twisted.

Penny was again stunned by all she had been protected from.

The girl doubled over, writhing as a pain racked her small body.

'You must come to my bed,' Penny said. 'We will make you comfortable until the midwife comes. I promise you will be cared for. And so will the babe.'

The girl braced herself on the wall. 'I feel as though I might die.'

'You won't die,' Penny said.

She vowed it. It wasn't fair. This girl going through such a terrifying thing. And Penny's husband didn't want children.

He had only made a mistake that first night they'd come back together. Every night since he had spent himself on the sheets. Penny would love a child and yet that wasn't to be.

This girl... This girl's body and life was being torn away from her because she was with child.

It was wrong. It wasn't fair. Not to either of them.

Most especially not to the girl.

'Perhaps you'll give me your name now,' Penny said, helping the girl into the bed.

'Mary,' she said. She closed her eyes, a tear running down her cheek.

All the anger and bravado that had been with her the other times Penny had met her was gone.

Penny sat with the girl, as her pains became greater, closer together. She stepped out into the corridor with Rona as the hours advanced. 'How early do you suppose she is?'

Rona shook her head. 'I don't have bairns of my own. I don't know. I can't tell by looking at the girl.'

'I'm worried for them both.'

Rona looked at Penny, her expression softer than Penny had ever seen it. Things were never easy with the prickly housekeeper, but she seemed united with Penny, in this at least.

'It would probably be a gift to the girl if the bairn died,' Rona said, looking regretful as she spoke the words.

But Penny had a feeling the woman was right. For where would this girl go back to, with a baby in her arms? How would she be able to face her family? Her father?

It was such a terrifying thing.

But Penny wanted the baby to live.

Penny wanted life for them both.

Watching another human being experience such physical distress made Penny's stomach churn.

By the time the midwife arrived, the girl was in extreme pain, gripping the bedclothes and thrashing back and forth.

Her hands gripped the sheets so tightly that Penny feared she might harm herself.

'Is there anything that can be done?' Penny asked the midwife.

'It's just the way of things. And she's a bairn herself,' the woman said, disdain in her tone. 'She's not prepared.'

'No,' Penny agreed. 'She's not.'

'The man who did this to her should be thrashed.'

'He should be killed,' Penny said. 'If The MacKenzie had any idea where he was his life would be forfeit.'

She knew that. In her blood.

For Lachlan was not an abuser of women. Far from it.

'Ah, lass,' the midwife said, shaking her head sadly. 'Men don't often see this as a terrible crime unless it happens to their own wife or daughter. Even then.'

'He would,' Penny said, conviction burning in her chest.

'A welcome difference to the previous Laird, then,' the woman said, her mouth in a grim line.

'So I've heard.'

The hours went by in a slow, tense fashion, until the girl's pain seemed to be utterly unbearable.

'It's time, lass,' the midwife said. 'Time to push.'

The girl was wild-eyed and it was clear she didn't understand, but then nature seemed to take over and she grunted, her eyes wild.

Penny grabbed hold of her face and looked at her. 'You're not alone,' she said. 'We will not let harm come to you.'

Calling from a strength inside herself that left Penny in awe, Mary pushed with all her might.

And then she continued like that, without making any progress for what seemed like hours.

Penny was exhausted, she could not imagine how the girl felt.

'Is it always like this?' she whispered to the midwife.

'There is sometimes more trouble than others,' the woman said. 'This babe doesn't want to come. I'm going to have to try to help.'

Penny didn't quite understand, but she soon learned. The midwife positioned her hand in such a fashion that she tried to ease Mary's pushing as the girl bore down with all her might.

'I can feel the baby's head,' the woman said.

Penny could offer no help there, but she could hold Mary. As her own mother should have done. Could be there for her. Could show compassion.

Could offer something other than blame and scorn.

'Good lass,' the midwife said.

Another push and Penny could see the baby's head.

Then it was suddenly over. The babe out in the world and Mary sagging with exhaustion.

There was no cry and a deep sadness expanded in Penny's chest.

It had taken so long. And it was early.

Penny wanted to weep for the injustice of it, but she couldn't.

Instead, she simply sat holding on to Mary's hand.

And then there was a sound. A whimper, more than a cry, but it soon grew, thin and tenuous, filling the room.

She looked at the baby and saw that, though it was dusky, it was moving.

'There we are,' the midwife said. 'There we are.'

'Does it live?' Mary asked.

'Yes,' the midwife said.

Mary let her head fall back against the pillow, a tear tracking down her cheek.

'I'm glad,' she said.

'Please hold the babe,' the midwife said to Penny.

Penny took the babe, wrapped it in her shawl. The midwife began to give care to Mary. She finished with the rest of the delivery, worry etched in her face.

'What can I do?' Penny asked.

'Nothing,' the woman said. 'She's bleeding. There are herbs I can give to try to slow it. But… Sometimes…'

'No,' Penny said. 'I won't let her die. She's been given nothing. No help at all. No kindness. She cannot die without ever…'

'These herbs should cause contractions in her womb. It helps slow the bleeding.'

The midwife made tea on the fireplace in the room and Penny did her best to guide Mary in drinking it.

The bleeding lasted through the night. By the time it was slowed, Penny knew her bed could not be saved. But as long as Mary could be, it didn't matter.

She heard a voice out in the corridor. Her husband's.

He'd returned.

Penny's body was stiff from being held in unnatural positions for too long and her eyes were gritty.

She stood, making sure the babe was secured in his little nest upon the bed. And then she went to the door.

'The village girl, Mary McLaren. She's had her baby.'

Lachlan looked as though he was gazing at the horror of battle. Penny looked down at herself and realised that she bore the marks of the particularly difficult medical event.

'I'm not hurt,' Penny said. 'It's not… I don't know if she will survive. Mary or the babe.' Emotion caught hold of her chest and it heaved on a dry sob. 'No one has slept and it's been so many hours…the girl doesn't deserve this.'

She felt herself sway and then suddenly found herself being lifted up off of the ground, held close to her Highlander's chest.

He began to walk back towards his bedchamber, where he closed the door behind him. Then he stripped her of her dress, all her bloody garments going to the floor. She shivered. But she found that she was not embarrassed, because she was far too focused on the exhaustion of her body.

He called for a tub to be brought in and for hot water, and wrapped her in a blanket to conceal her modesty as the staff went about doing his bidding.

'But Mary…'

'She will be seen to,' he said. 'Don't worry. You look as if you're about to fall over dead.'

She felt as if she were. But she also felt guilty for abandoning the girl in such an uncertain moment.

'You will not be able to help if you cannot see straight,' he said.

When the bath and water were produced, Isla offered to stay, but Lachlan sent her away. 'I will care for my wife,' he said.

He picked her up and deposited her naked body into the tub of warm water.

His hands were gentle as they skimmed over her skin and an ache of loneliness opened up inside her.

Sadness.

For she had adored this man's hands. When they gave her pleasure, she could find power in it. Could find a way to make a balance so that she wasn't left trembling and wrecked. But today had compromised her defences in a way that frightened her. She was small and reduced. She had never felt so much fear, not even when she'd discovered she'd been sold to Lachlan in the first place.

Now he was touching her and his hands were

tender, rather than arousing, though they still created sparks over her skin. He was large and she was tempted to lean against his strength.

'I just want to help,' she said.

'You may not be able to,' he said, but there was no cruelty in his voice.

'The baby is so small.'

'I've seen what happens with small bairns. It is just the way of things.'

'It's not fair,' Penny said. 'That all they should know is suffering.'

'Lass,' he said, his voice tender, scraping against raw places inside her. 'The world is harsh and cruel. It doesn't care if bairns get a chance to live. Or if girls get a chance at happiness.'

She knew he meant that. Down to his soul. Down to his very bones.

'I don't want to believe it,' she said.

She felt emotion rising up inside her. Emotion that reminded her of the day her mother had died. But there was…there was hope still. For Mary and the babe lived. And while they lived there could still be hope. Hope.

She closed her eyes and let Lachlan's rough hands smooth away some of the pain inside her. Let the warm water soothe the ache that had taken over her muscles, for it had been a day that was long and painful, and it was not over.

She cared for the both of them and couldn't simply stop because she was exhausted.

She didn't like it, for there was no place to put emotions like this. There was no way to stop them and Lachlan being kind was only making it worse.

But she was too tired to fight it. She could only surrender to the warm water, surrender to his hands. Surrender to this. To them.

'You are a soft thing,' he said, his voice rolling over her, even more soothing than the water. 'I forget that you haven't seen quite so many hard things of the world.'

'My mother died,' she said softly. 'I know about death.'

'You're supposed to bury your parents,' he said, his voice rough.

She did not normally press him. Their conversations stayed carefully around the edges of the deep, sad things that had hurt him in the past.

But she wanted to press now.

'It doesn't matter,' she said. 'Didn't your mother's death hurt you?'

'The manner of it, aye.'

'I was five. I was five when she died. It felt a lot like this. Confusing. Unfair. And I felt helpless. I didn't know what to do. And there was nothing to do. It was such a stark and horrible thing. I couldn't fix it. She was gone. I just wanted to save her and it was too late.'

She thought of every little animal, of every plan she had spearheaded since. All the way down to this. To trying so hard to save Mary and the baby.

It was the lack of hope she had never been able to accept. That she might never be able to do something to fix the situation. That she truly was helpless. That she truly was a pawn.

And had she been fighting against that from the moment Lachlan had stood in the great hall of her father's house? Hadn't she been trying to find a way to be active, to fix, to repair, to do something about this yawning void inside her? The one that she had contained inside a shiny jewellery box. But that could not be.

It could not be. And she had tried. She had tried so hard. But she was failing by inches. For her heart was bruised and battered and she knew that she must never cry.

But Lachlan hadn't locked her in a room by herself. He had drawn her a bath. He was here. And he was holding her.

What would he do if she wept?

And why did she want to see? She had found answers to her loneliness over the years. Had made friends by following people around and chattering at them. But this was something different. This desire to sit here and share silence. To allow his hands to create emotions, to soothe and to arouse. And why was it that the man who had brought her the jewellery box, that symbol of her own survival, why was it he who challenged that very way of living?

Why did he make her wish there was more?

This.

This tenderness.

Being held while her heart was sore…

It was as if she had been waiting for this all of her life.

And she hadn't known that. Hadn't wanted to know. For with the comfort came vulnerability. And with that vulnerability came fear.

How could she trust this part of herself to a warrior? To the barbarian who had bought her for revenge?

But this didn't feel like revenge.

It felt like nothing ever had and she wanted to bask in it. In him.

All while her soul trembled with fear over what might become of Mary and her child.

'When my mother died,' she said, speaking slowly, 'I wept. I cried from the very depths of my soul. Each sob was painful, because they came from somewhere so impossibly deep. My father hated the sound of my grief. He said not to cry because she was in heaven and if I did that I was a heathen with no hope. But I missed my mother. I missed her. And I couldn't stop crying. In his anger he took me to my room and he locked the door. Locked me inside. I couldn't come out until I learned how to lock away every last one of my tears. I know about death. It still isn't fair.'

Her throat went thick, her eyes filling with tears. Shameful tears. Tears that she was supposed to be able to keep inside. But she was so tired. She was so afraid. And weary with the lack of justice in the world.

She wasn't alone.

She could talk and someone was here to listen. And maybe…maybe she could cry. Just maybe.

A tear slipped down her cheek and she shuddered. Shivered.

'Lachlan,' she whispered. 'Kiss me.'

Because anything was better than feeling this. Anything was better than surrendering to this. And she found herself being lifted out of the water by her strong, wonderful Highlander, and he held her against his chest as he kissed her and kissed her. As he took her deeper into the carnal, sensual world that he had created inside her. One that existed apart from that place where she locked her feelings away.

Because this was theirs. She wasn't alone here.

But it wasn't about power, not this time.

Not about skill.

This was about being in that room with someone else. Crying and having a person there who would listen.

He laid her out on the bed, looking down at her as if she was a sumptuous feast.

And she shuddered. Shivered.

He slowly divested himself of his clothes, revealing his beautiful body to her. She would never tire of him.

There was something in the moment that felt like a surrender. There was something in the look on his face, in the tender paths his hands had just traced over her body, that made her feel safe in the surrender.

It didn't make her feel weak.

Rather, it made her feel brave. Strong.

She could surrender. She could choose to surrender, she didn't have to hide. She didn't have to push her feelings down deep. She didn't have to lock them away.

Because she was not a child.

And she had not been put in a wooden box with her mother that day. No matter that the room had felt like a coffin, it wasn't. Because she was alive, no part of her dead. Yet she had let part of herself be buried because of fear. A need to protect herself. A need to make sure she was never alone with her pain the way she had been that day.

But she wasn't alone here. She was with Lachlan. And so she wept as he trailed kisses over her naked skin. As his head moved down between her thighs and made a feast of her, creating a helpless, swirling sensation inside her that she didn't turn away from. No. She embraced it. Embraced him. Let his tongue and mouth push her higher, further, than she had ever imagined she could go.

It was like flying.

You helped me save the bird.

That injured bird. The injured bird with the crippled wing who had been grounded, his injuries preventing him from soaring high. But he had been restored.

And now, so was she.

Like a bird who had found flight once again.

It was magic.

They were magic.

He licked her until she shattered and in the pieces of herself she found beauty. Brilliant, sparkling glory in that shattering.

And when he thrust into her body, she gasped. It wasn't an invasion this time, though, and it wasn't a power play. It was a joining. A coming together in answer to the hollowness inside her.

And all it had taken was for her protection to be down. For her walls to have cracked and crumbled.

Then she could feel it. Could feel him.

Each glorious inch of him reaching places inside her that transcended reason.

And where those walls had once stood he rebuilt something different.

The woman she might have been.

Not just a woman who had escaped from her father, not just a woman who had learned how to survive.

But a woman untouched.

A woman who didn't have to fear laughter or tears.

A woman who had gone so far past the concept of innocence and ruin.

A woman who feared no pleasure or pain as long as her warrior was with her.

And it wasn't only his strength, but the strength he had found in her.

All through showing care. For it was the softness in his battle-battered hands that had created this.

The tenderness in his touch, in his voice, that had allowed her to open up.

When it was over, he lay with her, tracing shapes over her bare skin.

'If I had known that your father locked you in your room that way… I would've killed him before I took you.'

'No one needs to die,' she said softly. 'I survived.'

'A person can survive many things,' he said. 'It doesn't mean they should have to.'

'Neglect can't kill you,' she said softly.

'No, lass. It can. I know you've heard how my father used his fists on his mistresses. About how he killed one. It's true. He did. He never raised a fist against my mother. He never did, because she was the Laird's daughter. But his neglect, his transgressions against the clan, they contributed to her despair. That despair caused her death.'

'I had to live,' she said softly.

'Why?'

'I don't know. But something in me always believed... When I took care of the animals that I found, I believe that I was making enough of a difference. I know that it was a small thing, a silly thing, but it felt as though it mattered. It made me feel as though I mattered. And when you would walk with me, when I spoke to you, I felt real.' She closed her eyes. 'I grieved when you left. As though you were dead. I didn't cry. I haven't cried since I was five years old. Not until today.'

He pulled her into his arms, held her against his chest. And she listened to the ragged beat of his heart beneath her ear. 'I will tell you this,' he said. 'You were the only person who spoke to me like an equal for those years. And perhaps that's the real reason I came for you. You felt as though you might be mine.'

She said nothing to that. Exhaustion began to take hold and she found her eyes fluttering closed.

But the last thought on her mind was that he felt an awful lot like he might be hers.

Sealed with tenderness, kisses and tears.

She had dreamed of a different life. In a stately, civilised manner home with a man who put propriety above all else.

Lachlan rarely seemed to have a concept of propriety.

But he had a fierce, deep sense of protecting what was his.

And right then, she was very glad to be counted as his.

Chapter Fifteen

Lachlan had expected to hear of the bairn's death by morning. But it lived.

As did the girl.

He didn't care for the worry that it put on Penny's face. Not in the least.

His wife was too soft. Too hopeful in the face of something Lachlan had seen all too many times.

The babe was... It was far too small.

And he knew full well that good intentions would not keep a child alive. Nor hopes or prayers or dreams. For if they could, his mother would have kept all of her children, and perhaps she would have lived.

If she would've but had more to live for.

She'd had one son and that son had failed her. And he had tried...

He saw that soft, cherubic face in his mind again.

Not one of his brothers or sisters.

The bairn that he'd found near a battlefield while in the army, badly injured near his dead mother, a peasant girl, from the look of things, who had been brutalised by French soldiers.

He had tried.

And Lachlan had profited from saving a peer, but he had to ask God, had to ask whoever might listen, with a quiet rage in his heart, why a dissolute, titled man might survive grave injuries, but an innocent child hadn't been able to overcome them. He could still remember the little boy's whole body being bright with heat. When he had been certain the injuries would not take him, and the fever had.

He had been at war for six years by then. And he had seen atrocities that left scars on his soul.

But he understood why Penny had saved all those small creatures at her estate.

Because sometimes it was those small things that made you hope. They made the world feel bearable. That little boy...

Saving him had become the most important thing in the world to Lachlan.

And he had failed.

That failure stayed with him. And it also taught him better than to hope when there was little to hope in.

The world didn't care.

Perhaps God was too busy to trouble himself with the very small, even when they were innocent.

But this morning in the castle, the bairn lived.

Still, he knew better than to trust in it.

He could understand why it was a necessity for the girl and child to stay here. They could not be moved. Not in their state.

'Her father will kill her,' Penny said when they took breakfast.

'I will not allow it,' Lachlan said.

'I thought you could not control what a man did in his own home.'

She brought his own words back to him and they shamed him. Her blue eyes were level and unyielding. He had known his wife was strong, but she'd demonstrated that strength in new ways every day. She was becoming Scottish. Part of the clan.

'I will not allow harm to come to them,' he repeated.

The days passed and the babe continued to live. Mary grew in strength.

It was time to decide what to do about them.

But along with Mary's healing, his wife had changed.

She was quiet more often. Sometimes she simply sat near him. She would touch him, her head on his shoulder, her hand on his thigh.

He did not know what to make of the change. Neither did he dislike it.

She was doing a great deal of caring for the babe. It seemed to him the mother only took him for feedings, otherwise Penny had taken to carrying the child around.

Yes, it was time to discuss finding a permanent home for the girl and her child.

He understood that she couldn't go home—the issue of Dugan McLaren was one he was going to have to solve. But first Mary needed to be cared for.

She would be protected in the castle, that was true. But perhaps he could find placement for her in another clan, though the matter of her attacker troubled him.

She had said she didn't know him, which made him suspect it had been someone from a different clan.

He believed that to be the case, right up until she was beginning to move about the castle and she passed into the great hall while his men were present.

Her eyes locked with Callum's and he saw fear there. Utter terror. Her face went white and she stumbled back.

Then she collected herself and walked quickly back towards the stairs that would take her to her bedroom.

Lachlan said nothing. But he watched the face of the man for a good while, trying to read it. Trying to see evidence of what he suspected written there. Guilt. Fear. Something.

The man remained blank. That began to arouse suspicion in Lachlan above all else.

For what man would pretend the woman had not fled from him in fear?

One who did not want it noticed.

One who wanted to be able to deny that he was the reason why.

When Lachlan saw Penny later, he approached the subject directly.

'Has she said to you who her attacker might be? Or has she stuck with the story that it was a stranger?'

'She's never mentioned it again.'

'I suspect Callum.'

'But Callum is… He's your cousin.'

'He is. And one of my detractors. Certainly no supporter of yours. The way his eyes follow women around the room troubled me. And I find I've a concern about what he's done to Mary.'

'Lachlan…'

'I will not allow it.'

'Perhaps we should help her escape.'

'No,' he said, his voice hard. 'He will face justice. If it is true, then he will face justice.'

Accompanied by Penny, he went into the bedroom that Mary and the babe occupied. She was holding the child, her expression blank.

'The man,' Lachlan said without preamble. 'The one who got you with child. Was it Callum MacKenzie?'

'I told you,' she said, looking away, 'I didn't know him.'

'The fear on your face when that man was in the great hall says otherwise, lass.'

Mary's face went mulish. 'It is best for myself and the bairn if it's a secret.'

'Why?'

'I do not have to explain to you how it is for a woman,' she said, looking every inch a child and not a woman at all. 'There is no help for me. My own father would kill me. My mother blames my own actions.'

'And I do not,' Lachlan said. 'You and the bairn are under my protection. And I do not allow rape to happen within my clan.'

'He's too powerful…'

'I am The MacKenzie,' Lachlan said. 'There is none more powerful than I. Was my cousin, Callum MacKenzie, the man?'

'I…'

'He was,' Lachlan said.

'He will kill me,' she said, her voice hushed. 'And the baby.'

'He will not,' Lachlan said. 'For dead men can do nothing.'

There was no justice in the world, none but that which Lachlan would bring about himself. There was a snake in the midst of his men and he would not allow that to continue. He would not allow it to go on. He would allow for none of this.

He was Laird. And he would see justice done.

Penny was frozen with terror for all the hours that Lachlan was away.

She had no idea what her husband intended to do. But she feared, not only for his safety, but for his soul.

When he returned, a great shout was heard out in the courtyard.

All of his men were assembled and he had Callum MacKenzie walking in front of him.

Penny ran outside. 'Lachlan,' she said. 'What is it you intend to do?'

'I will make an example of this man,' Lachlan said.

It was then she realised that half the village had trailed into the courtyard.

'This man,' he said, pointing at Callum with his broadsword. 'This man used his strength against a woman. A *child*. He forced himself on her. I will not allow this to continue. This will not be tolerated. Not while I am The MacKenzie. For this is not the reign of Angus Bain. Your pleasure is not your master. *I* am your master.'

'You cannot do this,' Callum said.

'My word is law,' Lachlan said. 'I can do what I please.'

'A trial…' Graham said.

'It is not necessary. Especially among my men, among the gentry, I will discipline as I see fit.'

'You bastard,' Callum spat. 'You prize the life of some bitch over a man who shares your own blood?'

'I prize justice.'

'This isn't justice,' Paden said. 'It is an execution.'

'Laird, surely…' Even William, the boy Lachlan had brought back with him from war, looked at Lachlan with uncertainty.

That seemed to spur Lachlan on. 'Surely an example will be set and you will all know—I do not grant mercy. Not in these matters. If a woman or child is harmed here, the man responsible will be held accountable.'

'Lachlan,' Penny said, rushing forward. 'What do you intend to do?'

'Listen to your Sassenach. Even she doesn't want you to do this,' Callum said. 'This is not the way of things.'

'The way of things is wrong,' Lachlan said. 'At least under the hand of my father.'

'Lachlan,' Penny said.

He turned to her, his expression fierce. And he lowered his voice. 'You would have him live? He would do the same to you as soon as look at you, all men like him would. You would have this dog continue to use women as he sees fit?'

'No,' she said softly. 'But surely…'

'We keep him in the dungeon for the rest of his life?'

'I don't know,' she said. 'But your soul…'

Something flashed in his eyes. Shock. 'No one has ever paid a care for my soul, Penny. I was a soldier for ten years, there is more blood on my hands and blackness in my heart than you could fathom. It is too late for me.'

'Someone else…'

'This is my clan. Why would I pass the spilling of blood on to another man? You would have me put this on someone else's head?' Penny stood back, her heart hammering.

She knew she couldn't stop him.

Callum had raped Mary. Got her with child. The girl had nearly died. And even now she had nowhere to go because of what he'd done. But it pained her, this heavy weight that her husband must carry.

And she didn't want it. Not for him.

She wanted to spare *him*.

That horrible look in his eye, dead and determined, all emotion gone… It was much like the way she had trained herself to be before she had found a way to open herself up. Before she had found a way to weep.

His heart was scarred over and it was carrying him now. This man who understood this concept of justice, but never mercy.

And where was the mercy deserved for a man like him?

It wasn't Callum that she worried for.

It was Lachlan.

For Lachlan was the one who had to live with all this blood, all this pain. But the man had been at war for ten years and she knew he saw this differently.

'Go inside,' he said.

'No,' she said.

'There is no reason to expose you to this. Go inside.'

'Lachlan…'

And she felt that if it were his duty to rid the world of the man, then she must bear witness to it as his wife.

'I said leave,' he said.

Callum was down on the ground, his position that of a man defeated. But then, when he looked up at Lachlan, there was spite in his eyes. 'It's that Sassenach that you've brought to us. She's made you soft. For what is a woman for but a man's cock? If a woman's going to wander around offering it, why shouldn't I take it?'

'She did not offer,' Lachlan said. 'Do you deny that?'

'Since when does it matter?'

'Since I am Laird.'

'An Englishwoman's dog,' he spat.

Then he moved towards Penny. Penny tried to move back, but Callum had retrieved a sword from the ground and was barrelling towards her.

The rest happened in the space of a breath.

Lachlan moved faster and raised his broadsword. Brought it down in one fluid movement.

Penny looked away, her heart nearly exploding through her chest as she heard the sickening slice of blade through flesh. The sound of the man's head separating from his shoulders.

Her heart was thundering so hard she could scarcely breathe. Lachlan's strong arms were around her then, holding her from falling on to the ground. Keeping her from collapse.

'William,' he barked. 'Deal with the body.'

'Yes, Laird,' William said.

Penny was shaking, trembling.

'I told you to go inside,' Lachlan said. Holding her arm, he propelled her on with him, into the castle.

Her heart was throbbing in her chest, her emotions tangled together. She didn't know what she felt. She touched his shoulder and he turned to face her when they were inside the great hall.

Blood was splattered over his bare chest, up to his neck. It reminded her then of when he'd come back and found her in the castle after delivering the baby. Stained with the evidence of life. Of what…of what had to happen whether it was easy or good or not.

He had protected her. Saved her.

He had been determined to protect Mary. He had not been intent on executing Callum to prove his strength or might. It had been to put a stop to harm because the man was unrepentant. Saw no sin in his actions.

She was perversely grateful, however, that he had made a move for her. For it made Lachlan's actions those of a soldier in battle and not an executioner.

'I would have felt no guilt for it,' he said, his tone hard.

'I know,' she said, her chest squeezing tight. 'But I would have cared that you'd had to do it. I would have wept for you.'

'No one weeps for me.'

'I will.'

'There is no justice but what you make, lass. The world doesn't right these injustices. You must do it yourself with steel. My father did not protect this clan. He did not protect his wife. And I… I have seen things end badly. I have no great faith in the world to right its wrongs on its own. Nor do I labour under the delusion that I can always prevent it with my own strength. This, this I could do. Do not waste your sadness on me.'

Something twisted inside her then. And she felt…new. Looking at him, she didn't worry for his soul, not at that moment, because this was a man who knew his conviction. He was a man who would give his all to protect those who were weaker than himself.

A man who would protect her with everything he was.

He was not a man who would lock her away because she cried. He was not a man who would ever harm the innocent. The vulnerable.

A man with all the strength in the world, all the power, and he would use it justly.

She trusted that. Deep within herself she trusted it.

'You need to wash,' she said.

She took his hand in hers and he followed. Which she knew was a choice, because he did not have to be led anywhere by her. 'The Laird needs to bathe,' she said.

With great speed, the staff had seen to preparing the water for him.

It was set out in the centre of their room and

she took care in taking his clothes off his body, washing him clean of any blood.

'Thank you,' she said softly, as she sat next to the tub. 'Thank you for protecting us.'

''Tis justice,' he said.

'You know many men would not see it as such. They would not consider what he'd done a great crime.'

He looked at her. 'My mother despaired of her life. There was no escape. There was nothing for her. I would not have my people live in such desperation. Men…physically we are stronger than women. Where is the victory in overpowering one who could never fight back? It is a coward who takes joy in oppressing those weaker than himself. If a man wants to fight, if he craves violence, then he should find an opponent who might just as easily kill him.'

'When you were at war…'

'The brutality we saw, committed not just on the battlefield. There was a woman…' He hesitated slightly before pressing on. 'She was long gone from this world by the time my men found her. I will not tell you what she looked like.' His voice was rough, laden with the horror of what he'd seen and she could understand, then, why the death of a man who'd committed crimes against a woman would never linger in him for a moment. For this…this ate away at his soul. 'I have seen a great many atrocities, lass, and very few things are grim enough to cause me to lose sleep. But that… My dreams are haunted by that.'

She moved her hand slowly over his chest, to soothe. He put his hand over hers and she looked down at his scarred knuckles. 'It is not the bodies of dead men I see in my mind. It will not be Callum's lifeless body that lingers with me in my dying day. It will be the pain of girls like Mary. Of my mother. Of that nameless woman. It will be the weakness of men who should have been strong. And all the ways in which I was too late to stop it.'

'But you stopped it,' Penny said. 'You did.'

'The gesture coming a bit too late as we have a sickly girl in the room next to ours, with a bairn that may or may not survive.'

'He gets stronger every day.'

'You can never put your trust in these things, lass. Trust me. Now I do not wish to speak of these things any more.'

'Would you like supper?' she asked.

'Aye,' he said.

There was some great satisfaction in taking care of him this way and she wasn't certain where it came from.

But maybe it was just that same thing that had driven her to care for wounded creatures. It made her feel as though she mattered.

She might not be able to mete out justice in quite the way Lachlan did. But she was his wife. The Laird's lady. She was part of the clan. And she felt that, deeply, for the first time. In full support of her husband and the decision he had made today, hard and unyielding though it had been.

It was a statement. And they had come back to the clan under grave circumstances. And it meant that they could not tread lightly. He could not.

Even against his own blood.

She had supper brought up to their room and they ate together. They didn't need to talk.

But her connection with him felt strong. They didn't need to be touching. He didn't need to be inside her. She didn't need to chatter endlessly. She could simply sit and be near him.

A revelation.

She felt very suddenly inside herself. In a life that was hers.

A castle that felt like hers.

With a man who felt like hers.

This place was harsh. And it was different than anything she had ever been exposed to. It forced her to be stronger. It forced her to be different.

At the same time, time with Lachlan forced her to be fragile as well. To open up deep, compassionate places within her own heart.

Her interactions with Mary and her baby touched her in that way as well.

For the first time in her life, her world felt big. More than that, she felt powerful within it.

It was a gift, a change that she had never expected.

'Are you quite ready for bed, my Laird?'

'Past ready.'

And she went to him gladly.

Chapter Sixteen

There were grumblings among his people. While many supported the action he had taken against Callum, there were factions, even within his own men, who were bitterly angry. They did not think that a woman's chastity should be prized over the life of a man. Particularly when a woman's chastity had not even been proven.

He was beginning to feel concern for Mary's safety. She was ensconced in the castle, and growing healthier by the day. But they would need to find a position for her and he knew it could not be back in the village.

It had become customary for he and Penny to take their late meal alone in their room.

'Have you spoken to Mary about where she might want to go?'

'I think she'd like a domestic position somewhere,' Penny said. The place between her brows pleaded. 'I've written a letter to Lady Beatrice Ashforth. The Duke's sister.'

'Yes,' Lachlan said. 'The Duke. It has been a while since I've heard you speak of him.'

'It has been a while since I've thought of him,' she said.

He did not know why, but that gripped him with a fierce, possessive pleasure.

'And what did you ask this friend of yours?'

'Initially, I had intended to ask her about household positions. If she might be able to provide a reference, or give me names of those who might be willing to hire a girl from Scotland. But then... Instead I asked about school.'

'School?'

'She's young. She could go to a school that might train her, give her an education that she could use to take a position as a governess. She could have more options available to herself than simply being a scullery maid. Perhaps she'll choose that life. But when I thought she might die the thing that grieved me most was that she didn't have a chance. She didn't have a chance at a better life. She didn't have a chance to know what it was to be loved. To choose anything beyond this... This position she was born into.'

'That is the life most people must contend with,' he said softly. 'Not everyone is spirited off to the Highlands, after a broken engagement to a duke, a duke who would have vastly increased her circumstances. Whichever path you'd taken, your life would have changed. You have experienced extraordinary events.'

'It does not surprise me that you consider yourself an extraordinary event,' she said, a sly smile touching her lips.

'It is the way of things, lass. Most do not escape fate.'

'You did. A destitute Scottish boy who made his fortune, who survived nearly a decade at war. You're allowing this clan to escape the fate that your father consigned them to. Shouldn't Mary have a chance?'

'You're forgetting the bairn.'

'I haven't forgotten,' she said softly. 'But that is… Have you noticed she does not hold him?'

'I have not noticed the girl or the babe more than necessary.' It wasn't true. For he had seen how pale and weak Mary was and had watched her increase in strength, but had also seen that her interest in her child did not grow. The child still did not have a name. Not uncommon, for life was harsh and the chances of a baby dying were great enough that often the naming of them was delayed.

'I want her to choose. Because she had no choice in any of the things that brought her to where she is. I want her to be able to choose.'

'Do you expect word from your friend soon?'
She nodded. 'I hope.'

Word came early the next day. With Beatrice writing to say that she could find a position for Mary at a school, thanks to the influence and generous donations of her brother.

His wife began to weep.

'Always caring for wounded birds,' he said, dashing a tear away from her cheek.

She went immediately to Mary's room.

'Mary,' Penny said. 'I've had a letter from a friend of mine. She's sister to a duke. In England.'

Mary's eyes went round. 'A duke.'

'Yes. She has found... There is a position available to you at a school in London.'

'A school? What school would take me? No school wants a fallen woman who can't read or write...who has a child.'

'That you cannot read or write is not a concern. We can find you a position in a household with your baby if that is what you wish. But if you don't want the baby to stay with you...'

The look on the girl's face was one of such deep, pure emotion Lachlan had to look away. It was anguish, but it was hope.

'I can't leave him...'

'How old are you, lass?'

'Thirteen,' she said.

Everything in him turned. He didn't regret the death of Callum, not in the least. The man was worse than a devil, and he could burn in hell as far as Lachlan was concerned. Burn in hell for touching a child.

'I had to become a man when I was thirteen,' he said. 'When it became clear my father was not one. Eventually, I made my way to England and I made my fortune. You have been forced to a burden you should not have been. But what you do now…it is your choice.'

'The baby…'

'He'll be cared for,' Penny said.

'My parents won't. And, I wouldn't want him with them, even if they were willing, I wouldn't want them to have him.'

'If it was what you wanted,' Penny said, her tone careful, 'I would care for him.'

Lachlan took a step back. But Mary's eyes filled with tears. 'You would take care of him?'

'I would.'

'Would he be yours?' The girl's voice was filled with so much hope, it was nearly as sharp as any sword, as gutting as any bullet could have ever been.

'Only if that's what you wanted.'

'I tried to get rid of him,' Mary said. 'I felt terribly guilty about that, after he was born and I saw him. But… I can't take care of him. I don't know how. And I never imagined that I might be able to go to school. That I might be able to learn something…'

'You can,' Penny said. 'And if you really want, if you work at your studies, you might be able to find work as a governess.'

He could see a whole world of possibility in Mary's face. 'Not live in a house full of children like my mother. Not getting beat for the rest of my life by my husband. Learning to…to read and write and to get a real job. In London…'

'I just want you to be able to choose,' Penny said.

'I never knew I could choose. Not anything. I've never been able to.'

'You can now. And whatever it is you choose…'

'I want to go to school. If he can be taken care of… I don't know how to do it. I've been here, with no work to do, and I don't know how to soothe him when he cries and I don't know how to hold him right. And it is not his fault, but his father… His father hurt me. When I look at him I think of that.'

'You shouldn't live that way,' Penny said.

'Thank you,' Mary said.

'All I want is for you to make the best that you can with that choice,' Penny said. 'And don't look back. Don't wonder if you made the wrong choice.'

Dread built in his chest. The thought of this tiny, vulnerable child being in his care. Of Penny loving him. Of Penny...

If she lost this bairn, what would it do to her?

Lachlan waited until they left the room to turn to his wife. 'You do not mean to keep the child?'

'Why not?'

'You did not ask me.'

'You said to me, while we were on the way here from England, that I would likely be able to find myself a baby.'

'I did not say that.'

'You did.'

'If I did, then it was because I was simply thinking you might hold a child on occasion. Not because you were going to take in a foundling.'

'If your issue with children is your bloodline, then why can't I have someone else's baby?'

'So, is this what it is? You're offering her this position so that you can take the child?'

She looked stricken. 'No. How could you ask me that?'

'It seems to me a reasonable enough question, lass.'

'I do want the baby. I love him. And I'm much more prepared to take care of him than a girl of thirteen. I have a husband with all the money and power in the realm.'

'And you did not ask that husband what he might think of it.'

'It's a baby. And you made it perfectly clear you want nothing to do with them. But you told me that you were withholding a child from me because you didn't want to carry on your bloodline.'

'Do what you will, Penny,' he said, anger rolling through him. 'But this is not my responsibility. I have plenty enough to see to without taking on an abandoned child.'

'He's not abandoned. She's making the best choice that she can, for both of them. If you could have seen the desperation on her face when I first spoke to her. She didn't want this. And even now, it's clear that she has struggled to bond with him. That she hasn't. It isn't fair what she's been through.'

'Do what you will,' he repeated. 'But I'll have none of it. I have nothing to do with it.'

'I didn't think you were an unreasonable tyrant. I knew how badly your father had hurt you. How badly he hurt all the people here. And even though I don't believe your blood is tainted, Lachlan Bain, I could understand why you do. But what I don't understand is why you…why you're angry with me about taking this child in.'

She didn't understand. For she had not seen the things he had. The way the loss of her babies had destroyed his mother, year after year. The vow he'd made to that wounded child, on a battlefield years ago, that he could not keep.

That strength, love and power could not keep a bairn on this earth. No matter how deep it was.

She said she knew. She didn't.

'If you wish to take this on, I cannot stop you. I won't. But you're sheltered, Penelope, and you still believe that everything will work out right for you in the end because it has. But I know how quickly fever can take something that small. And when your heart is shattered over the death of a child...'

'Lachlan, you can't... We cannot guarantee that things in life won't hurt. Just like you could not know for sure if you would succeed here. But it doesn't mean you didn't try. I cannot guarantee that the child will live two years, ten years, thirty years. But... This kind of closing off yourself...that's what my father did. And he couldn't stand my emotions. He couldn't stand them, so he shut me away. And then I ended up shutting away pieces of myself for most of my life. And I missed them. But here... Here I have found myself, and I will not go back. I won't stop love simply because it might harm me. I cannot do that.'

'On your head be it.'

And he turned and left his wife standing there. If he were a man who could feel guilt, he might have felt it now.

But he couldn't.

His wife was still the woman who had saved that bird.

But he was not the man who had helped her.

And he never could be again.

Chapter Seventeen

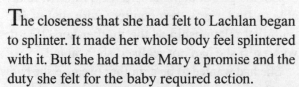

The closeness that she had felt to Lachlan began to splinter. It made her whole body feel splintered with it. But she had made Mary a promise and the duty she felt for the baby required action.

After Mary was bundled up and sent tearfully away to England with one of Lachlan's men, and also with Flora, who had found a position in London, it only got worse.

Because then Penny began to take over the care of the baby in earnest. It was up to her to name him. But she was having difficulty thinking of a name. Her father certainly didn't deserve a namesake. Lachlan wouldn't want one. And his father…

Well. There was no chance of that.

She had spent the past two days walking the halls, holding him and repeating different names.

The midwife had helped her find a wet nurse and they had got the woman situated in the castle. Penny was sorry that she couldn't feed the little boy, if only because she was desperate to find some way to let him know that she was his mother.

His mother.

She had lost her own mother so young she could barely remember her, and the word *mother* was tied to beautiful, soft feelings, which often gave way to the sharpness of grief.

But the gift of being able to be a mother, to be able to find a way to reconnect with that word, with that relationship as the mother herself... It was a gift she had not realised she wanted.

She had wanted to be a mother because she had simply assumed it was something she would do. Because it was a given that a lady of her standing would become a wife and mother.

When Lachlan had told her she wouldn't be, she'd been forced to contend with why that hurt.

And the reason became bright and brilliant while holding the baby one afternoon.

Because it brought her closer to her own mother. Because it made her understand the way she had looked at Penny. And made her feel as if she might have been loved once in the way a parent ought to love a child.

It was a week into her being the child's mother, when she finally thought of a name. And right at that same moment, she realised that she had not thought of the little box inside herself where she used to keep her feelings in all that time. She had simply felt them. She had felt love and concern and worry and despair, so deep and real over these past days.

She had felt happiness, joy, deeper than she had ever known it.

It astounded her that with that joy she could also feel some of the deepest pain she'd ever contended with. Over the fact she wanted Lachlan by her side for this. Wanted him to be united with her. For they had become family. Clan. And now this child was part of it and there was a wedge between them. She wanted all of them to be family.

She wanted Lachlan. By her side, always.

But she felt it. She didn't hide from it. And she wasn't confused by it.

He was not withholding his body from her. He was as ravenous for her every night as he had always been. But she could feel a distance there. And he didn't speak to her the way that he often did. Their silence no longer had that sweet sense of the companionable.

She was part of him enough to feel the distance and to know that it was real. She didn't have to know why.

There was a particular torture in having his body and knowing she no longer had his soul with it, for she'd experienced the difference. And now that she knew…now that she knew, it was devastating.

'I've named him,' she said, as she held him during supper that night.

'Have you?' He could not have sounded less interested if he'd made an effort to.

'Yes. Camden. It's Scottish.'

His expression was dry. 'Thank you. I didn't realise.'

She narrowed her eyes. 'It means winding valley. I wanted to give him a name that was connected to this place. To the clan.'

And one that felt like the true journey of her heart. Through a winding valley that was sometimes dark and frightening, fraught with peril, but was beautiful and worth the journey, no matter the cost.

'Not an English name?'

'He's not English,' she said. 'And neither am I.'

He paused, his broad shoulders shifting. 'You still sound English enough.'

'I'm part of this place. I'm part of you. Even if you're not very happy with me for the moment.'

He arched a brow. 'I'm not unhappy with you.'

'You are.'

'What have I done to make you think so?'

'You know.'

'Am I not sitting with you and having a meal?' He made a broad gesture over the food as if to suggest his grandness.

'You are. But it's not the same.'

'Do I not give you my body every night?'

'For all I know you give your body freely to whores as well. It used to be different between us. And you know that.'

His face turned to stone. 'Do you give your body to whores?' she asked. 'Even though I asked… I told you not to?'

'No,' he said.

She let out a sigh of relief, and looked down at Camden, brushing her thumb over his downy soft head. 'You like me a great deal more than you pretend. And right now, you're a great deal angrier with me then you're admitting.'

'It's just I've nothing to discuss when it comes to the lad.'

'So he'll grow up without a father?'

'I cut his father's head off and did us all a favour. I would have done well to grow up without a father.'

'Is that the problem? Do you not think you'll be a good father? Because you will. I know you will. The way that you take care of the clan, the way that you defended Mary… You're a leader, Lachlan, in a way your father never could've been.

And his blood is in your veins. So I don't believe that blood is weak. Because in you…in you it has become something entirely different. You believe in honour. And you believe in what's right.'

'Aye,' he said. 'I do. I believe in taking that which my father corrupted and restoring it. And giving it, along with the burden of leadership, to the people. I had intended for it to be Callum, now not so. But there are men among the chieftains and I will choose one of them, and their descendants, when I see who is worthy of it.'

'Honourable,' she said. 'But that's only relinquishing responsibility in the end. It's just fear of what you can't control, isn't it? And I understand that. I came here with my feelings locked away tight. And can you blame me? For nobody in my world ever treated me with any care. The only one who ever did… It was you, Lachlan. And then you were gone and I was left devastated yet again. But there is no good that comes from living that way.'

'There is plenty of good that comes from it,' he said. 'See the good that I've done here? That's what comes from it.'

There was something strange behind his eyes, though, and if she didn't know her hardened husband quite so well she would've thought that it was fear.

Fear. Was it possible the man was afraid?

* * *

Camden had a particularly difficult night and she chose to sit in her bedroom, which was now the nursery, holding him close, rather than allowing Rona or one of the other maids to see to him. The wet nurse came when he was hungry, but otherwise, Penny sat with the baby.

Perhaps Lachlan was afraid of being like his father. Or perhaps it was something deeper, yet more simple. She looked down at the tiny delicate baby and thought of what Lachlan had told her.

That babies died.

And she wondered if that was what truly frightened him. Loving something only to lose it.

For Lachlan did withhold his love.

He might care for her, but he didn't…

What a foolish thought.

Love.

She had never imagined she would have a husband who loved her. It was such an uncommon thing that you might find a person you could marry who might also love you. Whom you might also love.

A whisper of something went through her heart. Like an arrow. She chose to ignore it.

She simply continued rocking Camden. But it was Lachlan whom she thought of. And all the great distance between them.

And while she didn't push her feelings away, she refused to give names to them.

To do otherwise would cause far too much pain.

Chapter Eighteen

He could hear screaming. *Wailing.*

It pierced through his sleep. His dreams shifted, morphed half into memory. And he saw him. A tiny, helpless boy lying next to the body of his mother.

Crying and crying. Blood all over him. No way to tell if it was his or hers.

And he held him close. That tiny, fragile thing. He held him close to his chest.

'I promise,' he whispered. 'I promise to protect you.'

He woke with a start. His eyes open in the darkness of the room, but there was still wailing.

It was coming from the room next door.

And his wife wasn't in bed.

He got up, stumbled to the door that connected the two spaces and opened it.

This room was empty, too, of everything except for the bairn.

Camden.

Camden, she had named him. For the valley. For the land that belonged to his clan. For this new place that she claimed to have adopted. As she had done this child.

The image of Penny, devastated and grieving, tore at him. But he was still in a strange fog. A place somewhere between sleep and awake. That was where these memories came for him.

And they were all mixed together with the baby that was screaming in front of him.

He approached the cradle, which held the child, and stared down at his angry, red face.

He reached down and one flailing fist connected with his finger. He stilled. The child's fist rested there and he didn't know what led him to shift, but he did, and the tiny fingers wrapped around his own.

A strange, primal surge of possessiveness ran through him and he took a step back, uncertain of where it had come from.

The child started to cry again.

The crying only reminded him of that boy.

He had not held a child since…since one had died in his arms.

Slowly, he picked the tiny body up out of the cradle, held it in the crook of one arm.

The baby turned his head back and forth, making small routing sounds, like a pig. 'You'll be disappointed,' Lachlan whispered. 'I've nothing for you. I don't know where your nurse is. Or your mother.'

His mother. If Penny was the boy's mother, he supposed that made him a father.

He had never wanted to be a father.

For reasons that had built one on top of the other over the years. For reasons that echoed inside his heart and never seemed to get any quieter.

For reasons that screamed at him even now, as he looked down at the tiny, improbably fragile being.

He had made promises before. That all would be well.

He had made promises to save a life he had not been able to save.

Babies died.

It was the way of things. He had learned that early. He had grown up in a house filled with such death. This very castle. So much loss within the walls of it. He had come to accept that. To expect it.

But the useless brutality of what he had come upon on that battlefield…

He had promised. And he had failed.

What promises could he make his own children? What promise could he make to his own son?

He knew he could not prevent disease or sickness any more than he could prevent a clear day from turning into a storm.

He would not be able to protect this child, any more than he would be able to protect Penny from the grief that would drown her if she were to lose the child.

He had never wanted to be a father.

The door to the chamber opened, and in came Penny.

'Oh,' she said. 'I'm sorry. I went to the kitchen to see if I could find something to eat. I didn't realise he would be so upset. He was fine when I left.'

Her eyes were round and she was staring at him with a mix of fear and scepticism.

'Take him,' Lachlan said. He offered the child to her.

'Just a moment,' she said softly. She began to move around the room, setting her tray of food down on the table by the bed. 'I've been with him all evening.'

'Did you leave after I went to sleep?'

'Yes,' she said. 'I'm afraid I haven't been getting much sleep. I might have to call the wet nurse.'

'Why is it that you tend to him quite so much?'

'I don't know how else he will know I'm his mother. I didn't give birth to him. I can't feed him.

I wasn't with him from the beginning in quite the way I am now. I just want him to know.'

'I'm sure that he does,' Lachlan said. He was not certain of any such thing. He knew nothing of babies and even less of what one might know or think.

'Why do you not want him?'

'Penny…'

'I want to know. I want to understand. Because you're a good man, Lachlan Bain. You care for all the people in the clan, yet you don't want to care for this child. And look at how easily you hold him.'

'All I know of small children is death,' he said. 'Loss.'

He went to her and handed the child to her. 'To me, that is what this means.'

'But some children live. Or you and I would not be standing here.'

'Aye, some do. But many do not.'

'Lachlan…tell me. What is it?'

His lip curled. 'Is it not enough my mother lost every bairn save me?'

'There's something else, I can feel it.'

So could he. Pain like a wounded, clawing beast.

A darkness that went somewhere past rage.

It wasn't the rage that bothered him. It was the grief. Useless and soft. As pointless as mercy. But if Penny wanted to know, if she wanted to take part in this…on her head be it.

'The woman I found. Raped and murdered by the French. They left her baby for dead as well. He'd been grazed by a bullet. A deep wound, but nothing vital hit. They left him by his mother's body to die. I picked him up and wrapped him in my shirt. I made a promise to save him. For days we marched on and I carried that child. Until he became hot with fever. He died, Penny. There was nothing I could do. My promises were empty. I cannot promise you this bairn will live, nor any. I could not stop it if sickness took him. Nor can you.'

He never spoke of this. It had happened before young William had joined the company. He didn't know where any of the men who'd witnessed it were. It was a failure he carried alone. The one that rested heaviest of all.

For while he felt guilt over his mother's death, he'd had no way to return. He felt anger over that, most of all, for it was Penny's father who had prevented his return.

But he'd been able to take his revenge against that enemy.

Nameless French soldiers…

He'd slain many on the battlefield and somehow it had done nothing to make that boy and his mother feel avenged. The stain was on his hands, no matter how much he tried to make it otherwise.

'Lachlan, you tried.'

Three more useless words he could not fathom.

'And it did nothing. It would do nothing to protect you either.'

'I'm not your mother,' she said quietly. 'More importantly, you're not your father, so you could never push me to be.'

That hooked into something deep inside him and he realised that he did worry about that. About her sinking into a state of despair should she encounter such loss. His mother had been left with nothing to live for. Nothing.

He didn't want Penny to experience the same.

And when had he begun to care about her feelings?

Perhaps because it was much easier to consider her a pawn when he had not known the whole woman. And he did now. Courageous, fierce and beautiful. He had found her silly. He found her pursuits of saving creatures to be a mark of that silliness. But he could see now that it spoke to something deeper. And he had not asked for that. Had not asked for any manner of insight into who she was.

Because it didn't matter. It shouldn't. A man in his position was most definitely in want of a wife, but he did not need to know that wife. He did not need to care about that wife. There was a lot of ground between that and the abuses his father had dealt out. And no need to cover it. He could not afford softness, but that did not mean cruelty.

Because there was enough cruelty in the world as it was and if a man was soft he could hardly keep it out of the walls of his castle.

He knew that to be so.

For what had softness ever gained him?

It could not bring that boy back from the dead. Any more than it could protect the one here now.

He turned sharply and walked back into his bedchamber. His blood was stirred from being woken from sleep and he should never have gone into the bairn's room. That was her domain, not his. It was not up to him to care for a wee babe.

Women's work. And if the woman needed a child to keep herself occupied, that was her concern.

His was with the safety and protection of them, of the clan.

She was his. And they would both do well to remember it.

He could not sleep. He prowled the room for the better part of an hour and could hear Penny and the wet nurse moving about the room.

Then, she finally came back in.

'You could have stayed,' she said, 'if you weren't going to sleep.'

'I don't want you caring for the babe at night any more. You must move him in the room with the wet nurse.'

'I want to take care of him.'

'It is impractical. There is a reason a woman is here to see to his needs. You are the wife of the Laird. It is not your responsibility.'

'He's my baby.'

'He is a foundling.'

'He's mine,' she said. 'As if he came from my own body. As you will not dictate to me how I care for him.'

'Aw, but, lass, I *will* dictate it to you. Because I am your Laird.'

'You are my *husband*,' she said. 'And I don't know what has you in a state.'

'I am The MacKenzie. I create the state.'

She frowned ferociously. '*You* are an arrogant sod. And it is well past time you slept.'

'I'm not a bairn that you can put down to sleep,' he said.

'Then don't behave like one.'

Anger fired through his blood, for she had no right to speak to him in such a manner. And there was no reason for her words to feel as pointed as a dagger. No call for it to feel as if she was speaking directly to his soul. This clan was his. This castle was his. She did not determine the rules.

'You do not dictate to me, Penny.'

'And you don't seem to understand that this is not simply about a child. You hold yourself back. Not just from him. From me.'

'Perhaps you have forgotten,' he said, 'as you have grown so comfortable here in my care, but you are my captive.'

'Am I? I rather thought that you were mine.'

'You mistake me,' he said, 'because I have not been cruel to you. And I will not be. But do not mistake that for care.'

She drew back, as though he had struck her. And that only made him all the more angry because, if he had struck her, she would not be able to stay standing. And he would not. He didn't think she understood just how well she had been treated. He owed her nothing. She was an Englishwoman with a father who was barely better than his own. She was defying him with the child and he was allowing it, to an extent.

'You would be a good father,' she said softly. 'You would be a good husband. I know you think you've been a husband to me and you have. But not all of you. You're fighting it. You're fighting your feelings and you're fighting me.'

'I'm fighting nothing. It's you who are fighting the way of things. The truth of things. You do not wish to live with the true state of the world, with the state of this life. I'll allow you the babe, but do not push me further.'

'I think that perhaps the real problem is that you do care. And you want more.'

Penny could see the moment that she had pushed her husband one too far. The banked fury in his green gaze would've been terrifying if she had not known that he would never harm her.

Physically.

Emotionally, however, he had the power to devastate. And she knew it. He had the power to destroy her with a few carefully placed words and she knew that he would not hesitate to do so if it came down to it.

Then, he closed the distance between them, all that fury like a green fire.

'You forget,' he said. 'You forget what you're here for. You forget what a wife is for.'

He wrapped his arms around her, his hold rough.

He had never treated her like this, not even in the beginning. For in the beginning he'd had a care for her innocence. Now that was gone.

She could see that he had been tested past his limit.

But she... She had not been.

She was not the innocent that had first been

taken by Lachlan Bain, she was not that girl. She was not the girl who had been locked away, weeping and wailing in her bedroom, unaided by her father or his staff.

She was not even the girl who had mourned the loss of a servant boy who had been her only window into humanity. Because that boy was before her, buried beneath this mountain of a man, but she knew he was there. Because she had seen a glimpse of it when he'd held the baby.

He could pretend that he had no connection to the child. He could pretend he didn't want one. But she had seen it.

He was not made of stone.

He might wish that he were and she had the feeling that he did.

When he spoke of the woman who died on the battlefield, of the baby, the baby he'd held in his shirt, she could see his pain.

She could see that it wasn't a lack of love that he possessed. It was too much. A deep well of caring that was far too great for him to contend with.

The boy who had come all the way to England to try to save his clan. Who had been too late to save his mother.

The boy who had—like her—tried to find hope in small things.

It was why he had let her trail around after him, she was convinced of that.

It had not been an accident and had not simply been because he was trying to patronise his master's daughter. No. It had been more. It always had been. And at every turn the trust he had tried to have in humanity had been abused.

The way that her father had cheated him.

It was only on a battlefield covered in blood that he had found any sort of salvation.

It was no wonder he could not find faith enough to allow himself to care.

And this was where her strength was tested. This was where she proved that she had been changed by all of this.

Because as he held her against his chest, all his fury pouring down over her, it would be easy to shove her love, to shove her fear, down deep, to not let him see any of it.

But she would not turn away from her feelings.

Oh, she had thought she loved the Duke. Because of his manners. Because of his family.

Because he represented a soft, gentle life which had felt like the stuff of dreams after her hollow, cold upbringing.

But she had not needed gentility. She had not needed safety.

She had needed wildness and adventure, and all of the things that she had never imagined she would be strong enough to endure. She needed his ferocity.

Because only this, only this hardness, only the strength, could have demolished the walls inside her.

She could have lived a quiet life with the Duke. Protected, cosseted.

But in the end, it would have been little different than the neglect.

A slightly softer prison, perhaps.

But she would've never found herself.

For she was strong and she was fierce. She was enough to be the bride of a warrior. To be the lady of this castle.

To stand and defend her child. And to fight for her husband.

For his heart. To fight for the battle of all that he was.

Because they both deserved to be whole.

She had seen marriage only as an entry to a new life.

Because as a lady her destiny was to be with her father until she was with a husband. And so to leave her father... There had to be a husband. She had known only that she wanted different. She had not known that she wanted everything. But she did. Everything.

Love.

Not that sweet sort of pleasantness she had imagined finding at Bybee House. Days spent needlepointing with a cat. But this wild, untamed ruggedness that cut swathes of tenderness through her heart. That made her exposed and vulnerable as much as it made her strong.

Love.

This bright, brilliant, terrifying thing that made her strong enough to stand against the Highlander.

This man had been to war. And he had never truly left. For he was fighting. Fighting against himself.

Against what he sought to destroy, a weakness in his blood that she knew wasn't there.

Not in this man.

And she would show him. She would show him not only her strength, but his own.

He kissed her, hard and punishing, and she knew that he was trying to take this thing that had built so much closeness between them and force a wedge. But she wouldn't allow it. She didn't need books any more. She knew his body. And she knew all the ways that she could make it hers just as well as he knew how to make her body his.

And so she met him. She thrust her tongue deep into his mouth, wrapping her arms around him, pushing her fingers through his hair. She bit his lower lip and he growled. She found herself being propelled backwards on to the bed, his large body covering hers. He tore at her dress, her stays, her chemise, shoving it all down her body and throwing it down the foot of the bed like insubstantial gauze.

He had only been half-dressed, so it took her less time to divest him of his garments, leaving him as naked as she was. His arm was like a steel band around her waist, and he pinned her to the soft mattress, her breasts crushed to his broad chest as he continued to kiss her as though it might save them both.

Or damn them both.

He seemed to be on a path to hell and wanting to drag her along with him so he could prove the point.

Perhaps that they were too different. Perhaps that this was not sacred after all.

But it was.

In all of its forms. For between them, this passion could not be corrupted.

He kissed her, deep and hard, then, with his arm still wrapped around her, he turned her, wedging his cock against her bottom, moving her half-ruined hair out of the way and kissing a hot trail down the back of her neck. He pushed his hand between her thighs, teasing her swollen flesh with his fingertips.

'Still you're wet for me,' he murmured against her ear. 'Wet for a monster. How does that make you feel?'

She drew her head back and met his gaze. 'Strong.'

He growled again, manoeuvring her on to her stomach before drawing her up to her knees, his chest over her back. 'Let us see how strong you are, then.'

He positioned his hardness at the entrance to her body, slick and ready for him. But she had not taken him like this before.

This was what she had read about. This was what she knew.

The way animals came together. Not face to face, or with the female riding astride, but this base coupling, which between the two of them she knew was designed to make her feel as if they were distant.

She arched her back, moving herself against him, urging him to thrust inside.

He gripped her hips, hard, and then slammed himself home. He controlled the pace, the depth, and it was punishing.

She turned to look back at him and their eyes met. The desperation that she saw there told her that his dominance was only a façade, for he was no more in control of this than she. He might be the one with the physical strength to control the movements, but he was just as captive to it as she was.

Hope bloomed inside her. Bright and brilliant.

For she was not a captive now.

She had been a captive in her life with her father, hoping to move to a life of more acceptable captivity beneath the rule of her husband.

But the Duke had wanted her only because he had seen her as easy. She had helped his sister and his sister liked her. It would create peace in his house and it removed him from having to engage in the marriage mart.

She would only ever have been a pawn to him, though he never would have said that to her.

Those manners, after all.

But Lachlan...

He wanted her.

He needed her.

He was wounded and needed to be healed, and she could see that she was the one who would be able to accomplish it.

He could not minimise her power. Not with his strength, not with his control. Because it was too late. The bond had been created between them and he needed her.

And she had seen it.

As if he could read her realisation, as if he could read her thoughts, he grabbed hold of her hair, pulling her head so that she could no longer look at him. Pin prickles of pain broke out on her scalp, but it only reminded her of how powerful the desire between them was. For even that pain twisted and became need.

For even that made her slicker, made her hotter, brought her closer to the edge.

Ruin.

No. This was not ruin.

It was salvation. For them both.

'Lachlan,' she said, whispering his name like a prayer.

And he fractured. His movements became harder, more intense, and the depth of his hardness moving inside her body combined with the pressure built a deep, aching spiral of pleasure that built and built, so deep inside her she thought she would never be able to withstand it when it broke.

Then it did, her body pulsing around his, drawing from him his pleasure, making it her own.

They shattered together. And, somehow, it made her feel whole.

He moved away from her, breathing hard, and she knew that he had reached his completion inside her. She was happy for it. Pleased with the loss of control. She knew he would not be.

He swore a vile oath.

'Don't you know by now?' she asked.

'What?'

'Don't you know by now that the blood in your veins is not tainted by your father? The blood in your veins is infused with everything you've done. With everything you are.'

'Do not tell me the way of the world, lass. You are a child. A child who never left your estate until recently. You know nothing of the world.'

'I know about grief. I know about hope in the face of hopelessness. I know about staying strong when everything crumbles around you. I have seen sadness, despair. I have felt it. I know what it is to live small, you're right about that. But I know what it is to live big, too. I have done that. Here. With you. And I... Lachlan, I didn't know that I can have so much. I thought that I would count myself fortunate if I could find a way to survive in comfort. But here I have learned to live. And I... I never expected love, Lachlan. Ever. And when you stole me away from the life that I had planned for myself... You told me you would even deny me children and I was in despair. But it is the strangest thing, because it is through that that I found the deepest, most true part of my heart. I love you. I love you, and I had no expectation that I might love a husband. I do. Different than any sort of love I've ever felt. Different than I thought love could be.'

'No,' he said, his voice hard. 'There is no place for love here.'

'There is every place for love here. This is such

a vast, untamed place. A winding valley. It is the perfect place for it.'

'But I am not the man for it. I'm not the man for your love. I don't want it. I can't return it.'

'Why do you think that?'

'Because it is the way of things, lass. I am The MacKenzie. I have to be strong. I have nothing in my heart. I have fire in my belly, and that is the best that can be asked.'

'Lachlan,' she said. 'You love your people. You loved your mother. And I believe you loved that child you tried to save...'

'Love is useless,' he said. 'It only turns you into a grieving sack of pain. My mother loved. She loved my father for his sins. She loved every one of her children who died and she loved me, who failed to return to her in time. What did love give to my mother?'

'I'm sorry,' she said. 'I'm sorry about your mother. I think love made my father grieve in a way that hurt me, too. He loved my mother, for if he did not, I don't know that he would've minded if I cried. I think it reminded him of his own pain and he didn't want to feel it. But isn't that the real problem? That we don't let ourselves bleed? That we don't let ourselves feel? That is a prison. It's a prison that feels hopeless. At least pain is something. I think the real problem is when we feel nothing.'

'No,' he said. 'The problem is when we forget our purpose. Feelings cloud purpose.'

'And what of your anger? What of your revenge?'

'Perhaps it did cloud my purpose,' he said. 'Because I brought you here. And perhaps this is no place for you.'

'Lachlan…'

'You are my wife and will continue to be the lady of this manner. But we do not need to share a bedchamber. We do not need to share a life.'

'So that's it. I challenge you and I'm sentenced to a life living beside you and not with you?'

'It is better,' he said. 'You have your purpose. You have your child.'

'It isn't enough.'

'How can it not be enough?' he raged. 'How can it not be enough? You were content to go and live with your Duke and you would've had no more from him. Is it the title you miss? The balls?'

'You're right. I would've had nothing more with him and I wouldn't have minded because I wouldn't have wanted more. I wouldn't have expected more. Not for myself. Not from myself. But with you…'

'How?' he asked. 'How have you discovered this with me?'

'Because you brushed my hair. Because you

got the jewellery box. Because you tried to rescue that boy when many men would've left him as a casualty of war. Because I see who you are and you can tell me that man is dead, but I know he is not.'

He only stood for a moment, looking like stone. And she let tears fall from her eyes. Let them spill down her cheeks. 'Because I have all these tears for you,' she whispered. 'For us.'

'Do not waste your tears on me,' he said. 'I neither want nor need them.'

He didn't leave the room. He didn't tell her to go. Instead, he laid down on the bed, as if he was going to sleep, as if he was going to ignore everything that had just happened between them. And she realised she had no escape. No reprieve. If the man wanted to retreat inside himself, there was nothing she could do. She could not leave the castle. She could not leave him. And she didn't want to, because she loved him. But while he had done enough to reach her, while this thing between them had broken down the walls inside her, she had not done enough to breach the walls in him.

And that was a kind of despair that she feared might be all-consuming.

She dressed herself and, refusing to be moved from her bed, laid down on the other side of the mattress. But the space between them might as well have been furlongs apart.

For his roughness and their passion had not succeeded in putting distance between them.

But his denial of their love had.

And she did not know how she would ever find a way to repair it.

Chapter Nineteen

They had neither spoken nor touched for two days. Every night, she would lay down in her nightdress beside him and turn away.

But what had been said needed to be said. Love.

He had no wish for her love.

Love.

He could think of nothing he wanted less.

The distance between them was so great he was not terribly surprised when she did not join him for supper. But when he found the baby wailing in his room and Penny did not come, he began to feel concerned.

The wet nurse came and looked from Camden to Lachlan.

'Where is the lady?'

'I've not seen her.'

'It's unusual,' the wet nurse said, picking up the babe and putting him to her breast.

It was more than unusual. He could not imagine his wife leaving when the baby might need her.

'See to the babe,' he said.

He walked out of the room, and made his way down the great, long corridor, searching for Rona. 'Where is Lady Bain?' he asked.

'I've not seen her. Not since mid-morning.'

He continued to search. Not only was there no sign of her, there was no sign of Isla, her maid. Of course, they could have gone down to the village, but Penny had not been doing so, not since the birth of the baby. And certainly not since the execution of Callum.

Something felt wrong.

Had she left him?

No. She might leave him, but she would never leave her bairn. For all that he'd said to her the child was a foundling, he did believe her when she said he was like a son of her own body. He had seen it in the way she had taken care of him. He continued to search the castle and the grounds. And he was about to carry on to the village, when he noticed a flash of blue in a thicket in the courtyard.

He made his way to the blue and what he saw made his stomach tight with dread.

Isla.

Crumpled on the ground, blood on her head.

He knelt down and could see the girl was breathing, but only just. She was unconscious. He picked her up, holding her to his chest as he carried her towards the castle. The girl was small, insubstantial, and it was no effort for him to carry her. Still, his heart was hammering, because he knew. He knew that if Isla was in such a state, then Penny was worse, or…

A great, wrenching pain nearly cleaved his chest in two.

No. He would not think of it.

He could not.

He set Isla down in the great hall. 'Rona,' he said. 'We need a healer. Someone. Anyone.'

The housekeeper's face contorted in horror and she went to her knees by Isla's still form. 'What happened?'

'I don't know.'

'Where is Lady Bain?'

'I don't know that either. I'm going to trust you to make sure Isla is taken care of. But I have to go and find my wife.'

Lachlan's sword was already strapped to his hip and he went outside, ready to give orders for his horse to be readied.

But there were men who were not present.

And his suspicions were deeply roused.

'William,' he said. 'Ready my horse.'

'Aye,' the lad said.

He put his hand on the lad's shoulder. 'Where is Paden?'

'I saw him earlier,' he said. 'Going into the wood.'

'Was he alone?' Lachlan asked.

'Aye. But he had…he had something large concealed in a cloak. On his horse.'

Lachlan bit back a curse. 'Be my eyes here. You report back to me anything you hear. Do not make your loyalty to me explicitly known.'

'I think there is no chance they wouldn't guess it,' William said. 'I wouldn't be here, I wouldn't be part of this clan if not for you.'

'And I trust in your loyalty. But make it seem as if you might move with the wind. If it be changing.'

'What is it you think is happening?'

'My wife is gone. I found her maid unconscious. And Paden has vanished. I have my suspicions. But I will see them confirmed. And if I am correct, I will turn all the flowers in the courtyard red with the blood of those who dared touch my wife.'

Penny's head ached. She could not remember what had happened. She couldn't remember where she was. It was difficult for her to open her eyes, but when she did, she found that she couldn't have remembered where she was, because…she had no idea. And she was certain she had not been brought here awake.

Dimly, she became aware that her feet and hands were numb. That they were tied.

She couldn't move.

She shifted and that was when she saw him.

Paden.

'What have you done with me?'

'You're awake,' he said.

Her only response was to blink.

He made a dismissive sound. 'You won't be for long.'

'What are you doing?'

'I'll give you no explanation. You have your part to play in it.'

And here she was, being treated like a pawn again. Bound and lying on the ground in the middle of a forest and not being told why.

Of all the things to anger her, it was a strange thing.

But that was perfect. For if he did not think that she mattered, if he did not think that she mattered or could accomplish anything, then he might let his guard down and underestimate her.

It was the look of hatred on his face that rattled her. It was savage and much more intense than anything she had seen before.

Dimly, she could remember that she and Isla

had been attacked, ambushed, outside the castle. Isla…

'What did you do to my maid?'

'She might live,' he said. 'You, though, you probably won't.'

Her heart felt torn in two. And it wasn't even so much fear of losing her own life as it was leaving the life that she had at the castle. Camden. Lachlan.

She *loved*.

Whole and bright and brilliant for the first time in her life.

And it didn't matter if Lachlan loved her back, she loved him. And she had spent the last two days withholding that from him because she was wounded. And what good had it done her? It hadn't done her any. It was foolish. So utterly foolish.

Two days wasted when she could've loved him. And what had her spite been for? Trying to protect herself. Again.

Yes, he had hurt her. But he'd been trying to hurt her. He'd been trying to drive her away because it was all he knew how to do. Because he was a man who had experienced terrible pain and he hadn't been able to break through that yet.

Apparently her own breakthrough was imperfect.

It didn't matter. Now none of it mattered and, if

she could go back and do it differently, she would. If she could go back and simply love him, with everything she had, with no thought to her own protection, then she would. Because he was the conqueror of her heart.

Joyfully. Intentionally. She had allowed him to claim her and was happier for it. Or she would've been, if she hadn't been so determined to make his rejection about her.

Yes, he had tried to make it so. But he was protecting himself.

For he was not so endlessly brave as all that.

He was afraid of all that he could not control. And all the evils of the world that he could not keep at bay.

Then she had been kidnapped.

Who knew what would happen?

'You're using me as bait, aren't you?'

Because if he had wanted to kill her, it would've been easy. But, no, he wanted to kill Lachlan. And there would be no way he could accomplish that cleanly.

'Bait. The start of a revolution. The start of a war. If the clan believes that you have been murdered by Clan Darrach, all the better.' A grin lifted his lips. 'I couldn't challenge him at the castle now, could I? And a man who has survived a decade of war would make for a terrible challenge. But if he sees his woman bound with a sword at her throat, he'll be forced to surrender. And then, when the clan hears of your murder, of Lachlan's...we will blame it on Clan Darrach and my path to Laird will be clear. It's what Callum would've done if he could think of anyone but himself and his own prick. But, no. He was angry, but he didn't act. If a man doesn't like the direction his clan is going, then he should take action for himself.'

'You're a coward,' she spat. 'Not even brave enough to challenge Lachlan in a real fight. But Lachlan cares about the clan.' Her chest went tight. 'Above all. You've misjudged him.'

'Nay, lass, I don't think I have. And his weakness, like Callum's, will be his end. I will take the power. And all the Laird's money is to go to the clan. He's willed it so.'

And then he would have it all. Lachlan's money and power and both of them out of the way.

'I'll kill that bairn of yours as well,' Paden said. A chill went down her spine. 'Callum's whelp. There need not be any more blood MacKenzies in the castle. No one who might challenge my claim.'

'My husband sought to take care of the clan. And nothing else. My husband has spent his life working to get here so that he might do right for his people. *You* are nothing more than a self-seeking bastard.'

'Some fine English lady you are.'

A surge of rage went through her, of power. 'No, I'm no fine English lady. I'm Lady Penelope Bain. Of Clan MacKenzie.'

And as she lay there, her body aching, she didn't even know what to hope for. Because if Lachlan came, then he might be killed.

But if he didn't…then she certainly would be.

She whispered a silent prayer.

Please, if you love me, stay away.

For if he loved her…he might sacrifice for her.

He had to live. Because if he didn't live, Camden wouldn't live.

She needed them both to live. And this was why people feared love.

Because loving someone as much as she loved them hurt. Even while she was facing her own end, her worry was for them.

'Don't bother to pray for deliverance,' Paden said. 'It isn't going to come.'

Despair rolled through her. But then she looked up and saw a bird on the branch of a tree, bobbing his head, hopping back and forth. An absurdly cheerful thing in the face of all this.

But it meant something.

Because it was the bird that had made her sure that Lachlan was good all those years ago. And it was the memory of that that had given her faith in him in the present.

He would come. He would come for her.

And they would triumph.

Because there was no point of the world where it could be otherwise.

Lachlan might not be able to believe in hope.

But she believed in him.

And now, that would have to be enough.

Chapter Twenty

Lachlan's blood was fire and he didn't know who among his own men he could trust. So he rode out into the woods with his horse and his sword and the rage that fuelled him.

There was a sign, easy enough for even a casual tracker to follow. Evidence that a horse had gone this way recently. And it could be from any number of men, it was true. But he had to trust that it was leading him to Penny.

Penny.

And what if she died? What then?

He had told her, revenge was not a dream, it was a plan. And that was what he had tried to fashion out of his life. A plan.

A goal divorced from feelings so that he did not become his father.

So that he did not become his mother.

There was too much at stake.

But it did not insulate him now. Because somewhere along the line Penny had become a dream. She had slipped beneath his skin, beneath his defences. And though he hadn't wanted it, it was so.

He followed the path that William had set him on. When he came to the end of the trail he stopped and saw the broken branches just off there. He knew that he'd found them.

He drew his sword and rode into the clearing.

And there she was. Bound.

Suddenly Paden was behind her, his sword at her throat.

The smile on the man's face was savage. 'There you are. I was expecting you.'

'I will gut you like the treasonous dog you are,' Lachlan said.

'I don't think you will.' Disquiet filled Lachlan's gut. 'I'm not sad to be found by you, Lachlan. I have men in wait. Did young William send you this way? Your man. It may shock you to learn that your own man betrayed you.'

That hit him with the force of a bullet.

'No,' Lachlan said.

'Oh, yes. Young William is from Clan Mac-Connell. His mother left home when there was nothing left, went to Clan MacKenzie for protection. Your father killed her.'

Fire swept through his veins. 'I've nothing to do with what that bastard did.'

'It doesn't matter. William wanted revenge. I do have it. At my hand.'

'Leave Penny be.'

'I have no quarrel with your woman. If it weren't for you, she would be nothing. She wouldn't be here. But I also have no fear over cutting her neck.'

He pressed the blade against her throat, drawing blood. Penny's eyes were wide and fury rose up in Lachlan's veins.

'Drop your sword, my Laird.'

He tightened his grip on the weapon. 'You play a dangerous game.'

'You can let me kill her. And while I finish you could easily kill me. It is only a problem if the lass is worth your life.'

And here it was.

Weakness.

Because he could not let them harm Penny. Because he should care about the clan, only the clan. And his own life mattered only as far as it benefitted the well-being of his people.

But *she* mattered. She was the sun and the stars. The way he could guide himself. Without her, he was only a blade. Nothing more. Without her, he could not be the leader that he needed to be. Without her...

It didn't matter. None of it did.

Without her it was lost. Whatever he'd been

trying to win. What did the clan matter—rock and dirt and tradition—if there was no heart?

And Paden was right. He had identified his weakness. For his weakness was this woman.

This was love.

And love was exactly what he'd feared.

Still, in the face of it, in the face of the very reason he'd sought to keep his heart free of love, mercy and forgiveness...

He dropped his sword.

Penny let out a short scream, a tear trailing down her cheek.

Two of his men came out from behind the trees, wielding their swords.

Lachlan held his hands out. 'Release her.'

'No,' Paden said. He kept his sword at her throat and the men began to advance on Lachlan. In a flash, he knew exactly what he must do. The blade bit deeper into Penny's throat and blood trickled down her beautiful skin.

He saw red.

He would have only a breath, then he would lose her.

But he would not allow her to be lost.

He roared and charged at Paden and the man froze, clearly unwilling to kill her quite yet as she was his only means of controlling Lachlan.

A mistake.

Lachlan wrapped his fist around the blade, ignoring it as it sliced into his palm, and wrenched it away from her throat, pulling it from the man's grip. Bloody, he pushed his fist into Paden's gut. And when the man fell back he took up his sword by the handle and separated his head from his shoulders in one fluid movement.

By then, his men were on him, but Lachlan rounded on them. One blade went through his shoulder and he let out a vicious yell as he turned and drove his sword first through one man, then the other.

And he waited. Waited to see if there were more.

And through the clearing, he saw him.

William.

The lad standing there, holding his own sword. He did not have the posture of a warrior, in spite of having been a soldier. He looked like what he was: a boy. Narrow in the shoulders and fearful in the eyes.

Lachlan felt not one moment of regret for ending Paden, or the other two. But running William through did give him pause.

'Don't,' Penny said. 'He's a boy.'

'I was a man when I was his age. And he nearly cost us your life.'

'Lachlan…this is what revenge does.'

Those words caught him in his chest. 'Aye,' he

said. 'And he will learn what happens when your revenge does not go as planned.'

'He can't do anything to you.'

He ground his teeth together. 'I don't show mercy.'

He approached the lad and William began to tremble.

'My mother…' he said.

'I did not lay a hand on your mother, lad. And if you wish to quarrel with me, then you will quarrel with me. But my wife's blood has been spilled and if you think that I will give forgiveness for you trying to avenge your mother by spilling the blood of my wife…'

'I'm sorry,' William said and dropped his sword.

'I cannot abide a coward,' Lachlan said. 'You should at least fight me. Stand in your convictions.'

'Lachlan, please,' Penny said.

'*Why?*' Lachlan asked. 'Why should I spare him?'

'Because he doesn't know another way. That's all this is. Vengeance in fighting and violence. He was never given another way.'

'I saved his arse. I brought him back home. If it weren't for me he wouldn't be here. He was given another way. He chose vengeance.'

'So did you. You used me for your vengeance. Don't be so prideful that you don't see that.'

Mercy.

He looked down at his sword, red with the blood of men he could not allow to live. He had lived his life without mercy.

Except for the babe he'd tried to save.

Except for the bird.

And the bird and the babe had given him more than killing ever had. He could not explain it, only that he felt changed.

For he had stared down the worst of what it might mean to have a heart and he'd chosen to love.

And in his weakness, he'd been most powerful of all.

Lachlan lowered his sword. 'Where is your clan?'

'I didn't lie to you in England,' William said. 'They're gone.'

'Then you've nowhere to go. Because if you come back to Clan MacKenzie, it's a cell that will be awaiting you.'

'Laird…'

'I'm sparing your life. But you will not show your face in Clan MacKenzie. And do not even think about spreading poison to the other clans, because I will make it known what has happened.'

The boy looked as though he might weep.

'I didn't want her to be hurt,' he said.

'You only wanted me killed.'

'Paden said there would be money and power enough for everyone. And you keep all the power to yourself.'

'Look what you've done with a small amount of it. Ask yourself if every man ought to have power. Or if some of you do not possess the fortitude to wield it.'

The boy lowered his head. 'I'm sorry. I've nowhere else to go…'

All of a sudden he saw the boy differently. He saw himself. Reckless and angry and willing to make sacrifices of the innocent in order to see his vengeance played out.

For had he not done so with Penny?

She had not transgressed against him, but he was happy to catch her up in his revenge against her father. For anger was a sword being swept broadly across a battlefield, catching all in its path as enemies.

And there was only one cure for it.

He had seen it in Penny. The way she treated the members of the clan, those who lived in their household. The way she had given so much to Mary. The way she loved Camden as her own.

The way she was with him. For she had no reason to be a wife to him, no reason to show him care when he had swept her up in his vengeance.

Love.

Mercy.

He had been bound and determined to show none, but more punishment, more anger…would not heal this boy. And he might have set out a consequence, but what would he gain? What would the world gain?

This was what Penny had shown him, from the beginning, only he'd been too stubborn to take it in.

Sometimes you saved the bird. Because whether it lived or not, you had tried. Because whether it got you anything in return, it was good for your soul.

And only Penny had ever worried for his soul.

'Return to the castle,' Lachlan said.

'Laird…'

'Tell Rona you've need of food and sleep.'

Tears filled the boy's eyes. 'I betrayed you…'

'And we are not dead. None of us. So we have a chance to change course. William, I have never been a man to show mercy. I have seen the world as a merciless place. It can be. But if I am not willing to show mercy in it, how can it ever be more?'

The boy nodded, his expression grave. 'Go back, lad,' Lachlan said.

The boy did not have to be asked twice.

Then Lachlan turned to Penny and ran. He

knelt down on the ground beside her, gathering her up against him as he undid her bindings.

'Lachlan,' she said, weeping against his chest.

'You're safe, lass,' he said.

He looked at the bodies around them. Safe. She was safe. 'William sent me here,' he said, grimly. 'Knowing that they were waiting.'

'He knew that he could use me to make you drop your weapon.'

'Because even Paden saw what I did not,' Lachlan said.

'What is that?'

'How much I love you, lass.'

'Love?'

'Aye,' Lachlan said, his heart feeling as though it had nearly been ripped in two. 'I do love you. And I realised just how much when I had to face the fact that he could use you to get to me. There is no denying it. There is no protecting my heart. It would be better for The MacKenzie to have no vulnerability. It would be better for him to feel nothing. For I should've thought of the clan and nothing more. But I didn't. I couldn't. I love you. And right when I realised what a grave mistake it was, I accepted it.'

'Lachlan…'

'I sent William back to the clan.'

'You did?'

'Yes. I have never shown mercy, not in all my

life. But you have shown me that…lass, I cannot make a world that is safe. One that will shield you or me or the bairn from all harm. But I can create a world around us that is better. I thought only the sword, anger and revenge could bring about change, for I thought they were the strongest forces. But that is not true. You have shown me this. Change comes in small ways. In giving chances and choices. Mercy. In loving when it is too much to bear. I love you in that way. It is too much to bear.'

'I love you, too,' she said, the words coming out on a sob.

He brought her into his arms, lifted her up off the ground.

'You can't carry me all the way back.'

'Aye,' he said. 'But I can.'

'You were stabbed in the shoulder!'

He shifted, feeling the sting and tear of the wound. 'Aye,' he said. 'It doesn't much matter. Not when you're all right.'

'How did you know you could do that? How did you know you could defeat all those men?'

'I didn't. But I survived ten years battling the French. And while a Scot was always going to be a greater challenge… I've done well surviving to this point.'

'I suppose so.'

'And I had nothing to live for then. Nothing but

a vague idea of revenge and honour. Now I have you. I have you to live for, Penny. And I had your life to save. So there was no choice.'

'I knew you would come. I was also afraid.'

'I wonder if it would've been kinder for me to leave you. You would've never had to be afraid with your Duke.'

'No. But I would never have loved him either.'

He stopped walking for a moment. 'Penny,' he said. 'I didn't have a lot of faith in the world to begin with. But what little I had the war did a good job of taking away. And I thought…if I could save that bairn…'

'But not even that.'

'Not even. And somehow I got it in my head that not having feelings would protect me. That it would protect everyone. But my father loved nothing. He loved nothing but power. And that's what allowed him to act as he did.'

He kissed her lips, softly. 'But I love you. And it's what allowed me to do what I did tonight. I love you and it makes me stronger. It makes me weaker. It makes me vulnerable, but you've shown me that perhaps a leader must be vulnerable sometimes in order to truly lead.'

'You let William return to the clan.'

'Aye. And if not for you, I wouldn't have even let him live.'

'He's only a boy.'

'And I wouldn't have cared.' He cleared his throat. 'And truth be told, what I said to him echoes in my own heart. That the woman I used... the woman I used for my own dark revenge loves me and wants my life saved. That counts for something.'

'You're a good man, Lachlan Bain. And I always knew that part of you was still there.'

'It wasn't,' he said, taking hold of her hand and putting it over his chest. 'It wasn't there. It was with you. All this time. I'm starting to wonder if I came back to your father's house to collect my heart. For I think I left it there a long time ago. And you took care of it in my absence. I want you to continue to care for it because you have it.'

'I love you,' she said. 'And I never even knew that I wanted love.'

'I knew that I didn't. But you've changed me. And you've shown me that love is what makes the world matter. Because without it...there is revenge and there is honour. But there is no joy.'

'No.'

'Do you want to go back to England? I don't want you to go, but I feel as though I have to give you a choice. Because I took it. Now I need to give it back.'

'No,' she said. 'I choose you. I choose this. I choose the clan.'

'And I choose you,' he said. 'Not for revenge. For love.'

And as they walked back to the castle, the anger and pain of the last years began to fall away. For all that hurt, all the loss, had made him. And love had never been part of the future he planned for himself. But now he knew that it was what he needed.

Penny was what he needed.

Lachlan Bain was a patient man. But he had no real idea of what he'd been waiting for.

It had taken a chattering Englishwoman to show him.

He could only hope she had the patience to continue showing him.

'We must get back,' he said. 'To our son.'

Her blue eyes filled with tears. 'Yes. We must.'

Epilogue

❦

Lady Penelope Bain was eating toast when she suddenly had the urge to cast up her accounts and, upon doing some counting, discovered that she was pregnant with the barbarian's child.

'Are you upset?'

Over the past months much had changed about Lachlan in the way that he was with her. The way that he was with Camden.

Life at the castle was different, bright. Isla was back in her position and healthy as ever. They'd had letters from both Flora and Mary, who were happy in their new positions. Mary's letters had been written for her, at first, by other girls at the school. But the most recent had been done in her own hand.

Her life was changing. One word at a time. One lesson at a time.

Her life was changing because of love.

As Penny's had. And Lachlan's.

Love had overtaken fear and he no longer held himself back. But…she wasn't entirely sure if he had banished reservations about the two of them having their own child, though he no longer took extreme precaution to prevent it.

'It has taken time,' he said. 'But you know, it was never my blood I feared. I feared losing something I loved. For I did, as a boy. Time and time again. And when I failed to save that bairn…'

'You didn't fail to save him. You were the only chance he had. Without you… No one would've held him in his last moments.'

She watched as something in her mountain of a husband cracked.

'I had never thought of that,' he said, his voice rough.

'You didn't fail. You tried. You cared. That's hope, Lachlan. And it is the most powerful thing in the world.'

'Ah, lass,' he said. 'You give me so many more reasons to hope. Reasons to love. And I'm grateful.'

And hope they did, for years to come.

They had five children after Camden, all grew into boisterous, spirited men and women.

It was Camden Lachlan asked to one day be Laird.

'But my blood,' he said. 'It isn't yours. Or my mother's.'

'Aye,' Lachlan said. 'But the love inside you is. And I have learned that that is the only thing that matters.'

And that night, when he lay down beside his wife, he set about proving that very thing, again and again.

'How strange,' he said after, as he held her, 'that the one thing I thought I should not have has been the only thing I needed.'

'What is that?'

'Your love.'

'I love you, too,' she said, then she made a thoughtful face. 'The Duke really did have lovely manners.'

'You don't like lovely manners,' he growled.

'You're right. I don't. But I *love* you.'

* * * * *

Historical Note

One of my favourite pieces of research for this book was on the role of the Scottish soldier in the Napoleonic Wars. As the Wars are an important piece of Lachlan's back story, I wanted to dig into what it might have been like for him.

Highlanders were associated only with rebellion at the beginning of the Wars, but eventually their bravery and fierce fighting style—particularly that of the Forty-Second and Ninety-Second Regiments—earned them respect within the military. Bagpipes and kilts had been banned by the Dress Act of 1746, but the ban was lifted and, while kilts were not everyday dress at that point, they became a symbol of Scottish pride and were worn by Scottish soldiers during the Wars.

It is said that they rode into Waterloo to the sound of bagpipes, shouting, 'Scotland for ever!' I knew that would be exactly Lachlan's sentiment—so, although kilts were not in fashion during Lachlan and Penny's time, I felt it was reasonable that Lachlan would wear one, as any man wears his military uniform even when he's finished his service.

MILLS & BOON

Coming next month

THE HIGHLANDER AND THE WALLFLOWER
Michelle Willingham

Regina sank into a chair, burying her face in her hands. She didn't know whether to weep or groan with frustration. 'Why did you come, Lord Camford?'

'Because you didn't read Lachlan's note, nor any of mine. You refused my calls, and I had no other way to tell you that the laird married someone else.'

'His governess,' she predicted, feeling as if the bottom had dropped out beneath her. She had burned his letter without reading it. And he had been trying to call off the wedding. Dear God.

'Aye,' Camford answered. 'I am sorry to be the bearer of such news.'

Her emotions gathered into a tight ball of humiliation, but she managed to say dully, 'The wedding is off. We'll send the guests away and be done with it.' She already felt miserable, and the last thing she wanted was to face everyone else or see the sympathy in their eyes.

But then, this was what she deserved. She had been using the laird as a means of escaping her problems. She hadn't wanted to marry him, and it was now quite evident that he hadn't wanted to wed her either. If only she had opened his letter or allowed Camford to pay a call, she would have known the truth.

The viscount came close and knelt at her feet. 'I know

that you wanted to marry him to escape London. Because you're afraid of your father's blackmailer.'

She didn't look at him, so afraid she would break into tears. He took her hands, and she felt her heart begin to pound. 'But there is no reason why *I* cannot give you what you're wanting.'

What did he mean by that? Regina stared into his green eyes, uncertain. Then Lord Camford said, 'Marry me, instead. I will take you to Scotland, and you can escape London as you wanted to. I will also ensure that no one ever blackmails you or your father again.'

Continue reading
THE HIGHLANDER AND THE WALLFLOWER
Michelle Willingham

Available next month
www.millsandboon.co.uk

COMING SOON!

We really hope you enjoyed reading this book.
If you're looking for more romance, be sure to
head to the shops when new books are
available on

Thursday 23rd July

To see which titles are coming soon, please visit

millsandboon.co.uk/nextmonth

MILLS & BOON

LET'S TALK

Romance

For exclusive extracts, competitions
and special offers, find us online:

- facebook.com/millsandboon
- @MillsandBoon
- @MillsandBoonUK

Get in touch on 01413 063232

For all the latest titles coming soon, visit
millsandboon.co.uk/nextmonth

MILLS & BOON

HISTORICAL

Awaken the romance of the past

Escape with historical heroes from time gone by. Whether your passion is for wicked Regency Rakes, muscled Viking warriors or rugged Highlanders, indulge your fantasies and awaken the romance of the past.

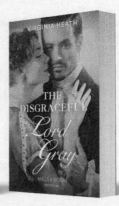